KINSHIP COVE: MATES & MACARONS

VOLUME ONE

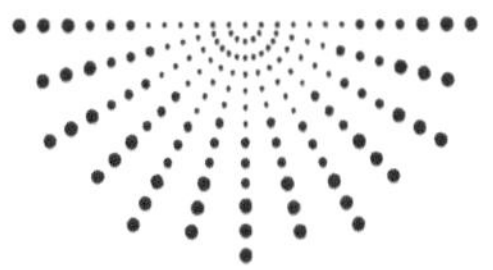

ELLIS LEIGH

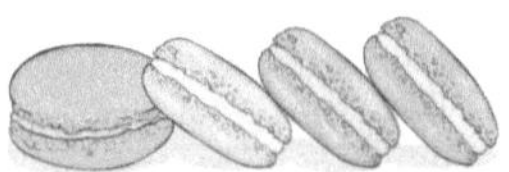

CANDIED WOLF

KINSHIP COVE: MATES & MACARONS

At the Cake-ily Ever After bakery in Kinship Cove, three sisters are about to meet their matches and prove that a man with a little silver in his hair can make one heck of a mate...if the fates allow it.

No more dating shifters—at least, that's what I promised myself after the last one met his mate while dating me. He wasn't the first—fate seemed to enjoy smacking me upside the head whenever I dared to cross the species line. So when a handsome wolf shifter with a few extra years of experience comes walking into my bakery, I shouldn't agree to go on a date with him.

Especially not because he's only in town for the biggest wedding of the year.

The one where his son is the groom.

The one between my last boyfriend and his fated mate.

Did I say fate liked to smack me upside the head? Try burying me in the rubble of my past mistakes instead. Like father, like son had never been so wrong...or so right.

1

COCO

There was something about being invited to an ex-boyfriend's wedding that really made a girl question every single decision she'd ever made in her entire life. It was like a game of if this, then that. If I'd done this instead of that, then I'd have that instead of this. Maddening. And also really, really distracting. And disheartening. And…every other dis word I couldn't think of.

I mean, sure, owning a small business with my sisters was pretty cool. I'd even leveled up last year and bought a house. A charming little bungalow on a quiet street lined with big trees that covered the sky like a green canopy as you drove down it. Very fairy-tale like. My house even had a white picket fence. On paper, I had my life under control: accomplished, career-driven, successful. On paper, I should have been really, really happy, but paper sometimes lied.

In this case, my paper didn't *overtly* lie; it was dishonest by omission. It neglected to mention the one area where I was truly lacking. My love life, which was an abysmal wreck. Romance was one aspect of my existence that I simply could *not* get right, no matter how hard I tried. And I tried. A lot.

I was pretty sure I'd dated every eligible bachelor in town—and by eligible, I meant human and shifter alike. No species-specific dating for me. No, sir. I kept the playing field clear, kept my options wide open. Of course, Kinship Cove, where I had always lived, wasn't your normal small town—it was rife with paranormal activity and tended to attract men and women who could turn into animals. When I was a kid, I'd called some of them werewolves. As a teenager, I'd learned the correct word was shifters and had strived to learn as much as I could about the ones in my community so I could be a good neighbor and friend. As an adult, I called them friends, peers, and the men I should have known better than to get mixed up with—bachelor mistakes number six, twelve, and eighteen.

Eighteen being the one about to get married in the biggest wedding ceremony Kinship Cove had ever seen.

A wedding my sisters and I—owners of the Cake-ily Every After bakery—had been hired to provide desserts for.

A wedding my ex—who'd literally broken up with me via email after finding his fated mate—had just invited me to. Over text message.

"The man needs to learn to make a damn call or send a letter." I tapped my fingers on the counter, trying hard to think up the proper response. *Kiss off* was definitely too harsh and totally unprofessional. *Are you joking* seemed too rhetorical. And *Gosh, I'd love to* was simply... not happening. Where were my sisters when I needed them?

"You keep frowning at your phone and your face is going to freeze that way." Misty, the woman who ran the front counter and kept all the customers—both shifters and human—under control, just laughed when I rolled my eyes at her. "What could possibly be so bad as to make the bubbliest human in Kinship Cove frown?"

I wasn't feeling very bubbly.

"I got a text." I set my phone down, still unsure how to respond to the message. "It's from Nico."

The look she shot me would have scared a lesser woman. "What does *the dog* want now?"

Dog. Because he shifted into a canine. Misty hadn't liked Nico from the start, had said he shouldn't have been leading me on, seeing as how I wasn't his fated mate. I'd ignored her, not unaware as to how shifters found their partners. Heck, the other two shifters I'd dated had found theirs *while* dating me. I'd thought the first one was a fluke. Figured the second was quite the coincidence. It couldn't—wouldn't—ever happen again. So I'd rushed into a relationship with the wolf shifter, choosing to believe I was safe from all that fate stuff.

I'd been so very, very wrong.

After two months of getting over Nico and a pretty badly scarred heart from how things had ended so abruptly, I could admit that I should have taken her advice. Fated mates would always win, no matter how much the shifter cared for their non-mate partner. That was why I'd vowed to stop dating shifters. No sense starting something the fates would finish when they tossed that beast their true fated mate, like they had with Nico. And Justin. And Charles.

Seriously, I should have rented myself out to lonely shifters. I could almost see the ad—date Coco Chance for a month or two, and you'll find your mate. Guaranteed to work or your money back. You just have to pretend you love her, and she has to fall for you too, so her heart can be shattered into a thousand pieces when you leave. Mention this ad for a discount!

Ugh. No thanks.

Apparently, I took too long to answer her because Misty suddenly said, "I don't know why you keep talking to him. No, wait, I do—you're a good person."

"Thanks."

"You're also an idiot."

"I retract my thanks."

"That's fine, but he's mated. *Ma-ted.* Not married, though he will be soon enough, and not just in a relationship. He's attached in a way most humans will never understand. The fates threw him a bone he couldn't possibly resist—there's no coming back from that."

As a woman who could shift into the cutest, softest, and yet meanest fox I'd ever seen, she knew what she was talking about. Me? I was still learning. Growing up in a town where mythical creatures walked among you was one thing—dating them was an entirely new ball game. One that sent your world sideways at every opportunity. And I'd suffered through three such opportunities.

Never again. "I don't reach out to him."

"But you answer when he texts."

"Well…yeah. How do you not?"

"Uh, I don't know. Maybe just *not*." Misty sighed, looking as if she were being forced to remind a wayward toddler why they couldn't play in the street. Me playing the part of the wayward toddler, of course. "Look, Coco. You're nice."

That didn't sound complimentary. "And your point is?"

"You're *too* nice. You're all sweetness and light around here, and it makes my job really damn difficult."

"Me being nice makes it hard to run the counter?"

"No. You being so fucking nice that you allow your ex-boyfriend— who dumped you the second he spotted his fated mate—to keep chatting you up even though he knows his mate will cut his balls off if she finds out makes my job of leading you three wild women through the world of shifters difficult."

"That's not what we pay you for."

"If I didn't step in now and again, you'd end up making some pretty gnarly mistakes. Like that time last summer when the hottie with the black hair was hitting on you? When you looked as if you were going to just melt into his side without asking him his species?"

"That just seems rude."

"Honey, in this world, rude is what keeps you from dating a skunk shifter. Do I need to remind you how that would have gone?"

Ugh. No. She didn't. "Okay, fine. I'm an idiot for being nice. I just can't help but acknowledge someone when they talk to me."

"Texts aren't talking—texts from ex-boyfriends are either booty calls or future mistakes. Maybe both. Ignore him."

I thought about her words for a long time, long enough to have finished a batch of my famous éclairs and for my sister, Madeleine, to arrive at the shop. She dove straight into the business of making the groom's cake we'd be supplying for the rehearsal dinner tomorrow night. Me? I thought about ignoring Nico. For what felt like hours.

But I couldn't stop thinking that Misty's advice was wrong.

"What now?" Misty said when she caught me frowning at my phone again.

"I just—"

"Do *not* tell me you were thinking of texting Nico back."

"Well, I mean—"

"No. Just no. You can never, and I mean ever, text him again. There is no good reason why you'd ever need to."

This was going to be awkward. "It's an invitation."

"To what?"

"The wedding."

Her face went flat, but her eyes—oh, her eyes were bright and hard as they stared at me. I knew that look—her fox was hanging out really close to the front of her mind. That little vixen had a mean streak a mile wide. I wasn't the biggest fan of having caught her attention.

Voice harsh, every word enunciated and slow, Misty said, "He texted you an invitation to his wedding."

Not a question, and yeah, okay. When she put it that way... But his bad manners didn't mean I had to act the same way. "I should probably RSVP, right?"

"That man has some balls, I'll tell you that." Misty huffed, pacing along the back counter and looking almost frazzled. Even the ever-calm Madeleine watched her warily, earbuds in and probably having no idea what we were talking about but knowing something had gotten to our solid and sure customer service person. We'd had lines out the doors and people screaming when we'd run out of their favorite cookies, yet I'd never seen Misty frazzled.

This was new territory. "Misty?"

"I'm thinking." She mumbled something to herself, still pacing. Still looking like a woman without a solution to a problem. Definitely new territory. Madeleine disappeared into the back, probably pretending to look for something in the storage room. Smart girl, though we'd have to have a little talk about her abandoning me with a crazed fox shifter. Not cool, Madeleine. Not cool at all.

"Maybe I'll text Ginger." My other sister, and the one with the most experience with men. Quite literally. The woman had no shame and an endless supply of both dating horror stories and successes. "She might know what to do."

Misty didn't answer me, so I did just what I'd planned—sent a text to my wildest sister and hoped for the best.

Me: I think I broke Misty.

Ginger: What did you do now? I'll be there in two minutes to put her back together.

Me: Nothing intentional. Nico texted me again, this time to invite me to his wedding. Thoughts?

The bubbles indicating she was responding showed up immediately, her answer popping up in seconds.

Ginger: He texted you an invite? Classy. That gives you the green light to fuck his dad after the ceremony.

I really shouldn't have been surprised by Ginger's answer. Shouldn't have been, but I was.

Me: That really isn't where I was going with this.

Ginger: That's where I'd go.

Now *that* didn't surprise me at all. I kept my eyes on Misty as I prepped the tray of éclairs to put in the front case. She didn't look any calmer, which meant this really bothered her. It bothered me too, but at the same time, it really wasn't all that shocking. Nico had always liked getting my attention, and I… Well, I fell for his lines every single time. At least, I used to. Before he found his fated mate and left me without a word. Except for a few text messages afterward that I'd answered just to be polite. And an invitation to his wedding. His *wedding*. As if he hadn't been in my bed just two months ago. Before *Bam!* Fate.

I was such an idiot.

As I finished lining up the delectable, chocolate-covered treats, the bell over the front door rang through the bakery. It had to be Ginger—she'd said she'd be here in just two minutes. With Misty out of commission and Madeleine hiding, I needed my sister to talk me through what to do about this situation. I needed a reply that would strike the perfect balance of *Piss off, you wanker* and *Jolly good time.*

Just less British.

I hurried out to the sales floor carrying the tray of éclairs. "Misty's still broken, and I am not having sex with a dad. That's a nonnegotiable."

"I guess it's too bad I have a son, then."

I slipped and wobbled hard, meeting deep, dark eyes as I bumped into the counter. As he smiled at me.

And then I died.

Not literally—that would have been way too dramatic for me.

But he was so…

I nearly dropped the tray.

Thankfully, the man grabbed the end and righted it before we had a baked-good catastrophe. His arm bulged—actually bulged—with the movement, as if the muscles were trying hard to get my attention. They truly didn't need to try that hard at all. This guy—this customer—was the living, breathing epitome of the word *man.* Tall and thick, with broad shoulders and a tapered waist. His simple black button-up shirt clung to his arms, the sleeves cuffed and rolled in that way that made me drool.

Arm porn was a real thing, apparently.

The higher sleeve also showed off a little ink peeking out from one side. Giving him a tiny hint of danger. Just enough to make my heart flutter. And he wasn't some young, cocky kid either. He had salt-and-pepper hair and scruff. A true silver fox right here in my bakery.

And I'd just said I wasn't having sex with a dad.

Open mouth, insert foot.

"Are you all right?"

The tone of his voice sent a shiver up my spine. "I'm so sorry. I thought you were my sister."

"Ah, well, that explains things."

Another smile, another shiver, and another slight bobble as I attempted once again to make my way to the display case. Why wouldn't my knees work the way they were supposed to?

"Allow me." He gave me a smile as he took the tray from my hands and set it on the top of the display case. "You know, I'm not sure whether to take the fact that you thought I was a woman as an insult or not."

He turned and crossed his arms over his chest. His very broad, very defined chest. Those cuffed sleeves slid up a bit, showing just that much more skin and ink and…

"Women don't have muscles like that." *Open mouth, insert whole darn leg.* Why on earth had I thought speaking was a good idea? My face warmed, and I bit my lip as his grin grew wider.

"Thank you for noticing."

As if there was any way not to. But he was a customer…and a new one, at that. I'd definitely never seen him around, which meant he was likely in town for the wedding. *Calm, Coco. Stay calm. Businesslike. Professional.*

"Is there something you'd like to taste?" That sounded far less professional—and way dirtier—than I'd intended it to. "I mean…would you like to eat something?"

Shut up, shut up, shut up.

He hummed, uncrossing his arms and looking me up and down. "I really only stopped in for a coffee, but a taste sure does sound intriguing."

Oh lord, fire. I was on fire. My face, my neck, my chest…lower. Pure fire.

"I recommend the éclairs," I said, my voice way too low and breathy. "They're a personal favorite."

"That's a lot of *sweetness* first thing in the morning. I'm not sure I can handle it."

The way he said sweetness almost did me in. There was an odd sort of implication in that word, a promise of some kind. As if he knew he could handle *it* just fine and wasn't meaning the sugar rush. "You'll never know unless you try."

"You make a compelling argument." He looked over the tray, humming again. "Tell you what. I'll make you a deal—I'll buy one of these delicious looking éclairs and a cup of coffee. I just drove into town and need a little something *sweet* before I get to work."

"Of course. But what's my part in the deal?"

"You can accompany me to dinner this evening."

Not a question but not really a demand either. "Oh...I—"

I spun as Misty slammed through the kitchen door, the fox shifter no longer looking frazzled but definitely pissed off. "Give me your phone. I'll text that asshole back for you. And he'd better not be expecting you to drop to your knees and..." Her eyes went wide, her mouth falling open as she looked over the man before me. "Shit. Sorry. I just—"

A rumble sounded, a vibration I couldn't place. One that called to me, made me want to rub up against the man behind me and curl into his arms. I even took a step back as if to do just that...with a stranger. A *customer*. What was wrong with me?

At my tiny misstep, Misty crossed her arms, still staring at the customer even as the room went silent once more. Her eyebrow winged up high on her forehead, the look on her face one that I'd seen before. One that screamed attitude. "New in town?"

I looked back at the man in question just in time to see his lips quirk and his shoulder rise on a casual sort of shrug. "Here for the wedding."

Of course he was. Which meant he wasn't sticking around. A sad sort of cloud passed through me, one that made no sense. I didn't know this man, and yet his leaving hurt as if we'd been friends for years. A fact that would probably make him think I was an absolute loon.

Not of the shifting variety—bird shifters were rare even in the Cove.

"I should get back to work," I said, shaking the thought of men shifting into eagles and turkeys from my mind. "Misty, the gentleman would like an éclair and a coffee."

She blinked, looking from me to him and back again. "If you say so."

"Wait." My silver fox grabbed my arm, his touch gentle but warm. "I probably didn't ask properly, but it's been a long time since I've done anything like this. I'd really like to see you again. Will you have dinner with me?"

Oh god, oh god. His eyes. They owned me, made me want to strip right there and do dirty things to him. Made me want to tell him yes to anything he wanted from me. But my brain threw up a roadblock…or twelve. "I don't even know your name."

Smooth, Coco. Real smooth.

"It's Magnus." He let go of my arm and held out a hand for me to take. "And you are?"

"Coco." I grabbed the proffered hand, letting him tug me toward him. Gasping quietly when I was close enough to feel the heat rolling off his body.

"Fitting name for someone so delectable. Now, how about dinner?"

I couldn't speak, could only nod, which seemed to be enough of an answer for him.

"Excellent. If I can just—"

"That no-good bastard of a man." Ginger rolled into the bakery like a storm, not even giving Magnus or me a second glance. "How dare he text you out of the blue like that? I'm still for the fucking his dad plan, but I know you'll want to be all responsible and polite and stuff. How we're sisters, I have no idea. Well, hello there."

She stopped, giving Magnus a smile most men would have fallen all over themselves for. I had to fight back the urge to jump in front of her.

I also had to fight back the urge to growl at her, but that was likely just a weird reaction to…something.

"Ginger, this is Magnus." I took a step closer to him, unable not to. "He's in town for the wedding and stopped in for something sweet. This is my sister, Ginger."

I shivered as his fingers brushed the back of my arm. "Good morning, Ginger."

"Good morning to you too. Can't say we usually get such handsome men in here this early." She kicked that killer grin up a notch, making me lean just that much closer to Magnus. "Is there anything else I can do to make your day a little brighter?"

I was going to punch her.

But Magnus stayed cool. He also kept a solid hold on my arm. A possessive one. "Actually, I was just about to exchange information with your sister here. She's agreed to have dinner with me tonight."

Ginger's eyes brightened, and her smile grew. "Oh, well, that's just wonderful. She needs an evening out on the town with a handsome man. It's been a while for her, if you know what I mean."

"Ginger," I groaned.

Magnus chuckled. "Well, I promise to show her a good time. I really should get to work, though. Coco?" His grin dropped, and his eyes grew heated when I turned and fell into his gaze. "I'll need your phone number."

This was so crazy—so fast and unexpected and not at all something I would usually do. But everything about this man felt right to me— everything drew me to him. I could sit back, not agree to the date, and forever wonder what had made me feel so much, so fast for a stranger. Or I could take a chance and see what happened.

As much as it went against my nature, I was ready to take a chance.

"Right. Of course."

"And, Coco?"

"Yeah?" Oh my lord, he was so close. Practically surrounding me in his...mannishness. Was that a word? Did I care? Pretty sure it was a no to both.

Magnus leaned in enough to whisper right into my ear. "I'm hoping you'll keep an open mind on the whole dad thing. Maybe not for tonight, but..."

But...and then nothing. Not that I needed him to expound on that but. The implication was clear. I'd be having sex with a dad if things went well. Just not Nico's dad. I was more than okay with that.

I was also fighting hard not to simply say yes and ask him to take me home with him. Hard enough to babble, "You should really try the lemon donuts."

He blinked. "I should?"

"They're my favorite."

"Then I will."

Lemon donuts. What in the world was I saying? *Focus, Coco. Fo-the heck-cus.* "And, Magnus?"

"Yeah?"

I rose onto the balls of my feet to move closer, to breathe him in as I whispered in his ear, "I'm not anti dads in general."

His hand brushed against my hip as if he wanted to pull me closer. "That's good to know."

"And, Magnus?"

Another throaty chuckle. "Yes, Coco?"

"I'm really looking forward to tonight."

This time, he did grab my hip and pull me in closer. Close enough to press my breasts against his chest as he leaned in and said with a growl, "Me too. You have no idea."

No, I didn't—but I couldn't wait to find out.

2

COCO

You're lying." Magnus sat back in his chair, wide-eyed, looking like a man who'd just been told the world was flat by a scientist. I wasn't a scientist and the world wasn't flat, but my sister was what I considered to be an expert in online dating, and I'd just told him one of her most unbelievable stories.

"Totally not lying. She showed up, and the man was on a bicycle with no teeth and most of his belongings in a bag. From collared-shirt-wearing businessman to homeless meth head in an instant. I don't think she'd ever been so thankful to be in a public place in her life."

"That's just—" he shook his head and reached for his coffee "—bizarre isn't a strong enough word." Two sips and his eyes were back on mine. So intense, that stare. Almost possessive in the way his gaze held me captive. "Do much…online dating?"

Oh. *Oh.* That pause. Magnus said so much with that pause, and all of it sounded like jealousy. I had to fight to keep from preening right there in front of him. That such a virile, attractive man was jealous at the thought of *me* dating someone else? Huge compliment. "I let Ginger handle that. She's the online dating queen."

"So no swiping right for you."

"No swiping at all. You can't tell much about a person from a picture, you know?" My own jealousy reared its head, coloring my words green as I tried to keep my voice casual. "What about you? Swiping right a lot?"

His slow smile warmed something inside of me. "No swiping right for me either. I prefer to play the dashing superhero and save women from dropping trays of baked goods instead. Shows me in my best light."

"It really does. I was certainly impressed."

"Then I'll strive to be a superhero every day just for you." That look in his eyes became more focused, stronger. His hold on me tightening. "So Ginger handles online dating, but you have a second sister. Yes?"

"Madeleine. She's more of a…well, she's gorgeous and sort of shy, so she only tends to date people others set her up with. Even that's pretty rare, though."

"And you?"

"Me?"

"How do you prefer to meet the men you date?"

I couldn't help myself. "I like to accost them with éclair trays and see what they do."

He sat back, all raised brow and crooked smile. Looking almost cocky. "Tell me more. I simply have to know what sort of trap I fell into this morning."

"Well, see, if a man can save the éclairs, he's a winner in my book. If you'd have let me drop all those delicious treats this morning, I wouldn't be here now."

"Thank the fates for quick reflexes."

The fates. Not God. That one word made all my perceptions about him break apart and reform in another shape. One that morphed and rebounded in my head. *Thank the fates* was a term I'd heard around town a lot, and his saying it likely meant he was a shifter of some breed. Dammit, and everything had been going so well. I'd sworn off shifters after Nico. Now, there I was, flirting with certain disappointment once again. No matter how much I cared about him, no matter how much he might end up claiming to care for me, someday fate would throw his true mate in his path and *poof*…gone.

We had a connection, sure, but it was nothing like that of a fated couple. At least, I had to assume it wasn't. I didn't know what that intensity felt like, but I'd seen it a few times. Been close enough to it to witness two people fated to be together giving in to the pull. But this draw, this closeness I felt for Magnus, couldn't possibly be that. Had I been Magnus' mate, he would have said something. He would have told me or acted to make me his or…something. Even if I was just a human. I knew shifters and humans were sometimes paired up, and to be honest, I envied those couples. Shifters mated for life—no take-backs, no second chances needed, no falling apart. Sure, their relationships weren't always perfect, but that bond was unbreakable.

My heart, on the other hand, was not.

"Where did you go?" Magnus asked, leaning closer and looking a little concerned. "Your face just went through too many emotions for me to keep up with."

"Sorry. I just… So, you're a shifter."

He suddenly looked a little wary. "Yes. Is that a problem?"

Was it? The man was amazing—handsome and smart, funny and kind. Every part of me felt the attraction to him, especially my lady parts. They'd practically been calling his name since he met me at the front door to the restaurant looking so damned handsome. I'd regretted not allowing him to pick me up at home almost instantly, wishing instead to be alone and behind closed doors so we could get to know one another. With a lot fewer clothes on.

Stupid single-girl dating rules.

I'd been close to letting him pick me up like a gentleman, but Ginger had squashed that with one story of how an internet dater found her address and harassed her for weeks before the lion shifter next door finally had to put his fist down. Or paw, really. Whatever. I didn't have a lion shifter next door, so meeting Magnus in a public place had seemed like the safe option.

But there was nothing safe about Magnus. He was danger personified, especially to my heart. I liked him…a lot. Probably too much. Something clicked with us, something drew me to him. I loved the way he made me feel and the easy conversation we'd had over dinner. Loved the smiles and jokes and the mature way he acted. The man was witty, classy, and hot as hell...what more could I ask for? And if in a few weeks or months he found his mate and walked away?

Well, I'd lick my wounds when that time eventually came. Not literally. I wasn't very catlike.

"Coco?"

Oh, right. He'd asked me a question. "Yes. Sorry." His smile fell, and his face stiffened. It took me a second to rewind the conversation enough to realize I'd just answered his *Is that a problem* question about him being a shifter in the positive. Oops.

"No. I mean no. I mean...I'm so sorry. You being a shifter isn't a problem. I've dated them before."

He didn't look thrilled about that. "You have?"

"In this town? How could I not?"

"And you're okay with it?"

"Sure." Misty's words of warning filtered through my mind. "Wait, you're not a skunk shifter, are you?"

Magnus looked positively insulted. "Heavens no. I'm all wolf."

Like Nico. *Wonderful.* "I've dated a wolf before. I'm familiar—"

His sudden growl cut me off. I stared, unable to look away. Not afraid, really, more...turned on. That sound called to me in a way I didn't understand. I'd heard it in the bakery as well—not knowing then what it was—and I'd reacted the same. I wanted to cuddle up on his lap and snuggle him close. Wanted to rub my cheek against his and soothe the beast inside of him. Which could be awkward. We were at a nice restaurant, after all.

I could identify every shifter in the place, though. They were the ones who'd stiffened and turned in our direction even from across the room. The ones who could hear him. Who sensed the danger. My date was dangerous. That really should not have been so hot.

"Are you okay?" I asked, keeping my voice low so as not to attract any more attention than we were already getting.

Magnus coughed, his growl quieting. "Sorry. That just hit me the wrong way."

"What did? The fact that I've dated—"

"Yes."

"You didn't let me finish."

"I didn't need to—the fact that you've dated covers it."

This man. "You're jealous."

His eyes caught mine, looking hungry and predatory. His wolf likely staring back at me. "Of course I am. How could I not be with such a charming and beautiful woman as mine...date? As my date."

If only I could really be his. But this—us spending time together—would have to be enough. I could play the game if it meant getting more time with him. I'd just have to guard my heart a little bit. Keep a safe distance from any sort of emotional connection. Totally doable. "You're a charmer."

"I try. So I should take that as I'm succeeding?" He leaned closer, smiling again, reaching for my hand.

I gave it to him. "So far, yes."

"I'll take that. Maybe someday I'll get a resounding yes." He raised an eyebrow. "Maybe I'll get you yelling a few of them in a row."

"Naughty, sir. Very naughty."

"Only with you, my sweet Coco. Just you."

So...maybe that emotional distance wasn't as doable as I'd originally thought. It'd be fine, though. Perfect. I'd figure out how to deal with keeping him at bay.

Hopefully.

Magnus paid the bill when it came, insisting even after I offered to do so. He also held my chair for me as I rose and kept a hand on my lower back as we left the restaurant. All such simple things, but so important. So sweet and filled with manners many men no longer seemed to have. I was swooning hard.

"I had a great time," I said, standing on my front porch and feeling an awful lot like a teenager on a first date.

Magnus smiled, staring down at me. "I did as well. I hope you'll let me take you out again."

"Yes."

"Not a so-far yes, but a real yes? I must be improving,"

"It's the charm. It builds up."

"Good to know." He tugged me close, wrapping his arms around me as he leaned in. As he stole every one of my senses with his very presence. "I'd really like to kiss you goodnight, Coco."

Oh, thank god. "I'd really like you to."

So he did. With soft pressure and a light brushing of his tongue against my lower lip. With his hands growing stronger, gripping me tighter, pulling me in. And when I opened for him, when I parted my lips so my tongue could meet his, all sense of soft or light exploded into hard and fast and more.

Magnus stroked his tongue against mine, growling low in his throat and making me whimper. The sound spurred him on. He grabbed me by the back of my thighs and lifted me, wrapping my legs around his hips and pressing me against the front door. The wood felt cold against my back, but I didn't care. Magnus was hot enough to keep me warm. And his kiss...strong, full, and tasting of mint and the sweetness from the dessert we'd shared. He savored my mouth like a fine wine, licked and sipped and nibbled on my lips like they were the most decadent dessert. He kissed me like a man who truly enjoyed the act of kissing. A perfect kiss in a perfect moment with a perfect man.

Who has a job somewhere else and a perfect mate out there likely waiting for him.

That thought poured cold water all over my arousal. I pulled away, breaking the kiss and seeking space...literal space between us. Breathing was hard—as was Magnus—but I needed a moment. Needed to keep my head clear and back away from this wild sense of rightness I felt around him. We could date, I could take him to my bed, but I couldn't let go of my heart. Not again. Not after Nico had shredded it so thoughtlessly. Not after it'd taken so long to stitch myself back together the last time a shifter had torn through my life.

Space. Space was good. So why was I clutching Magnus to me?

"Coco?"

I shivered at the tone of his voice, wanting so badly to drag him into the house and do all sorts of naughty things to him. *Slow down.* "I should get inside."

Magnus groaned softly but nodded. "Of course. I'm sorry if I was too forward."

"No." I held on to his arms as he set me down, still wanting to feel him. Needing to. "It's not that. I just…I like you."

He squeezed my hips. "Not seeing a problem here."

Of course he wouldn't. And I wasn't sure how to explain my worries to him. "There's no problem. I just…want to take my time."

"Of course. Whatever you need—we'll go at your pace," he said, opening the door for me. "I have a feeling it's past your bedtime. Let me make sure you get tucked away in this charming house okay."

"Are you angling to come inside?"

Magnus growled and pinned me to the doorframe, looming over me. "I'll come anywhere you say I can, my beauty. But not tonight."

Breathing was so darn hard to do. "Not tonight."

Magnus grinned and ran a finger down my cheek, rubbing his nose against mine in the sweetest butterfly kiss. "Because you want to take your time."

That voice. I would have bet Magnus could get me off by talking in that deep, sexy voice alone. Past-me was a cockblocking brat. "Right. Time. I should…do that."

"Go to bed, Coco. I'll call you tomorrow."

He wouldn't, but I liked the idea of the promise anyway. "Okay. Goodnight, Magnus. I really did have a wonderful time."

"Goodnight. I'm calling you tomorrow. Be ready."

As if there were any way to be ready for a man like him.

3

MAGNUS

Mate. The word echoed through my mind, hard and rough against my senses. I'd met my mate. I hadn't expected to—not after all these years—but something about that bakery had appealed to me. Something had forced my hand and made me open the door. My wolf had practically demanded it. Thank fuck I'd learned a long time ago to follow his lead or else I might have missed her.

My Coco.

A gorgeous woman with long, brown hair and a heart-shaped face who radiated warmth every time she smiled. Curves for days on her, too —the kind that made a man want to grab hold and never let go. The kind that made him want to kiss and lick every dip. And that mouth… both the shape and what came out of it. The woman was pure temptation, a decadent dessert after a disappointing meal. And I wanted to devour her.

Only problem with that? She was human. *Human.* Which meant I needed to take my time, introduce her to me and my wolf a little slower than if she were a fellow shifter. I couldn't assume she felt the same strength of connection to me that I did to her or the same need to mate and complete our bond. For once in my very long life, I needed to take things slow. Give her time to learn me. To wait for the right moment.

23

All things I knew I absolutely *had* to do. All things driving me absolutely mad as well.

Which was how I found myself opening the door of Cake-ily Ever After for the second day in a row, unable to stay away. I'd woken up hard and aching, wishing she were in my bed. Wanting to slide inside her wet heat and watch her fall apart beneath me. I'd had to go for a run before I could even think about starting my day. My wolf had run us ragged, exhausting my muscles but not my mind. I couldn't forget the feel of her skin under my fingertips, the taste of her lips. The softness of her body pressed against mine. One goodnight kiss and a few stolen moments of grinding on the girl, and I was whipped. Owned. Mated.

It was about damned time.

"The handsome man returns." Ginger, the sister I'd met the day before, gave me a smile as she slid a tray of brightly colored cupcakes into the display case. "What brings you back here? And if you say anything other than my sister, I might just castrate you."

The fact that she said that with her grin still in place might have been scarier than if she'd been more serious. "Thanks for the warning, but rest assured—I'm here for Coco."

"Good. C'mon back—she's working on the macarons for an event order." She snagged a piece of waxed paper along the way, reaching into a case and grabbing what looked like a small bun of some sort.

"Breton butter cake," she said as she handed it to me. "Coco trained with a French pastry chef after culinary school. Her éclairs are to die for, but these are a staple."

I took a bite, wishing I could get a taste of my mate instead, but the sweet, buttery flavor knocked every thought from my mind in an instant. Okay, not every thought—I was a man who could smell his mate in the air for fuck's sake—but enough of them to focus on pastry for just a moment. "This is delicious."

"It is, and she makes them every day. If you're lucky, she might even make them at home for you." Her grin turned positively wicked as she backed through the door into the kitchen. "Hope you don't mind working out."

I rolled my eyes at her teasing even as I figured an extra run a day might be good for me. Between the sweets and the need bubbling up inside of me, a little exertion would go a long way toward keeping both me and my wolf under control. Besides, Kinship Cove was the perfect place to spend a little extra time in my wolf form. Between the woods, the other shifters, and the waterfront on the western side of the village, the place was made for a man like me. One who preferred a little freedom to get his animal on.

Of course, then I saw Coco standing over a tray of pink discs with a triangular white bag thing in her hand. All thoughts of being away from her even for a minute vanished. *Mate. Mine.*

"Hey, cookie lady," Ginger said in a loud voice. "You've got a delivery."

But Coco didn't look up. "Five minutes. I just need five minutes to put these together before the filling sets up too much and I can't get them to stick right."

"I can wait." I grinned and took a bite of the bun as Coco's head shot up. That smile, those dark eyes...fuck, she was beautiful. I wanted to toss her ass on the floor and rut her for days. Instead, I devoured her sweet baked good and looked her over. "You look gorgeous this morning, though that doesn't surprise me in the least. It's hard to hide such beauty."

Her smile set my chest on fire, and the slight flush that rose up her neck made other parts of me warmer as well. "What are you doing here?"

"I told you I'd see you tomorrow. It's tomorrow."

"You said you'd call."

"Seeing you in person seemed like a better idea."

Sweet. Sweet smile, sweet duck of her head, sweet little blush... everything about this woman was sweet. My mouth watered at the thought of finding out just how sweet every inch of her was.

She shook her head, biting her lip as if to hold back her grin. "I'm happy you're here, but I need—"

"Five minutes. Go ahead and finish your work. I'll wait for you."

That must have been the right answer because instead of going back to work, Coco rushed over to me. I barely had enough time to grab hold of her hips before her lips were on mine, her scent surrounding me, her taste on my tongue. I growled, unable to hold it back, wishing for more time with my mate…preferably with fewer clothes on.

"Hi," she whispered when she finally broke the kiss and settled with her hand against my chest. "I'm so glad you stopped by."

"I am too. Is it too forward of me to say I missed you last night?" I kissed her nose after she gave me a small head shake. "Good. Because I did miss you. Now, go get your work done so I can have you to myself for a while."

"Okay. It'll only be a few minutes."

"I've got all day for you."

She blushed a delicious shade of pink, almost as bright as the macarons she'd been making. Her smile grew, and I knew I'd done the right thing. Said the right words. I'd just made my mate happy, which was my biggest need. My wolf practically danced through my mind, his tail up and his back straight, the cocky fucker. Still, I couldn't blame him. Making our mate happy was all we wanted to do. Score one for the old man and his pain in the ass wolf.

As Coco settled in behind her tray of pink circles, the fox shifter from the day before came racing in from the back. Her eyes widened when she saw me, and she slowed her steps—a predator acknowledging a more dangerous one in its midst. Something in her body language caught my attention, made me think the woman might be more of an obstacle than a supporter of my mating with Coco. I needed to deal with her. Immediately.

"Good morning, Misty," Coco said, still focused on her work.

"Morning, boss lady. I'd ask how the date went, but considering you have a shadow today, I can guess."

I couldn't resist teasing my mate. "No, please. Ask. I'm dying to know how I did on the charming scale."

Coco chuckled softly. "You're doing just fine. It builds up, remember?"

"I definitely do."

As the fox walked past me, keeping her eyes on mine until she was through the swinging door that led to the sales area of the bakery, I finished my treat. And then I moved to follow her. The other sister had disappeared into the back of the kitchen and those macarons had Coco distracted, which meant I could get Misty alone to figure out what her problem was. No way could I pass up this chance.

I brushed off my hands and tossed the waxed paper that had been wrapped around the bun in the trash. "I'm going to order a cup of coffee. I'll be right back."

Coco only nodded, too deeply focused on her work to even look up. Good. That meant I had a few minutes so long as her sisters didn't pop up. I headed through the doorway into the shop area just in time to see the fox tie an apron around her waist.

"Am I actually making you a coffee or pretending to?" she asked, sounding more irritated than I would have liked. And my wolf definitely didn't care for her tone—I had to hold back the growl he threw at me.

"Let's go with actually," I replied, keeping my eyes on her. Making sure she knew who the stronger apex hunter was. "I could use an extra one this morning."

"Up too late thinking about your new mate?"

She wasn't far off. "Perhaps."

"Yet you weren't with her." She shrugged and moved past me toward the fancy coffee machine in the corner. "She doesn't smell like a woman who's been claimed by her mate."

"I haven't claimed her. I haven't even told her yet."

She looked over her shoulder at me, frowning. "That you're mates?"

"Correct."

Her eye-roll grated on me. "She lives in a shifter town. She knows how *this* works."

I paced. How could I not? "She's *human*. Knowing how shifter mating works and being caught up in the middle of it are two totally different things."

"Sure," the fox said, dragging out the word and sounding so damn sarcastic. "I'm going to guess she knows a lot more than you're giving her credit for."

"Maybe she does, but I can't take the chance that I'll overwhelm her. I want to give her a chance to know me before I get all...*mine.*" I growled, the idea of Coco belonging to me appealing to my wolf in the most primal way.

Misty tilted her head, furrowing her brow as she took me in. "I'm surprised you can resist the pull to complete the mating bond. Not many males can."

"It's not easy." That was an understatement. If my wolf grew any more agitated, I had a feeling even running myself ragged through the forests outside of town wouldn't stop him from racing straight for Coco's little house and taking a bite of her. Or a lick. But we couldn't. "She wants to take her time. And as much as I don't want to waste a single second, she's worth waiting for."

"That she is." Misty patted my shoulder, ignoring the way I flinched away from her touch. She wasn't my mate—I had no interest in another woman putting her hands on me. Not since I'd laid eyes on my Coco. Misty chuckled and hurried away, likely knowing she'd pushed me to the edge of my comfort zone. Sneaky little fox.

Concerned fox, too. "You realize she's like family to me, yeah?"

I shrugged. "Sure. Okay."

"And foxes—we protect our own." She stepped closer, looking me square in the eye. Not backing down. "My family skulk is one of the largest in the country. You fuck her over, and we'll all be coming after you."

A fox with an attitude. How novel. "Are you threatening me?"

"No. I'm making you a promise. Hurt her, and you'll be dealing with us. Treat her well, and everything will be okay between you and me."

I could actually respect that sort of ultimatum. "Treating her well won't be a problem. I plan to treat her like a princess."

"Good. Now, go take our girl out to brunch."

She rolled her eyes when my wolf growled over the *our* in her statement. I couldn't help it—Coco was mine, and I wasn't fucking sharing her. Ever.

4

COCO

Date one had been the dinner out where Magnus had walked me home and kissed me at my front door.

Date two had been a long and casual brunch at the diner down the street from the bakery—the one run by Misty's family.

Date three would be another dinner. Three dates in just under twenty-four hours—that had to be some sort of record. At least, for me. But that wasn't what I was concerned about. Not really. Tonight was date number three. Third-date night, which meant sex. Not demanded or required, but sort of back-of-the-mind planned for. The anticipation of what was likely to come had built within me all day, the sense that we'd be moving our relationship forward burning just under my skin. I couldn't wait, and yet I didn't want to take that step at the same time. Conflicted, thy name is Coco.

If I'd been Ginger, I would have jumped Magnus that first night on my front porch. She had a tendency to dive in head first and think about hitting the bottom later. If I'd been Madeleine, Magnus would likely have to wait forever to touch my naughty bits. I was pretty sure my younger sister was a card-carrying virgin, which was perfectly fine for her. Me? I was neither a first-date sort of girl nor a virgin. Hence the third-date rule that had somehow developed in my head over the years.

Three dates seemed like an adequate amount of time to get to know someone enough to make yourself available for…stuff. Naughty stuff. Naked stuff. I needed to shave my legs. And…other parts of my body. Just in case.

Whether I was ready to jump off the cliff into a relationship with Magnus or not, the desire was definitely there. I'd wanted to drag him inside with me and strip him down after our first date, but the idea of getting attached to him, knowing my history, slowed me down. How could I let myself fall for him—and I totally would fall for him—when I knew he'd just find his mate while with me? I was apparently a living, breathing good luck charm for shifters looking for their fated mates. Three times—*three*—the man I'd been dating had been struck by fate. That had to be some sort of record. Or joke. Three strikes and I was out —or so I'd thought.

The fear of Magnus leaving me for his fated mate still lingered, but my desire to be with him in every way was growing. Perhaps it was nothing more than denial, but I was in a full-blown "enjoy today what you'll have to pay for tomorrow" frame of mind. And I was going to enjoy every single *inch* of Magnus for as long as the fates allowed.

"The groom's cake is ready for tomorrow's rehearsal dinner. How are you doing on the five hundred macarons?" Ginger asked, her voice a little tinny as it came through the phone. I had my foot resting on the closed toilet, my leg slathered in foam, and a razor in my hand—not exactly the ideal schedule-planning situation, but we made it work.

"I'll be finished tomorrow morning. Most are already completed and stored. So the rehearsal dinner is pretty much set. What about the cupcakes for the bachelor and bachelorette parties? Last I checked, we needed to make another three dozen to meet the order quantity."

Ginger piped up at that. "I'm on those. The sweet and salty ones are already completed—I just need to sprinkle some pretzel dust over them before I call them complete. For the boozy ones, I've got cake soaking in liquor already. I'll only need to make the buttercream frosting and top those suckers, and they'll be done."

Good. The schedule for the wedding festivities was tight—we had to work ahead. "And those parties are the day after tomorrow, so we've got time there. How's the wedding cake coming?"

Madeleine groaned. "All the lace-like icing is taking me forever, and the perfect tiny roses the bride wants are going to get lost in the massiveness of this thing."

"But will you get it done in time?"

"Don't I always?"

Yeah, she did. That didn't mean we weren't going to check in to make sure. Each of us had our specialties—Madeleine decorated the things Ginger and I made. She had an artist's gift with fondant and buttercream, able to make cakes that looked as if they were spun from spider webs, carving faces or animals into what was essentially flour and eggs to create edible masterpieces.

Ginger mostly handled our cookies and cupcakes. She was creative much like Madeleine, but her talent tended to focus on flavor combinations and profiles our customers couldn't resist. The woman had come up with a bacon-maple cupcake that always brought a line of people to our door.

Me? I was a classically trained pastry chef, so I tended to stick to the French pastries and tarts that had stood the test of time. The things that required technical baking knowledge to pull off well. My specialty, though? The treat that had put us on the map as *the* bakery to go to? Macarons. We were famous for them, especially when the three of us got together to create them. Between Ginger's flavor combinations, Madeleine's decorations, and my talent at simply making a macaron with the perfect texture, we could build a cookie that made people beg for more. The ones for the rehearsal dinner tomorrow night would be no different.

"Okay," I said as I slid the razor up my calf for the final time. "So tomorrow is all about macarons. We can finish the cupcakes after those are ready for delivery."

"Deal," Ginger said. "So, can we focus on the more important event?"

My mind went blank. Nico's wedding was the biggest event of the year, and we had the contract to supply desserts for the rehearsal dinner tomorrow, the bachelor and bachelorette parties the next night, and the wedding cake on Saturday. There was nothing bigger.

I had no idea what needed to be discussed. "What are we talking about here?"

"Your date with Magnum."

"It's Magnus."

Ginger chuckled. "I think Magnum fits him better. Or does it? Do tell."

As if I would talk about his…oh hell, I totally would, and my sisters knew it. "I wouldn't know."

"Wait…what?" Ginger sounded horrified. "How have you not taken that pony for a ride yet?"

"Maybe she's waiting for the right time." Madeleine. Of course.

"Thanks, Mad. I am sort of waiting."

"For what? Christmas?" Ginger sounded affronted at the very idea. "He may have a little gray in that beard, but he's not fucking Santa Claus, Coco."

There was a ho-ho-ho joke in there somewhere, but I didn't have time to think it through. "I'm not waiting for anything in particular. I just…"

Didn't want fate to slap me upside the head again.

"Wanted to get to know him," Madeleine chimed in.

"Maybe." Not really, but it sounded good.

"So, you know him now?"

How to explain to Madeleine—the possible virgin—that I didn't, but I was ready anyway. "Sort of."

"I call bullshit. What does he do?" Ginger asked, sounding like a lawyer instead of a baker all of a sudden. "Why is he in town? Where does he live?"

"I…" Oh god, they'd never let me live this down. "I'm not sure."

"So you've gotten to know him enough to have sex with him, but you don't actually know anything about him." Madeleine's sarcasm might as well have been a whip cracking across the line.

"I never said it made sense."

"You're so transparent," Ginger said with a laugh. "You're afraid to get attached when you know he could find his fated mate at any moment."

Yup. Transparent. "You can't deny that it's a possibility."

"It's an excuse. You want the dick, get the dick. Lust makes sense. Sex makes sense. All that love stuff and soul mates and forever...that's the shit that doesn't make sense. Sex is easy."

"Says who?" Madeleine asked.

"Says me. And I bet Coco agrees, don't you, sis?"

I hated when they put me in the middle. I hated it more that Ginger might well have been right—lust and sex were easy. The hard part came when my heart got involved. Which meant I could have sex with Magnus, I just couldn't fall for him.

I had a feeling that was easier said than done.

"Look, girls. I know you're trying to help—"

Thankfully, I was saved by the bell. Quite literally.

"Oops, that's probably Magnus at the door. Gotta go." I hung up and wiped the last of the foam from my leg, hoping against hope that I'd sliced off every last hair. If not, well...there was nothing I could do about it now. I grabbed my phone and my purse and headed for the stairs, looking forward to another night talking across a candlelit table. To jokes and banter and Magnus' brand of wittiness to fill a few hours. But when I opened the door...

Woman down.

"You look amazing." Magnus gave me a smile, looking like some sort of movie star in his dark blue suit coat and pants with a crisp white shirt underneath. No tie, top two buttons open—casual enough for Kinship Cove but still dressy. Sexy as fuck, too.

"You don't look half bad yourself." I stretched for a kiss, shivering as his hand came down to grab my hip and pull me in close. As his growl vibrated against my skin. I couldn't help myself—I placed my hands against his chest and just...touched. Felt. Closed my eyes and absorbed the warmth of him. It was almost crazy how much I'd missed him this afternoon, and the reconnection felt good. So, so good.

I wanted more.

Magnus seemed to want the same. He held me tight, a soft rumble making his chest vibrate against me, before tapping my hip and stepping away. I swear, the man even had to take a deep breath. "Are you ready to go?"

No. "Yeah."

I locked the door behind me, wishing I had the guts to simply pull him inside my house and take him to bed. Wishing I could feel his rough hands on my skin. The weight of him on top of me. That sweet sting as he slid—

"You okay there, beautiful?" Magnus had a concerned sort of smile on his face as he dropped into the driver's seat of his car. He'd apparently already helped me into my own—my thoughts had been running too far off course for me to even notice. I took a deep breath, instantly regretting it because he smelled so good and he was so close and—

"Coco?"

Oh, right. "Yeah. I'm fine."

"You sure? We can cancel—"

"No." I nearly jumped out of my skin at the thought of not completing our third date. "I'm good. I swear. Just…distracted by you."

His smile spread slowly, his eyes twinkling. "You're the distracting one. Too damn beautiful for me to resist." He started the car, dropping his hand to my thigh as he pulled away from the curb. Making me shiver as his thumb slipped up under the hem of my skirt. The man was going to kill me, and we hadn't even made it to the end of my block yet.

I licked my lips, trying hard to speak past the desert my mouth had become as I asked, "What do you do for a living?"

He didn't seem prepared for that question. "I'm a project management consultant. Why?"

Because my sisters had gotten into my head. "Just curious, really. Where are we going, by the way?"

His grip on my thigh tightened, sending a spark straight up my spine. Making me need to bite back a moan as he said, "I made a reservation for us at that steakhouse out on the highway. They have a great wine list."

His fingers found their way between my thighs, his entire hand gripping me. Holding me in place. Teasing me. I was done with the teasing. "Magnus?"

His eyes darted my way before returning to the road. "Yeah?"

"It's our third date."

"Okay."

"I have a third-date rule when it comes to men."

He sat silent and still, almost tense. "What sort of rule?"

Time to be a big girl and tell him what I wanted. "A rule about sex."

Was that a twitch in his jaw? "Really?"

"Yes. And while I'm sure you made a reservation for us at a lovely restaurant—" I grabbed his hand, tugging it higher along my thigh. Slipping it well under the edge of my frilly skirt until we met the thin lace of my panties. "—I'm also sure your hotel has excellent room service."

The tires squealed as he made a U-turn. "Hotel, it is."

5

COCO

Magnus was perfectly controlled on the way to the hotel. He kept the conversation light, kept his hand on my thigh, and even helped me out of the car. He was an absolute gentleman as we walked across the parking lot and into the lobby...but then we made it into the elevator. As soon as the doors slid closed behind us, the wolf came out.

He pushed me against the wall with a growl, caging me in with his big body. "Are you sure about this, Coco?"

Was I? My body was, for sure. My heart had already buckled itself into a seat and sat ready to fall. The only wild card was my mind—would I be able to keep my guard up? To keep from sliding down the treacherous slope of the L-word? Did I have it in me to control my emotions so my heart didn't end up splattered all over the concrete? I doubted—I doubted hard—but I didn't care anymore. "Yes. I'm sure."

His growl changed to more of a low rumble, almost a purr, and his hands grew more daring as the floors rolled past. Up my thigh and under my skirt, pulling the fabric up, up, up. Slipping underneath the red lace hidden from him to tease where I was already so hot and wet. Where I wanted him so badly.

"Magnus," I gasped, arching into his touch. Needing so much more. So much.

37

"Once I have you, I'm never going to let you go."

If only that were true. The elevator came to a stop, and I grabbed his arms. Pulling myself away from him. "You'll have to catch me first."

He reared back, looking shocked. The elevator doors opened. I laughed and raced through them, having no idea which way to go but running for the fun of it. Wanting him to chase me a little. Needing to break the tension with something lighthearted. What I should have remembered was the old adage about never running away from a dog. Magnus charged after me like a man possessed, catching up fast, grabbing me by the arm, and yanking my back against his chest before picking me right up off the ground.

"My girl is being naughty. As if I wouldn't have caught you, beautiful."

I wrapped my arms around his neck, still laughing. "I wanted you to."

"Good. Because the idea of letting you slip away from me is abhorrent to my wolf and me."

Magnus carried me into his room, barely even slowing down to unlock the door. I couldn't blame him. The growl rumbling continuously against my shoulder had me harried and flushed, focused completely on getting naked. Getting him naked. Getting him inside of me. I wanted that more than anything, more than I'd ever wanted another man. And I wasn't willing to wait.

I pushed out of his arms, dropping to the ground and spinning to face him. Staring down the hungry wolf at the door as I retreated. As I egged him on. "I want you."

He cracked his neck, looking like a man on the edge. "Coco, you'd better stop. My wolf—"

"I want your wolf too."

His growl grew louder, his eyes brightening. Staring hard...at me. "Don't ask for what you can't handle."

He had no idea. I tugged my dress over my head, dropping it to the floor while still staring into his animalistic eyes. Giving him the most challenging eyebrow raise I could come up with. "I'm pretty sure I can handle you just fine, Magnus."

He stalked closer, his lips tipping up into a wicked smile that had my panties soaked in seconds. "I'm sure you can as well. After all, you're my—"

I didn't let him finish his sentence. Instead, I launched myself at him. He grabbed me in midair and yanked me against his chest, meeting my mouth with his in a fiery kiss that had me grinding all over him. Had me whimpering as he held me tightly.

"By the fates," he gasped as he broke the kiss to lay me down on his bed. "I don't know what I did to deserve a woman like you, but I'll keep doing it. Every single day, I'll strive to be worthy of you, Coco. You're everything to me."

Not everything...not his mate.

I pushed that thought aside and stretched out, loving the way his eyes heated as they took in the lingerie I'd been hiding under my dress. The secrets I'd kept concealed under the flirty little sundress. Third dates meant sex, and that meant going all in with just enough red lace and straps to hopefully keep him coming for more. For as long as I could keep him.

"Show me how much you want me," I whispered, tugging him closer. Needing to feel his weight on me. His presence.

Magnus crawled over me, still dressed, sliding between my spread thighs like he belonged there. Was made to be there. "Be sure, beautiful. I won't be able to let go of you once I have you."

"I never want you to let go." Because it would hurt so much if he did. When, not if. When.

Which was so *not* what I needed to be thinking about.

Magnus kissed me deeply, stealing my breath with the way his lips moved against mine, the way he stole my control with his tongue. I helped him take his clothes off, both of us laughing and twisting until there was nothing funny anymore. Until he lay naked on top of me, his hips spreading my legs, his cock hard and heavy against me. Ready. So very ready.

"You're mine, Coco," Magnus said as he thrust inside me. Not slow, not gentle—direct. One push, all the way in. And I loved it. Loved the way he stretched me, the way he filled me so full. The way he owned me with his thrusts.

If only...

Magnus pulled completely out of me, disappearing down my body.

"What the...oh god." His tongue. Sweet heavens above, the man's tongue might as well have been a weapon with the way he used it against my clit. Lashing, licking, flicking...teasing me higher and higher. Feasting on me as he pushed my legs up and out, opening me for him. Pinning me like a butterfly. His fingers soon joined the mix, his growl vibrating through me as he pressed in deep. As he curled those digits and hit a spot that had me gasping for air.

As he made me come with just his mouth and hand.

"Good girl," he said, climbing back over me and reaching to grab a condom out of his wallet. "Fuck, I want to come inside you so badly, but I know where that will lead."

To a commitment he couldn't make with me. "I'm on the pill."

He groaned long and deep, running his hand up and down the length of himself as he sat back on his knees. "Don't tempt me, woman. I'd say fuck it and ride you bare, but I can't. Not yet."

I didn't know why not, but it didn't matter. All that did—the only thing I cared about—was the way his hand danced along his cock. The way I had him trapped within my legs. He gave me a snarling growl and then he was back, hovering over me as he kissed me deeply. Thrusting into my pussy with a grunt and a growl that made me want to die. And the sounds between us... My god, had I ever been so wet? Had I ever been so turned on and ready? So needful for more?

I didn't think so.

Magnus groaned, moving faster. Snapping his hips into mine as he lost that hefty control. "Fucking heat. By the fates, beautiful—you're going to burn me up."

But I felt as if I were the one on fire—inside and out. Everything about this man set my soul on fire, had my heart blazing as he moved closer. As we came together. And his body—good lord, the man was made of muscle, all lithe and trim with a scattering of dark gray hair across his chest and arms leading down to the base of his cock as it disappeared inside of me. I couldn't stop touching, feeling, looking, tasting. Every inch. Every dip and curve. I wanted to learn them all. To memorize them. To never let them go.

"Mine, mine, mine," he chanted, and I lost myself. To the heat, to the stretch, to the feel of him against me. The words I dreamed of hearing for real. I lost my mind as my body convulsed underneath him, pleasure breaking over me like never before.

"Yours, Magnus. All yours."

And I was. The walls I'd convinced myself to build had crumbled at some point, and I was a mass of feeling, emotional want. I was totally and completely his. Even though I knew he'd break my heart soon enough. I was his in a way I'd never experienced. In a way I knew would linger long after he was gone. I was his. Period.

And I was doomed.

6

MAGNUS

Coco had an ass meant for touching, stroking, smacking, biting, and rutting against. I'd done all of that last night. I woke up hard and so very needful, so I locked her into my arms and pressed my aching cock against that phenomenal ass. Rocked against the softness on my journey for some sort of release as she slowly woke up. I wanted to roll her over and slide deep inside her again, wanted to cover myself in her scent and her in mine before we started our days, but my mate was human. I needed to take it easy on her. Needed to be soft and gentle sometimes. I'd fucked her hard last night. She needed a break.

Her hand landed on my hip, tugging me closer as she circled her hips into mine. "I have a better place for that."

Okay, so…she didn't need a break, after all.

Before I could respond, Coco rolled and pushed me over. I ended up flat on my back, staring up at the ceiling…until she settled herself over my hips. Then my eyes locked on her naked body over me. The way her wild hair hung over her shoulders, half covering those strawberry-tipped breasts. How her thighs spread over my hips, straddling me. How her body moved as she began rubbing all the delicious heat of her pussy over my cock.

Mine. But I couldn't say that. Not yet. I'd almost told her a few times last night. Almost let the cat—or wolf—out of the bag. I had to hold back. The thought of losing her, of scaring her until she pulled away, gutted me inside. I could resist the mating pull a little longer. Even if it half killed me to do so.

I grabbed her waist and tugged her up, dragging that delicious pussy all over my cock. "Well, good morning, beautiful."

Her smile stunned me, made me lose all sense of time and space. Where was I? What was I supposed to be doing other than making her look at me like that every second of every day? Why wasn't I inside her yet?

"I need to take a shower before heading into the bakery." She reached over and grabbed a piece of white fabric from somewhere on the mattress before pulling it over her head. My shirt. The woman wore my clothes and was completely covered in my scent. My wolf was happy. Well, as happy as he could be while lying flat on his back with someone over him. Alpha issues translated to mates, apparently. Still, I'd let Coco do anything to me so long as she looked that happy.

I grabbed her thighs, the growl in my chest unavoidable. "I think we should take one together. Save water."

She bit her lip and fell forward, her arms on my shoulders as she rolled those wicked hips over mine. As she moved just enough for my cock to shift down, to slide against the opening to her heaven. For the tip to slip inside her luscious heat. I couldn't resist the need to thrust. Just a little one because she was playing some sort of game that I definitely wanted to see the end of. But I wanted inside her as well. I wanted it all.

"Magnus," she gasped, as if she hadn't been expecting me to take advantage of her position. The girl would learn—I wasn't noble enough to behave. I took what I wanted most of the time, and at that moment, I wanted her body and mine to join. So I teased her with subtle strokes, with tiny movements of my hips. Just enough to stretch her opening with the end of my cock. Not enough to seat myself.

Coco had other ideas. As I rocked forward, she pushed back, taking all of me inside in one move. I nearly came right there. Nearly released a snarl that would have been heard all across town as I sank my teeth deep into her flesh to solidify our bond. My mate wanted me enough to seize control, needed my cock to satisfy her and wasn't afraid to just take it. And I would satisfy her—many times over if I got my way—as soon as I got over the shock of her heat enveloping me and the soft, suction-like pull of her pussy as she moved her body back and forth on mine.

So fucking perfect.

"Use me, beautiful. I want to watch you get yourself off." I slipped a hand between us to rub circles over her clit—something that drove her absolutely wild, as I'd learned last night. Once I had her moaning, keening and rocking and fucking herself on my hand and cock, I could only stare. Could only sit back and absorb every facial expression my mate displayed. I wanted to savor each one, to memorize every move and twitch that brought her closer to her pleasure. To her breaking point. I wanted to learn her signs and tells so I could keep her sated and happy in my bed. Our bed.

And when she came, when she caught her breath and squeezed her eyes shut as her body pulsed around me, I followed. Unable not to. Filling her as I groaned and gripped her hips hard. Wanting to fill her with more than just my come. My teeth lengthened, and my wolf howled in need of that one final mating bite. The big one that would join us forever. The unbreakable linking of our souls.

I couldn't deal with that just yet, though. I still hadn't told her she was my mate. I needed to, wanted to especially in that moment—with her all warm and sated, damn-near boneless as she lay on top of me with my cock still inside her. Yeah, I wanted to tell her everything, but I'd seen shifters dealing with human mates over the years. The shifter always seemed to end up chasing the skittish human at some point, and some never caught them. I didn't want to chase Coco. Well, I did. In fact, the idea of her happily running naked through the forest with me behind her appealed in many, many ways. But that likely wouldn't happen right away. She'd panic, pull away, and my wolf and I would be crushed. I'd spend every waking moment trying to win her back, but there was always a chance that she'd leave for good. That she wouldn't feel the same pull to me that I felt to her, and I'd lose her.

Not fucking happening.

"I need to shower, but my legs won't work," Coco said, her hair tickling my chest. Reminding me that I had her—even if only for right then, I *had* her. I just needed to figure out how to keep her.

I chuckled and grabbed her by the thighs before sitting up. "C'mon, my heart. I'll help you stand up so you can get ready for the day."

Not that I was thrilled she was going to wash off my scent. I'd just have to make sure she was covered in it again before she left. Such a hardship.

One shower, an abbreviated blow job that nearly had my wolf claws breaking through my skin, and a quick fuck against the tile walls, and we were ready to start our day. Well, mostly ready.

"Why are you doing that?" Coco swatted at my hip, laughing as she tried to move away from me. We stood at the elevator bank in the hallway, already outside of the little bubble of happiness we'd created in my room. I wanted to drag her back down the hall again, but she needed to work. I wasn't letting her move out of my arms, though. I fully intended to make sure every male in town knew she was mine, starting with all the shifters. That meant making sure she smelled like me.

"I don't want to stop touching you." I held her against my chest, rubbing my body on hers as she laughed. I couldn't help myself—she was so delicious and perfect and *mine*. I'd do anything to keep her that way.

Coco spun in my arms, looking up at me with a radiant smile on her face. Happy. My mate was truly happy. "Are you trying to make me smell like you?

I froze, unable to answer her. She was human—how did she know about scenting? "Yes, I am. Is that a problem?"

She shook her head before rising up to brush her lips against mine. "I think it's adorable that you want to let the other males know to stay away."

Adorable. Not what I was going for, but I'd take it. "You're mine, Coco. I don't share."

Her smile fell a little, but I was already in motion. Already pressing my lips to hers and slicking my tongue between them to capture her mouth. Already losing what little control I had around her. I had her pressed against the wall, my hand gripping her thigh and my cock trapped between us as I kissed her as if I were starving for her. And maybe I was. Maybe I needed to tell her how much.

No more fucking maybes.

"Coco," I said as I broke the kiss, resting my forehead against hers. "I need you to know—"

"Dad?"

My kid had the worst fucking timing in the world.

"Good morning, Nico." I tore myself away from Coco, turning to face the man I was only beginning to know and the woman he was soon to marry. "Good morning to you as well, Fiona. Ready for the rehearsal dinner tonight?"

But Nico wasn't looking at me. His eyes had locked on Coco, the surprise on his face turning my blood cold.

"Nico—"

"Wait… Coco, you're dating my dad?"

My wolf responded to his tone, to the volume with which he spoke to our mate. To the way she trembled against my side. My growl rumbled through the hall, but Nico ignored me. The ignorance of a wolf shifter raised only in the human world.

"She's dating my dad," he said to Fiona, shaking his head. "I mean, man…talk about sloppy seconds."

There was no holding back. I grabbed Nico by the collar and rushed forward, slamming his back against the wall when I reached it. My growl turned to a snarl, and my teeth lengthened. Son or not, he had no right to embarrass my girl that way. Not happening. "You are talking about my mate, son. I would choose my words carefully if I were you."

A door opened down the hall, and I looked up just in time to see Coco disappear into the stairwell. Running. From me. Just as I'd feared she would at some point. Fuck.

"Magnus, please put him down," Fiona said, sounding bored and tired. She'd grown up with shifters—she knew better than to make any sort of comments about another's mate. She also didn't deserve to have my son's past sexual history thrown in her face.

"You have not earned the mate the fates have given you, and I seriously doubt you ever will," I said, a growl rolling through my voice. "And you certainly have not earned the attention of mine."

I set him back on his feet as he stuttered and coughed.

"Jesus, Dad. I didn't mean anything by it."

Fiona's eye-roll might as well have been my own. "You only say that when you get caught being a jackass. You owe your father and Coco an apology." She gave me a small smile. "Congratulations on finding your mate. She seems like a really nice girl."

I grunted, still staring at my son. The man I didn't know well enough yet. The one I'd found out was part of me by accident. The one I was only starting to build a relationship with.

The man who likely knew more about my mate than I did. "Tell me everything about Coco and your relationship. Now."

7

COCO

His dad. Magnus was Nico's dad. I couldn't wrap my brain all the way around that one. Or wouldn't—it was totally embarrassing to have been caught in the hallway after sleeping with Magnus by his son whom I'd also slept with. Two generations…linked to me through sex.

I was going to puke.

I hadn't gone to work, instead, texting Ginger that I wasn't coming in. Not until later—after the storefront had closed. I'd finish the damn macarons for tonight from my own kitchen if I had to, but there was no way I was facing the town or the possibility of seeing either Magnus or Nico. I couldn't.

And Magnus…I'd really felt something for him. Something deep down in my soul. What we'd done hadn't just been sex, but that didn't matter anymore. I'd slept with his *son*. He'd never speak to me again. And even if he did, I couldn't be with him. Not after that. I couldn't come between the two men. I couldn't have Magnus because I'd had Nico.

Fate was a cruel, cruel bitch.

"You had better be dressed," Ginger hollered, storming into my bedroom with a frown on her pretty face. "What is this? What's happening? Why are we hiding? What did that man do?"

Madeleine crept in after her, much quieter than our brash sister. Looking more concerned than mad. "What happened, Coco?"

I grabbed a pillow and shoved it over my face, unable to look at them. "He's Nico's dad."

Ginger snatched the pillow away, climbing onto the mattress to hover over me. "Try that without this thing in the way."

I swallowed hard and closed my eyes for just a moment. "Magnus is Nico's dad."

Silence. Neither woman said a word for a solid ten seconds as they stared at me. It was Madeleine who broke it, surprisingly.

"That explains so much."

I bolted upright. "How does that explain anything other than that I slept with father and son?"

She shrugged one delicate shoulder. "It just does. Nico was sort of a jerk, and I never understood what you saw in him. But Magnus—he's kind and caring and absolutely perfect for you. Maybe there's a part of Magnus in Nico that was what attracted you to him."

Ginger snorted. "Half his DNA is from Magnus—that's more than a part."

"It doesn't matter," I said, trying to cover myself with the quilt but having to fight Ginger for it. "It's done. Over. Nico can run off and marry Fiona, and Magnus can go back to…wherever he's from. And me? I can sit here and be humiliated for the rest of my life. And celibate. Maybe I should join a nunnery."

Madeleine scrunched her nose. "We're not Catholic."

"And you look horrible in hats." Ginger sat down beside me with a huff. "Look, so you slept with father and son. It's not like you knew they were related or you did it intentionally. It's nothing more than a weird coincidence. You'll forget about it in no time."

But I didn't want to forget—if I did, that would mean I'd be forgetting about Magnus. About the way he had made me feel last night. About how much my heart beat just for him. The very thought broke something inside of me.

"I really, really liked him," I whispered as the first tears began to fall.

Madeleine settled in beside me and patted my hair, offering comfort in her own quiet way. "We know, Coco."

No promises. No empty words like *he'll come back* or *maybe things will work out*...because they both knew how unlikely that was. And so did I.

"I can't face them. If they come to the bakery, I won't—"

A sob ripped from my chest, a picture of Magnus looking at me with disgust slamming into my head. No, I couldn't face them. Couldn't deal with Nico's mocking or Magnus' disgust. None of it. I simply didn't have it in me to stand strong right then.

"No one is saying you have to face them at all, sweetie," Ginger said as she grabbed my hand. "I wouldn't even ask you to come to work, but we need you. The rehearsal dinner is tonight, and there's no way we can get the macarons done without you."

"Please," Madeleine added. "I can't make the filling taste like you do, and Ginger has no patience for almond flour anything."

"It's true. Almond flour is bullshit and hates me. All my macarons crack and dry out worse than some old spinster's vag." Ginger inched closer, cocking her head and looking serious. "We need you at the bakery or else we'll fail at this job. You can hide in the back—no customer service required. But please come make the cookies."

I had two pleading sisters and a heart that wouldn't stop aching no matter what. Maybe being busy would do me some good. "Fine. But no customers—none. I don't care who it is."

"Pinkie swear," Ginger said, holding out her pinkie as we'd done since we were kids. The three of us joined fingers, dissolving into giggles as we tried to hold on to one another.

Maybe this day wouldn't be so bad, after all.

Four hours, three hundred macarons, and way too much red food coloring later, and I had to admit—my day hadn't been too bad. Save for being caught post-sex by my date's son whom I'd also slept with and the fact that my heart was completely shattered from the idea of never seeing Magnus again. But, hey—I had my iPod blaring in my ears, and all the trays of pink macarons looked amazing. What more could I ask for?

Yes, that *was* actually the saddest thing I'd ever thought in my entire life. Positive thoughts and all that.

Misty popped back to check on me a few times, but my sisters shooed her away to the customer area. They were taking their promise of me not seeing anyone seriously—and that anyone included our foxy customer service person, apparently. That was fine with me—I wasn't ready to explain what had happened.

Of course, no plan ever went perfectly. Especially not when dealing with a wily fox. At one point, as I was lining up pink macarons to place into the delivery boxes, a hand appeared in front of my face and ripped out my earbuds.

"Hey," I squeaked.

Misty stood on the other side of the prep counter looking almost livid. "What the hell happened?"

I glanced around, not seeing my sisters. Of course.

"The duo of fox blockers is dealing with a wedding cake crisis," she said, looking almost smug. "You and I are alone, and you're going to tell me what happened before I assume the worst and call for my family to hunt down that dog."

I loved her protectiveness, I really did, but it was so misplaced. And I *so* wasn't telling her anything. I couldn't. "Nothing happened. I don't know what you mean."

The glare Misty shot me practically sizzled. "Oh, really? You have no idea what might have made you hide out like some sort of felon on the run from the law? Or what caused your sisters to block me from the back of the bakery because, and I quote, 'Coco can't deal with life right now.'"

Okay, that was a little much. "I can deal with life."

"But not me. And not Magnus."

My heart lurched at his name. "There's nothing to deal with there."

If her eyebrow rise could talk, it would be saying "Bitch, please."

"Really? Then why has he shown up at our door five times today, looking like a man whose heart's been shattered? Why does he keep coming back even after I told him you won't see him?"

Won't…couldn't was the better word. I couldn't face him after that morning. Couldn't deal with seeing the disgust on his face. Couldn't deal with having to listen to him end whatever it was we had. I simply couldn't. "He'll leave town after the wedding. Everything will settle back down."

Her face—always so expressive—went slack. "Leave town."

"Yes, leave town. Look, Misty—I know things are a little weird today, but I don't want to talk about it. I just want to get these cookies for tonight's rehearsal dinner finished so I can go home and drown myself in a hot bath, a bottle of Malbec, and maybe some sort of ridiculously sugary ice cream. Is that too much to ask?"

"You have no idea," she said with a shake of her head. "He won't stop coming to see you, and he's certainly not just leaving town. I'm going to kill him for not telling you."

"Telling me what?"

She pursed her lips. "It's not my place to say."

"Then skip it altogether because it doesn't matter. I screwed up. Either that or your beloved fates have a really sick sense of humor. Either way, it's over. There's no coming back from…what happened."

We stood staring at one another, silent…battling with our eyes. I refused to give in, and she refused to back down. At least until the ding of the bell announcing a customer chimed through the shop. Pulling the boss card might have been a low blow, but I took it.

"I think you're needed up front."

Misty scowled but turned, walking away without another word. At least not until she made it to the doors separating the kitchen from the sales floor.

"He won't stop, he won't leave, and that pain gnawing at your chest will only get worse. You don't want to tell me what happened…fine. But you will eventually. When you're ready, I'll still be here for you even if you are being a bit of a jerk right now."

I crumpled the second the door swooshed closed behind her. I *was* being a jerk. But I was hurt and embarrassed, and the last thing I wanted to do was relive this morning over and over again. Better to forget—to push everything out of my mind and let myself fall into my work.

Misty was right about one thing—someday, I'd tell her what happened. But she was wrong too. No way would Magnus keep coming after me. He had an entire life outside of Kinship Cove to live. He wouldn't give that up for me.

Especially not after finding out about Nico and me.

But I couldn't focus on all that. Instead, I slipped my earbuds back in and cranked up the volume. I still had cookies to finish. A job to do. The perfect distraction from the shambles my life had become.

Macarons to the rescue.

8

COCO

The day dragged by, the macaron-building only keeping my mind off the mess of my life for a few hours. Once done, I had nothing to do but wallow. My head and heart refused to let me ignore how much I missed Magnus, which was silly. I'd only known him two days—not even a full forty-eight hours yet. I should have been able to forget about him and deal with the lingering humiliation of being caught performing the walk of shame. By my current partner's son. Who was also my ex-boyfriend.

I mean, really...that *really* seemed to be where my attention should sit.

Instead, all I could think about was the fact that Magnus had come to the bakery looking for me. That he had wanted to talk to me after everything. That he hadn't stopped showing up and trying to reach me. Well, he hadn't stopped until it was time for the rehearsal dinner to start. Of course.

I sat in the kitchen of the bakery with the lights dimmed and the space silent. My sisters had already left for the night, along with Misty. They'd delivered the macarons and groom's cake—a sculptured confection of a wolf howling, of course—to the banquet facility where the rehearsal would be held. They'd probably made it home hours ago. Me? I'd stayed at the bakery, claiming a need to clean up. I'd really just wanted a little time to wallow before I had to deal with my empty house.

I was a full-time wallower, apparently.

The ringing of the kitchen phone interrupted the quiet I'd been sitting in. I almost didn't answer it—we were closed, after all—but not a lot of people had that particular number. Customers called the phone out front. It could have been one of my sisters needing something, which was the only reason I even considered picking it up. Still, I looked at the phone sideways as I approached it. I'd never dreaded a hunk of plastic more.

Deep breath. "Cake-ily Ever After Bakery, this is Coco. How can I help you?"

"Oh, thank the fates. Coco, it's Misty."

She sounded harried. That couldn't be good. "What's wrong?"

"The groom's cake isn't here."

It took me a solid five seconds for her words to make sense. All thoughts of Magnus and my own personal shame disappeared, and I rocketed into work mode.

"What do you mean, it isn't there?" I was in motion before I finished my ridiculous question, heading for the walk-in refrigerator at the back of the kitchen.

"Um, that it *isn't here*? As in, not at the banquet hall. I was making sure the macarons were set up on the trays the bride requested when I noticed the blank space in the display. I've looked all over for it—it's not here."

"That's impossible. Ginger was supposed to—"

What Ginger was supposed to do was take the cake over before heading home for the night. What she'd failed to do was take the cake over before heading home for the night. The wolf sat in the refrigerator, looking just as real and regal as ever. Madeleine had outdone herself—Ginger had failed miserably. "Shoot."

"It's there, isn't it?"

I sighed and grabbed the cake, carrying it to the packaging station.

"Yeah. It's not even boxed. What was Ginger thinking?"

"Pretty sure she was thinking about that dragon shifter she met."

Had I been dropped into an alternate reality? "What dragon shifter?"

"It's not important. Look, the rehearsal is starting soon, and people are going to notice a giant empty space on the sweets table. You need to get that cake here."

Work mode—deactivated. Me showing up at that building was so not happening. "No. I can't be there. You'll have to come get it."

"There's no time. There's barely enough time for you to put that cake in your car and drive over here."

She wasn't wrong, but still...I couldn't do it. I shook my head and closed my eyes, trying to drum up enough courage to face Nico and Magnus, to be seen. To walk into a room where almost everyone I knew would be milling around, knowing some of them likely had heard what I'd done. Kinship Cove was a small town, and people talked. Secrets didn't stay buried for long.

"Coco, please," Misty pleaded. "Your business needs you to pull on your big-girl panties and bring that cake over here."

I swallowed hard, whispering, "I can't face them."

"You don't have to, honey. Come in through the back—I'll meet you in the kitchen and take the cake. Less than a minute from when you show up to when you leave."

Less than a minute. To ensure the success of the business we'd built from nothing. Ginger may have screwed up, but that was likely an accident. If I didn't come through, it would be on purpose. I couldn't do that to myself or my sisters. "Yeah. Okay, I think I can do that."

"Good." She sounded so relieved. "Now, box up that cake and move your ass. You'll be cutting it close."

"On it." I hung up and got to work, making sure the cake was protected in a large, sturdy box before carrying it out to my car. The darn thing weighed a ton, so the process wasn't easy on my own. Still, I managed. And then I was off. Heading for the place where my ex was marrying his fated mate while his father—my current lover—looked on.

Not unusual at all.

I pulled up to the back door of the hall some twenty minutes later with one wolf cake latched securely in my passenger seat. My stomach churned as I hopped out of the car—less than a minute. That's all the time I needed to spend there. I couldn't possibly run into Magnus in under a minute. Not even if I wanted to.

And I sort of wanted to.

I missed him.

I was also apparently a glutton for punishment.

"Drop off the cake and go home. Less than a minute." I practically chanted to myself as I grabbed the cake and headed for the kitchen entrance. The cake was heavy, though, and so was the door. I had to kick the metal surface in the hopes that Misty was waiting for me on the other side. It swung open a second later, and I hurried through, utterly focused on hanging on to the blasted cake until I made it to the prep counter twenty feet away.

"Thank god you're here," I said once I was fully in the kitchen space. "Let me just set this down so we can look at it, then I'm heading home. I want to get out of this place before anyone sees me."

"But you look so pretty in your kitchen whites, Coco."

I stumbled, nearly dropping the cake as I spun to face the person who'd opened the door. Who wasn't Misty. Who was the last shifter I wanted to see...ever.

"Nico."

His lips quirked into a cocky sort of grin as if he thought the breathy way I said his name had something to do with wanting him. It didn't— the cake was really fricking heavy. I set the behemoth down on the counter and looked around, hoping Misty would appear from thin air. Or that the floor would open up and swallow me whole. Or for a horde of zombies to come racing in to distract the shifter.

No such luck.

"So this is the groom's cake." Nico sidled closer. "Did you make it?"

"Madeleine handles the cakes." Not that I should have to tell him that —he'd heard me talk about the bakery enough to know how our business worked. Not that he'd spent any time there. In fact, Magnus had spent more time in the kitchen in two days than Nico had in months. A heart-stopper of a realization and one that only pushed me to want this over with and fast.

I opened the box and stepped back, still proud of what my sisters had accomplished with the cake even if the man looking was one I had no interest in interacting with. "Madeleine created this per Fiona's request. I hope it's to your satisfaction."

He hummed, barely sparing a glance for the cake my sister had probably put fifteen hours into. "Well, I was hoping you'd handle everything. For me."

He stabbed me with a look and the sort of smile that had once made my knees weak. Not anymore, though. My feelings for him had long been sitting in the negative column of my mind, and today was no different. I wasn't feeling nostalgic or missing him—I was over it.

The person I was missing was his dad.

"Well..." No words for him or that ridiculous statement. None. "I should get going." I turned and headed for the door. For my escape. "Misty's here and will handle the cake presentation. Congratulations and thank you for using Cake-ily Ever After. If there's anything else you need—"

"I need to know why you chased after my dad."

Ice water. It pumped through my veins. "Excuse me?"

"You heard me." He came up behind me, grabbing my arms and tugging me against his chest. "You miss me that much that you have to go sniffing around the old folks' home?"

I jerked away, that ice water turning to fire in a heartbeat. "Magnus is not old, and I didn't know he was your father when I met him."

"But he is, and it's weird. So how about you just stay the hell away from him, yeah? Not that he'd give you the time of day after I told him all about us."

Oh. Oh no. "You...told him."

Nico shrugged. "He asked about us, so I gave him the full story. How we met, the dates we'd been on, how you liked it when I would bite your nipples while you rode my cock."

Dead. I was dead. As was any chance at reconciling with Magnus. Ever. "That's... Why would you do that?"

Misty rushed through the swinging doors at the far end of the kitchen, looking panicked. At least, until she spotted Nico—then she looked pissed. "Shouldn't you be rehearsing with your mate or something?"

He leaned closer, lowering his voice as he said, "I never was one to share my toys, Coco. And no man likes sloppy seconds."

Misty jumped between us, looking positively fierce in her anger. "Oh, hell no, you don't."

But the damage had been done—he'd told Magnus about us. *Everything* about us. He'd destroyed any chance I might have had. Burned it all to the ground and swept away the ashes. And he knew it.

"Nice guard dog." Nico shot Misty a grin as he backed away. "Good to see you, Coco. The cake looks awesome—I'm sure my dad is going to love it."

He disappeared through the far doors, leaving me alone with Misty.

"Tell me you don't believe that bullshit line."

I licked my lips, unable to speak. Not wanting to remember. I was going to be sick—he'd told Magnus about us. About our sex life. About things that should have stayed between us and never been shared. It had to have been in the last few hours—Magnus had been showing up at the bakery most of the day. He'd been trying to reach me. I'd ignored his texts and calls, and refused to come out of the kitchen, though. I'd...I'd screwed up so badly. Maybe if I would have talked to him first, explained what had happened with Nico and me, maybe he wouldn't have asked. And then Nico wouldn't have been able to sabotage...what? Magnus and I weren't anything to one another. We'd dated a little and had one great night together. There was no long-term commitment there. No promises of a future. There was only food and sex and great company.

And I was going to miss all that so much.

"Coco." Misty reached as if to grab my arm. "What do you want me to do?"

"Nothing," I whispered, taking a step back. Needing to escape. "It doesn't matter. None of this matters."

"What are you saying?"

"I have to go." I sprinted out the door, rushing to my car and hoping to be on the road home before I broke. Before the tears began to fall. Before anyone saw me crying behind the hall where my ex would be celebrating the upcoming wedding to his mate. I didn't want anyone to get the wrong idea—I wouldn't be crying over Nico.

I'd be crying over his dad.

MAGNUS

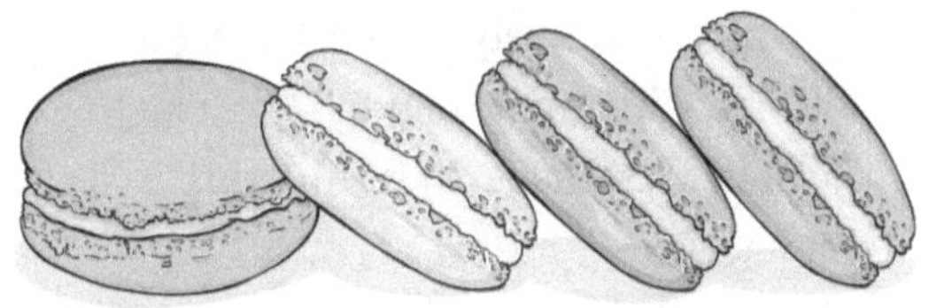

I'd never been so fucking pissed in my life. I'd been fuming all day, ever since Nico had interrupted Coco and me and she'd disappeared. I wasn't mad at Coco, though. Never her. More at myself—at my failure to tell her she was my mate so we could build our bond, at the fact that I couldn't convince her to even talk to me. I knew she was hurting, she had to be, and there was nothing I could do to fix it for her. If I'd told her she was my mate, none of this would have happened. She would have been confident enough in our connection to face down Nico. But I'd failed her by keeping the secret, and now she was suffering because of me.

So, no, I wasn't mad at her—I was raging against a situation that was really of my own making.

The fact that I was trapped at Nico's wedding rehearsal wasn't helping anything either. The banquet hall smelled like Coco. Not completely—not as if she stood in the room with me—but her scent was there. Lingering in the rooms, drifting along on the recycled air through the vents. It would catch me at odd times and yank me out of whatever I was doing. It was also driving me absolutely insane.

As was the man I had recently learned was mine.

"I mean, if you're that desperate, I'll give you my black book of girls. Not like I need it anymore."

My *son* was about to learn what battling with a real wolf shifter meant.

"Nico," I said, biting back a growl. "Drop it. Immediately."

He chuckled, catching the attention of his mate. Fiona was a lovely girl with a good head on her shoulders. She had also been raised in a shifter pack, unlike Nico. I had a feeling she'd be running things for a long time to come, which was likely the best thing for my son. He was a little too *human* at times. Like right then.

"Come on, old man. You have to admit this is more than a little weird. I mean…you had sex—"

The growl I'd been fighting reverberated through the dining room, making the shifters in the room go silent. Good—Nico needed to *hear* me for once. "What Coco and I did is none of your damned business. Do you understand?"

Nico opened his mouth as if to say something, but Fiona stopped him with a sharp, "That's enough."

My son's jaw snapped closed. Not for long, though. "Fiona, I was just—"

"Being an asshole." She stepped right up to him, looking fierce and filled with rage. I could relate. "You're not much of a wolf, Nico. You're not much of a son either—Magnus finally meets his mate after all these years, and you do nothing but try to come between them. That's pathetic. But beyond wolf and son, you're even less of a man and a mate for not thinking about your mate. Where did I go wrong that the fates saddled me with someone like you?"

The room had gone so silent. What was that human saying? You could have heard a pin drop. The shifters could have anyway, but still— silence. Everyone staring with rapt attention at the arguing couple. The ones who were supposed to be walking down the aisle in less than forty-eight hours. Talk about awkward.

When Nico didn't answer Fiona, she spun on her heel and stalked across the room, with Nico chasing after his retreating mate. Thank the fates for small miracles. I'd been putting up with his shit all damn day, had been stuck running back and forth from the hotel to the bakery to try to talk to Coco while helping Nico get ready for the wedding weekend. Nothing about this day had been easy, but hearing anything about my mate being with another man had definitely made things worse. And having to smell her without being able to see her, to touch her, to know she was okay, was agony.

I spent the next hour shaking hands, smiling, and generally being the father of the groom for a roomful of people I had no interest in dealing with. The shifters were giving me a wide berth, perhaps sensing the level of stress my wolf felt at being kept away from his mate. Or maybe I had one hell of a scowl on my face. I couldn't tell anymore.

"You really fucked this up," a woman said. Not just any woman—the one from the bakery. The fox shifter who'd been playing defense all damned day. And she smelled so much like my Coco, I nearly whimpered.

"Where is she?"

Misty shook her head, keeping her eyes on mine and looking pissed as hell. "She's not ready for you yet."

A growl slipped out. One I had to swallow back. I didn't want to upset my only link to Coco, didn't want to lose the opportunity Misty's arrival placed in my lap. So I pushed my pride as far down as I could, and I did the only thing I could. I asked for help. "What can I do?"

"Well, first, you can kick Nico's ass for opening his mouth. I thought she was getting better, that she was close to breaking. But then the dick-nozzle—sorry, I shouldn't insult your son—"

"It's fine. Dick-nozzle seems appropriate, given the situation."

"Good. So, dick-nozzle catches her in the back room and tells her no man likes sloppy seconds."

My heart nearly stopped. The only thing keeping it beating was the intense need to destroy Nico. Son or not, a man didn't get to speak that way to my mate. "I'll kill him."

"Yeah, but that won't get you Coco back, so let's tuck the killing away."

Not an easy task. "Fine. What else did he say?"

She shrugged, her lips pursed as if she'd just taken a bite of something rancid. "Something about not wanting others to play with his toys."

"Coco is *not* a toy."

"Well, no shit. Glad you're keeping up with me, dog." She leaned over and grabbed a couple of pink macarons from the sweets table, handing me one. "Eat that. Coco made it."

That was reason enough to eat the whole lot. I took a bite of the cookie. Sweet, crisp, slightly fruity—the cookie was an amazing feat of baking. It was also practically a piece of my mate. I could almost taste her in the almond flour, smell her in her filling. No wonder I kept catching whiffs of her throughout the hall—she'd left her scent on the cookies. I wanted to gorge myself on the macarons to hang on to whatever part of her I could. I also wanted to flip the table the cookies sat on and chase after my mate. Such a strange reaction to a cookie.

"They're delicious," I said, staring at the display of pink circles in confusion. Devour or destroy. Devour or destroy.

"You trash those cookies, and Coco will kill you."

Decision made. I tore my eyes away from the display, catching Misty's wink. "You sure do seem to have my number, fox."

"I've seen enough wolves meet their mates to know exactly how stupid they get about them."

Mate. My mate. Whom I'd failed. Well, fuck, the fox might want to skin me alive once I admitted my failings. Time to man up. "I didn't tell Coco that she was my fated mate."

Misty didn't look surprised in the least. "Yeah, I figured that out when Nico was able to get under her skin so easily. She has no idea how serious you are about her because you chose not to tell her this vital piece of information that affects the rest of her life." Misty's eyebrow raise might as well have been knives slicing through my heart. "You should have told her the first day. What's wrong with you?"

What was wrong with me? I'd spent a hundred years alone, growing older in my appearance as my mated brethren stayed young. I'd assumed the fates had forgotten about me, had chosen not to give me the gift of a mate. I'd seen matings go right and so very wrong, and I was terrified I'd screw up mine now that I had finally found the woman meant for me.

But that was a lot to admit to a woman I didn't really know, so I stuck with something she could understand. "She's human."

That earned me an eye-roll. "And she's lived in a shifter town her whole life. She knows exactly how these things work. She was also raised with shifters as family members—the man she calls uncle is the Kinship Cove pack alpha, for crying out loud. She's seen exactly what happens when a shifter meets their mate, and you didn't do any of the things she would have expected. You kept this huge revelation a secret from her to protect her but ended up hurting her instead. Right now, she's dealing with an intense pull to be with you, the fact that she might have ruined any chance with you because of her past, and the assumption that you're going to leave her behind when you meet your fated mate. Because that's happened to her three times."

Oh, my poor Coco. "By the fates."

"Exactly. You need to tell her the truth. That you're her mate, that nothing else matters but your bond, and that you're not simply going to vanish one day when someone better comes along."

There would never be anyone better. Not for me. "I'll tell her all that. Everything. The second I see her, I will lay my heart on the floor. There's just one problem."

Back to the raised eyebrow. Just one. "What's that?"

"She won't talk to me."

Misty's lips turned up in a wicked sort of grin. Just what I'd expect from a sneaky fox. "That's where I come in."

10

COCO

I swear, I wasn't staring at the clock. I just happened to notice when it turned from 7:59 to 8:00. Just happened to be looking at the cable box as I was pressing buttons on my remote and trying to find something—anything—to watch that wouldn't remind me of Magnus. I wasn't intentionally watching for when the actual dinner part of the rehearsal dinner had been scheduled to start. And even if I were, I'd never admit it.

Frustrated, I pressed the off button and threw the remote across the couch. The neighborhood was too quiet, everyone seemingly at the banquet hall to celebrate the impending nuptials of Nico and Fiona. Whatever—I was happy for them to have found their happily ever after. Mine? Well…I was pretty sure I'd lost any chance of living it out. I shouldn't have felt that way—Magnus and I had only known each other a few days—but something deep inside me told me he was it. My one. My lobster.

Ooh, maybe I could find some old *Friends* reruns.

Wait…no. With my luck, it would be the "we were on a break" ones. No. Darn that Ross.

My phone buzzed on the table, and I reached for it more out of habit than anything else. Misty was calling—not texting or Instagramming or WhatsApping, but calling. So weird. I swiped to answer anyway.

"If there's something wrong with that wolf, you're going to have to call someone else. I've surrendered to yoga pants and Ben & Jerry's already."

"There's definitely something wrong with that wolf, but you're the only person who can fix it."

That...wasn't Misty. Tingles shot through my body, every nerve coming awake at once. Magnus. On Misty's phone. I didn't know what to say, so I said nothing.

"Coco." Magnus' thick, deep voice made me tremble, and I was pretty sure a whimper even escaped me. Maybe he had been the one who whimpered. No, that was silly. It had to be me. He wouldn't—

"Coco, beautiful, open the door."

"What door?"

"Your front door."

I headed to the front hall almost on autopilot. Not wanting to obey but unable not to. Nothing made sense anymore except Magnus was talking to me and I didn't want him to stop. Ever. "You want me to open my front door?"

"Yes, beautiful. Open it."

"Why?"

"Because I can't wrap my arms around you unless you do."

Oh god. Magnus was here. On my porch. I walked faster, hurrying toward the white slab of wood and glass between us. Nearly crying when I saw his shadow through the curtains. Magnus. Here.

But then the memories of earlier—that morning at the hotel, running into Nico, sloppy seconds—came back, and opening that door seemed impossible. "What if I don't want to?"

"You do," he said, sounding so damn sure of himself while I trembled and fought to keep from panicking at the idea of seeing him. Of losing him. Of everything.

"What if I *can't* open it?"

"If you want me to role-play being the big, bad wolf and blowing your door down, we can do that. Your neighbors might not like it, though."

I pressed my hand against the glass, a tired smile pulling at my lips. "My neighbors are all at the rehearsal dinner. Where you should be."

"No, beautiful. I'm right where I need to be."

Perfect words. Exactly what I'd thought I'd needed. And yet... "Magnus?"

"Yes, Coco?"

"I'm too afraid to open it," I whispered.

"Oh, honey. There's absolutely nothing to be afraid of, but I understand. Why don't you step away from the door for me? Go press your back to the wall by the staircase."

I did as I was told, again unable not to obey him. Not sure why I couldn't just reach down and turn the little lock that would allow him entry. But I couldn't—let him in or ignore his instructions, even though his instructions included opening the door.

I was a mess.

Not as much as Magnus, though. The door flew open a second after my back hit the wall, and he was there—all big and bold and looking completely wild. His wolf in control. But what struck me wasn't the animal side of him. It was the dark circles under his eyes as if he hadn't slept in days, the frenzied stare he shot me. The way his hands trembled as he reached for me.

"I've missed you so much today, beautiful."

I'd missed him too. So, so much. But still, I couldn't move. Couldn't surrender to how much I needed him. There was so much wrong between us, so many ways this could end with my heart shattered on the floor like glass. Everything already hurt, and I'd only been around him a few days. How bad would it be if I spent months falling in love with him? If he left me after years because he'd found his mate? I couldn't.

I wouldn't.

"Magnus, I don't think—"

"You're my mate." He stepped toward me, and my world tilted sideways. *Mate?*

"What?"

"I'm so sorry I didn't tell you right away. I assumed you'd need time to get to know me before I laid something so heavy and intense at your feet. I didn't realize you'd been around so many shifters and knew exactly what mating means to us." He inched closer still, keeping his eyes on mine. Pinning me in place with a look. "I didn't know you'd already had your heart broken by a careless shifter who should have known not to play with it."

"Magnus, I—"

"I'm not playing, Coco. Not with you or your heart or any of this. You're my mate, the one person the fates deemed perfect for me. Nothing else matters—not Nico, not your interwoven pasts, not this damned spectacle of a wedding. All that matters is you and me." He ran a finger over my cheek, sending shock waves through my body. "I've waited so damn long to find you. I'll do anything for you."

I almost closed my eyes, almost turned away from him. The joy his words fueled soothed the ache in my heart, but could I trust it? Could I trust *him*? Could we get past...the Nico situation?

I couldn't take that step without knowing. "You're missing your son's rehearsal dinner."

"That's really not..." Magnus sighed, "My son's an asshole sometimes."

"I'm not going to argue with you there."

"He never should have played with your emotions the way he did, and he certainly shouldn't have said one damn word about you and me being together. He has no right to question fate." He inched closer, sharing his warmth with me. Wrapping me in his scent. "His mother was human and raised him like one. I didn't even know he existed until I ran across him on a business trip and recognized my scent within him. The shifter traditions and codes are practically lost on him because he wasn't raised with them, and that doesn't give us a lot in common. I've been trying to build something with him—some sort of relationship— for the last couple of months because I missed so much. Trying hard but... But Coco, he's a grown man. He's not a child who needs me to be in his life every day. I love him because he's a part of me, but I don't know him. And to be honest, what I do know, I don't like very much."

"But he's your son."

"And you're my mate. My future. You're mine forever…if you'll have me."

I reached for him, pulling him against me as I pressed my lips to his. How could I not after all that? I was his mate—his *mate*—which meant we would have a bond humans could only dream of. Strong, powerful, and unbreakable. Everything I could have wanted, I suddenly had in my arms.

And there was no way I was letting it or him go.

Without true intention, the kiss turned wilder. Magnus lifted me by my thighs, pinning me to the wall with his hips and assaulting my pussy with the thick ridge of his cock. I groaned and pulled him closer. Needing more. Not caring that the front door sat open and the world outside could see us. Let them. Most of my neighbors were shifters of one sort or another—they'd understand the draw of mates.

God, I couldn't stop thinking that word. *Mate.*

Magnus finally broke the kiss, his eyes bright as they met mine. His breaths hard and fast as he said, "I've waited over a hundred years to find my mate, and here you are. But I'm not a young man, Coco. I don't have the patience to play the sort of games my son would. So tell me you'll be mine—tell me we can figure this out. Because I've waited a century to claim my mate, and I don't want to wait another second."

This night had become magical. So much better than watching *Friends* reruns. "Yes, Magnus. To everything…yes."

"Thank the fates." He pushed off the wall, carrying me across the hall so he could kick the door closed, and then he was racing up the stairs as I laughed.

"You're going to throw your back out, old man."

His growl made my pussy throb. "I'm not old yet, beautiful. Just experienced. And I'm going to use everything I know about pleasing a woman to keep you satisfied and happy." He set me down when we reached my bedroom door, grinning down at me. "I like these pants, by the way."

"Because they're clingy?"

"No, because they tear easily." With a swipe of his hand, he ripped my yoga pants from my body. Ripped. My. Yoga. Pants.

Some things were not easy to forgive, no matter the motivation. "Those were my favorite."

"I'll buy you more. It's naked time."

Okay, well…that motivation was acceptable. "Yeah?"

"Yeah. How do you feel about me claiming you, Miss Coco?"

"Can't say I've ever been claimed before."

His growl reverberated through the house, his hands rough as he grabbed my hips and pushed me backward into my room. "No, you haven't. And no one will ever get the chance to again. You're mine, Coco. All fucking mine."

Words I'd dreamed about hearing. "Prove it."

So he did. Six times that night. He also claimed me as his mate. His partner forever.

His.

Period.

The snarl he released as he did it—as he bit down on my neck and came inside of me—might have been my most favorite sound ever. I silently vowed to make him growl like that every day for the rest of our lives together.

I might never watch another *Friends* rerun, but life with my mate was worth it. Magnus was worth it.

Unless the episode where Ross refused to pay for delivery on his new couch came on. That one was golden, and I could watch it with my mate. Magnus needed to learn the true meaning of the word pivot.

EPILOGUE

COCO

One month. That was how long it took me to let Magnus move in to my house. Not that we'd really spent much time apart since he'd claimed me as his—we simply made it official at the one-month mark. More so than just him having most of his books, his work computer, his toothbrush, and his almost obscenely large concert T-shirt collection at my place. Those shirts were awesome and so comfy, by the way. I had a bit of an obsession with wearing them—and nothing else. Due to my obsession, Magnus had developed his own obsession with taking them off me slowly. No ripping of the shirts. My yoga pants...well, I wished Amazon had a Subscribe&Save option for those. Magnus always replaced what he destroyed, but still—it added up.

If I didn't like what he did to me afterward, I'd probably be pissed about the pants. But alas...multiple orgasms had a way of erasing any sort of bad mood. So I continued to wear them, and he continued to rip them off me. Good times.

A scratch at the back door pulled me from my job of unpacking some of the kitchen accoutrements his movers had sent along from his former home out east. Two houses coming together meant having to make decisions about what stayed and what didn't. We definitely didn't need doubles of everything, so I'd been tasked with picking what we were keeping and what we were getting rid of. Most of his stuff was going simply because the kitchen was my realm, though he had a way nicer coffee press than mine. We'd be keeping that one.

Another scratch. Shoot. "I'm coming."

It had to be Magnus coming back from his run. His wolf had settled into Kinship Cove nicely, the surrounding forests and mountains giving him places to take off and let his instincts rule. The best part was that he tended to come home from those runs all wired and crazy. Needing me. Wanting to tackle me into bed and spend a few hours making me scream.

I didn't mind that one bit.

I opened the back door and grinned as a large, gray wolf padded inside. A mud-covered one.

"You're dirty, mate. Do I need to wash the wolf or the man?"

Magnus shifted to his human self, standing before me with mud covering most of his skin. So much skin. Naked Magnus was a sight to behold. Still. I might never get over seeing him in all his unclothed glory. Or, at least, I hoped I never would.

"If you're promising me time in the bath with you, then the man is in."

"And if I'm not?"

He growled and grabbed me, rushing across the room until he had my back to the wall. The ridge of his erection rubbed me in all the right places. "You don't want to be naked with me, beautiful?"

"I do, but not in the tub." Water and sex didn't work…not for me at least. Shower sex, yes. Bathtub, not so much.

"You just want me to fuck you against the shower wall."

Guilty. "Any wall will do, really."

His grin had my stomach clenching with want. "Like the one I've got you up against right now?"

"Yes." I leaned in for a kiss, groaning when he licked into my mouth. The man certainly knew how to kiss. Who was I kidding? The man knew how to do everything, including give me multiple orgasms against a wall. And on the floor. And in the shower. And in the bed. The couch. The porch. The car… I was a lucky, lucky human.

"I want you in a bed," he said before kissing his way down my neck. "I want to lay you down and lap that sweet pussy until you scream."

How was I supposed to say no to that? "Okay."

He chuckled, adjusting his hold on me while turning and heading for the stairs. But not before he grabbed my ass cheeks.

And ripped through my yoga pants with his claws.

"Oops," he said, looking completely unrepentant.

"You did that on purpose."

"Of course I did. Those pants make me want to get you naked."

"So give me a chance to take them off."

As he hit the stairs, I wrapped my legs around his hips and rode him as hard as I could. I was a rocking and writhing madwoman chasing my first peak before he even made it to the second floor.

"Patience, my mate," he said with a moan as we reached the top landing.

"You waited so long to find me. Don't make me do the same."

A hundred years he'd been without me—I couldn't wait for thirty seconds. That was okay, though. He liked me needy and craving him. Liked it enough that he laid me on the rug at the top of the stairs and shoved the shirt I wore up to my neck.

"No more waiting," he said before sucking my nipple into his mouth and making me groan. "We were apart for long enough."

We were—him a century, me not nearly as long. But it didn't matter. We'd found each other, and nothing would come between us. Not my past or his, and especially not his son. Nico and Fiona had left Kinship Cove to be closer to her pack. Something Fiona had wanted desperately, and Nico…well, he dealt with it. That woman definitely wore the pants in their relationship.

Me? I tried to wear pants, but Magnus tore them off.

Something I'd never, ever complain about.

SUGAR DRAGON

KINSHIP COVE: MATES & MACARONS

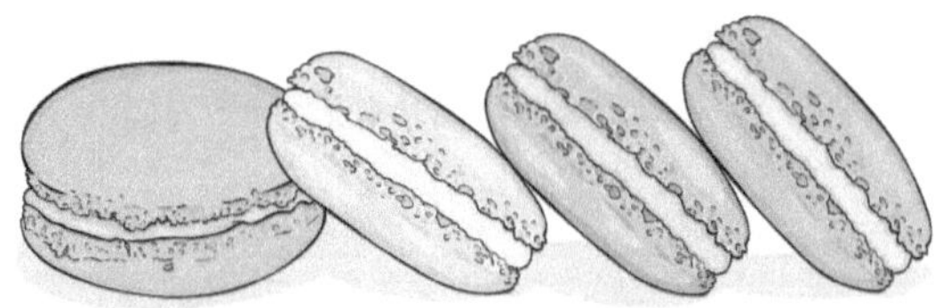

The next delectable treat from the Cake-ily Ever After bakery in Kinship Cove will have your mouth watering. This recipe for happily ever after includes one feisty baker with a short attention span and a dragon who's been hunting her for decades. All of the fated yumminess, none of the guilt.

Try everything once. That was my rule in life, food, and dating. I never missed the opportunity to have a new adventure, play with the right flavor profiles, or spend an evening with the perfect guy. Who needed Mr. Right when there were a thousand Mr. Right Nows running around? So, when a handsome man with heat in his eyes and a little silver in his hair came waltzing into my bakery, I knew I was in trouble.

He's annoying.

He's rude.

He's demanding.

And he just might be the perfect match for me.

Too bad he's a dragon shifter, and dragons don't do the whole fated mate thing. But maybe rules—mine and his—were meant to be broken.

1

GINGER

Bakeries were total guy magnets. Like how dogs and babies attracted women to single men in parks? Sweets and coffee lured the males living in Kinship Cove in droves. Which was why owning and working at the only bakery in town—Cake-ily Ever After, a name that was totally my idea—was such a win in my book. I had my pick of the men in the area, or I'd *had* my pick. Pretty sure I'd already been through the list of all eligible men who weren't either related to me, might-as-well-have-been related to me, or smelly.

Don't judge my aversion to smelly—being a human in a town filled with shifters of various species, the smell factor became a good measuring stick for a man's date-worthiness. Ever met a skunk shifter? How about a ferret? Yeah. My sheets cost too much to risk them to any sort of…lingering odor possibility.

The rest of the men? Dated them. Been there, likely done that. Maybe more than once, though I doubted it. I was a one-and-done gal at heart. I needed new blood, which was why the biggest wedding of the year for the shifter community happening right there in our little town was such a gift. New men from all over the country were showing up in droves, and our bakery was busy as all get-out. I basically had my pick of my favorite type of men—tall, dark, handsome, and only in town for a few days. They were all mine for the taking.

Except for one.

"The handsome man returns." I gave the seriously hot silver fox who'd just walked in the door a grin as I slid a tray of my fan-favorite unicorn cupcakes into the display case. No unicorns were harmed in the making of said cupcakes—and yes, I had to put a sign under the name to keep shifters from worrying. "What brings you back here? And if you say anything other than my sister, I might just castrate you."

I wasn't kidding, even if I did make sure to keep my smile bright. Magnus had strolled into our bakery the day before and taken a liking to my sister Coco. Enough of one for the two of them to have spent an evening together. Just dinner, though, according to her. No sex. Pity that, because the man was fine with a capital F-I-N-E. And not available to me.

He was also a good sport. "Thanks for the warning, but rest assured —I'm here for Coco."

Totally not available. "Good. C'mon back—she's working on the macarons for an event order."

I pulled a piece of waxed paper from the dispenser and grabbed a treat for him, one I knew from experience the men in the town appreciated. My sister could be racking up some serious mattress miles if she'd just put her skills to use. Baking skills. And…others. Both my sisters—the serious Coco and the quiet, slightly dreamy Madeleine— tended to be a little more reserved than me. Coco dated a little, but Madeleine didn't. Me? I made up for both of them. In spades. Just not with the guy Coco seemed to have fallen hard for. Now they just needed to fall a little more…preferably into a bed together. Naked.

And now, I was stuck thinking of the man naked. Of course.

"Breton butter cake." I handed Magnus the buttery bun, sending all my get-my-sister-laid energy toward it. Couldn't hurt, right? "Coco trained with a French pastry chef after culinary school. Her éclairs are to die for, but these are a staple."

He might have groaned at his first bite. Not that I blamed him. "This is delicious."

"It is, and she makes them every day. If you're lucky, she might even make them at home for you." I spun to back through the kitchen door, grinning widely. "Hope you don't mind working out."

His eye roll only made him that much more handsome. Graying hair, a body that screamed I work out louder than an LMFAO song, and a sense of humor? My sister had hit the jackpot with this one. The bitch.

"Hey, cookie lady," I hollered as soon as I'd led Magnus into the realm of flour and butter and all things delicious. Also known as the kitchen. "You've got a delivery."

My poor, harried sister didn't even look up, focusing on a tray of pink macarons instead. "Five minutes. I just need five minutes to put these together before the filling sets up too much and I can't get them to stick right."

Magnus answered her before I could. "I can wait."

Coco's head shot up, her dark eyes looking right at the man behind me. That was likely my cue to...be anywhere other than in their way. I slipped through the kitchen to the hallway that led to our walk-in refrigerator. We used the space for storage mostly—we owned more aluminum than a...well, business that made things from aluminum— though my youngest sister liked to hide out back there as well. I found her just outside of the refrigerator, looking almost lost as she stared at a pegboard covered in icing tips.

"Lost something?"

Her frown deepened. "I can't get the lace drops right on the wedding cake, so I thought I'd try a different tip. Are those new shoes?"

I turned my leg and lifted the heel of one foot. "They are. Do you love them?"

She shook her head, her eyes still not on the hand-painted red and brown clogs I'd spent the last three weeks tracking down. "They're beautiful. How long will they last?"

As in how long would I wear them before I tossed them in the back of my closet, never to be thought about again. "Until the next awesome pair comes along. Like always."

She shook her head. "You're never happy with what you've got. How's the wolf?"

As in the groom's cake. The bride and groom were both shifters—wolf shifters, to be specific—so the couple had requested a wolf howling at the moon to be carved out of cake for their rehearsal dinner. Clichéd but doable. The bride-to-be, a woman named Fiona, had laughed when I'd told her the same thing.

"Honey, we're shifters. Being clichéd is simply part of the game."

And so, a three-dimensional, howling wolf it was.

I'd never tell Coco this, but I liked Fiona. She was strong and independent, sassy and a little wild. She was also saddled with Coco's ex-boyfriend for the rest of her life due to some cosmic fate nonsense. Almost all shifters had to basically drop everything in their life the moment they met their so-called one true mate simply because the universe brainwashed them into thinking that person was perfect for them.

Such bullshit.

But I digress. "The groom's cake is done and tucked into its den for the night. I just need to finish a few dozen more of the cupcakes for the bachelor and bachelorette parties." Boozy cupcakes—rum and pineapple upside-down cupcakes, dark chocolate Rumchata cupcakes, angel food cake with strawberries soaked in vodka. Fiona knew how to throw a party, and I knew how to keep it going. Sugar and booze…perfect.

"So many things to keep track of." Madeleine shook her head and grabbed a tiny silver tip from the massive collection of other shiny silver tips. "I assume Coco's almost done with the macarons."

The cookies my sister was famous for. "Looked like it, though Magnus just showed up to distract her."

"The older man from yesterday?" Older—because he had a little gray at his temples and in his scruff. "They're cute together."

And sweet—he seemed like a nice guy. But… "Too bad they're destined for failure."

Madeleine swiveled on her heel in a slow-motion sort of way. Very horror-movie style. "He can't be that much older than her."

I blinked. Blinked again. "I never said anything about the age difference."

A flood of pink rushed up her neck, staining her cheeks. "Oh. I just assumed… Well, I was wrong. But still, why do you say they're destined for failure? Maybe they'll fall in love."

I hooked a thumb over my shoulder, pointing toward the kitchen on the other side of the wall. "That right there? All the googly-eyed sweetness? That's lust. And lust is fine—more than fine. It's amazing and powerful and perfect for a night or two, but you can't confuse it with love. You'll get your little heart broken if you do."

Head cocked, hazel eyes locked on mine, she pouted. "So, how do you know the difference?"

My younger sister was about as sweet and innocent as they came—but she was also quite likely a virgin. Not a bad thing, but I was far from claiming that status. This was a topic that needed to be handled delicately. "Love is…calm. Patient. It's quiet. All that swept-up excitement isn't love—that's lust trying to get your attention. Love doesn't need to preen."

"But what if it's love at first sight?"

Wannabe princess—not surprising. "That's just for fairy tales and those poor shifters trapped by fated mates. It doesn't exist for us."

Those perfect little bow lips of hers—goddamn, she really was the cutest of the three of us, and I hated her a little bit for it—turned down into a frown again. "I doubt you, Ginger."

I shrugged because, really, what could I say to that? She'd learn. Likely the hard way if she had some sort of Cinderella dream. The handsome prince and a shoe and him sending men to search a kingdom for his lost love. This was the age of Craigslist Missed Connections, Facebook, and dick pics. Who needed the shoe?

I grabbed a tray of cupcakes from the walk-in and headed up front, figuring I could restock the display case for the late morning/early lunch crowd. I'd been on a kick with my cupcakes lately—a savory and sweet one. The tray I'd picked featured maple French toast and bacon cupcakes, strawberry and pretzel ones, and my personal favorite, Frito caramel. I know, putting a corn chip on a cupcake sounded weird, but when said vanilla cupcake was filled with a decadent caramel sauce, capped with caramel buttercream garnished by a sprinkling of Frito crumbs, and finished off with an intact Frito and a caramel sauce drizzle, they became the ultimate sweet and salty treat. You'd eat one. Trust.

Still, the whole sweet and salty kick had been growing old. I needed to try something new, needed to experiment again and focus on something else. I needed my next obsession. Coco liked to say I had a short attention span, but I preferred to think of my desire for new and better and more as growing weary of the usual. The cupcakes could sell by the tray, but eventually, I'd get tired of coming up with a particular sort of combination and want to move on. So I would. I liked seeking new and different ways to explore flavor profiles, to mix and match things that most people would never put together. I liked to keep things fresh and new in both the business and my life. My dad had called me fickle—I considered myself adventurous.

"Oh, thank the fates you're here." Misty—our shop manager, customer service manager, and expert on all things shifter, being that she was one—rushed over as soon as I pushed through the swinging door into the store. "My mom needs me at the restaurant for a few, and I just sent Coco to an early lunch with Magnus. Can you cover for my break so I can go deal with my family before they burn the place down or something?"

Misty's family owned a little diner down the street from us. It was how we'd met her—she'd been working there as my sisters and I had been planning our business over coffee and homemade pie. She'd sort of hired herself when we'd finally opened, which had worked out surprisingly great for us. We baked, she sold the stuff, and everyone made a little money putting smiles on people's faces. Total win.

She also ran the front of the bakery like a military operation, so if she said she needed to leave, something really must have been off at the restaurant. "Sure. No problem."

"You're a godsend."

I gave her a smile and a wink. "That's what they all say."

Misty laughed and rushed out the door, leaving me alone with cases upon cases of yummy baked goods. Between them and the scent of strong coffee brewing, we'd see a hefty lunch crowd for sure. The day was nice and sunny, so I pushed open the front door, set up a fan to subtly waft the scent of the bakery outside, and I readied myself behind the counter. Trap baited.

It didn't take long to snag my first catch of the day. "Sheldon! How are you?"

Sheldon Pierce—wolf shifter, somewhat shy, liked to stare at my cleavage when we danced—gave me a smile as he tugged a woman behind him. "Hey, Ginger. This is my mate, Ali. We could smell something baking from down the street and thought a scone or two sounded like the perfect treat."

"Yeah, perfect." The woman gave me a shy smile. Guess there wouldn't be any more dancing for Sheldon and me, what with that sweet-looking girl on his arm. I almost felt bad for her—Sheldon wasn't exactly a rock star in the sack. I'd taken him home one night—just the one—and remembered being really freaking grateful when he left before dawn. In fact, I was pretty sure he'd never actually gotten me off. No completing the pass, making the touchdown. No scoring the winning goal, if you know what I mean. A lifetime of sex with no happy ending all because some mystical fates decided *this* was the perfect person for you? No thanks.

Not that I'd ever say that to either of them.

"Congratulations on your mating—I hadn't heard." I offered each of them my widest grin and moved behind the display case. "How about a couple of vanilla scones" —*because Sheldon was as vanilla as they came*— "and some coffee? On the house, of course. Consider it my gift to you on finding each other."

Sheldon looked down at his mate then nodded my way when he saw her smile. "Sounds great."

And so the hour went—men from town came in, most of whom I'd dated at one time or another, and I sold them something from the case along with a cup of coffee. Sometimes tea. Working the front was an exercise in flirting—because who could resist that opportunity?—and a trip down memory lane. So many men, so many past partners, so many nights good and bad. Lord, I needed to get out of town more. I was pretty sure I'd dated every eligible bachelor in it.

A few of the guys in town had wanted more than I'd been willing to give them—more of my time, more of me, more commitment. Those ones were either happy to see me, hoping I'd change my mind and go out with them again, or cranky. As if the fact that they couldn't hold my interest was somehow my fault.

Okay, so maybe it was a little.

Sort of.

It wasn't like I could control my brain, though. Nothing lasted long there—nothing held my attention and took root except for my sisters and our bakery. They were with me for the long haul, but the rest? Flashes in the pan. Distractions. Playthings to be forgotten about eventually. Maybe if they'd been memorable enough—

A man walked in and thoughts…gone.

Brain…fried.

Panties…wet.

Good lord, he was the hottest thing I'd ever seen. Tall and muscular but not thick, with a shock of black hair streaked with gray and the bluest eyes I'd ever seen. A silver fox who looked ready to eat me alive and fully capable of doing so. And totally new in town.

Jackpot.

"Well, hi. Welcome to—"

"You smell like cinnamon."

"I…well, I work in a bakery." I gave him my best smile, the one I'd practiced in the mirror as a teenager. The one that hopefully said *why yes, you're handsome and I'm available, so let's have a little fun* in a not-too-blatant way. "That's sort of bound to happen."

He dragged those eyes made of ocean waves over my body, something almost covetous in his gaze. "Cinnamon is my favorite."

There was no doubting the direction of his thoughts. "That might be the strangest pick-up line I've ever heard."

He shot me a cocky smile that made my knees weak and my breath catch. But then he opened his mouth.

"Who says I was trying to pick you up, Sparky?"

Attraction could turn to anger at the flip of a switch. Or at the possibility one might be rejected. Being pissed about the tossing out of a nickname I didn't exactly ask for was likely a much better look for me than the latter, though. "Sparky?"

"Yes, because your eyes practically shoot sparks when you're mad."

"I'm not mad."

"I bet." He darted a look at the case of pastries and lifted his chin. "I'll take one of those cinnamon crunch donuts and a cup of coffee. Heavy cream with a sprinkle of cinnamon, please."

"You really *do* like cinnamon."

"You have no idea."

Did he... The man had just made an innocuous statement sound filthy in the best possible way. I had no idea how he'd twisted such simple words into something that made my body begin to burn from the inside out. Seriously, no clue. What I did know was that I wanted him out of my shop. Technically, I wanted him out of my shop and in my house. Preferably in my bed. But apparently, he didn't want the same thing. Perhaps he was married—not likely, seeing as there was no ring on his finger, as if I wouldn't look. I wasn't an amateur.

This was Kinship Cove, though—home to hundreds of breeds of shifters. Maybe he had a fated mate sitting at home waiting for him. Yeah, probably mated. I mean...there could be other reasons why he wasn't interested in asking me out. I wasn't arrogant enough to think I was *every* guy's type. I'd just expected more than a dumb nickname and a complete shutdown from him for some reason.

Why did my chest hurt so much? Was I...sad? About a man not returning my flirtation? What the hell was wrong with me?

"You okay back there, Sparky?"

I blinked, looking down at the empty coffee cup in my hand. The one I'd been holding for at least a minute as my brain tried to decipher my body's reaction to Mr. Nickname-Maker-Upper. Or whatever.

"Yeah. I'm good." I made his coffee, grabbed his donut, and returned to the counter to ring him up, smile firmly in place. Not my flirty one that had taken me so long to perfect, either. He didn't deserve it. "That'll be four dollars."

The bulge of his bicep as he reached for his wallet totally did *not* steal my attention. Nope. Not at all.

"Four is an interesting number, don't you think?"

I tore my eyes away from his arm, wondering when I'd been dropped back into elementary school math class. "Huh?"

"Four." He handed me cash, his fingers brushing mine and sending tingles shooting up my arm. "Two plus two."

"So you passed kindergarten. Well done."

His smile turned to a smirk with the twisting of one side of his mouth. "Yes, kindergarten and beyond. Even biology. Physiology. Anatomy."

Oh lord. "You like to study bodies, then?"

Those deadly blue eyes tracked up and down my torso, devouring me with a look. "Some. I really like to study bodies interacting, though. The way they're meant to fit together fascinates me."

"I bet it does." I dropped his change on the counter. "Enjoy your donut and have a great day."

He shook his head, his grin only growing wider. "Thanks for the chat, Sparky."

"My name's not Sparky."

"Oh yes, it totally is." The jackass actually winked as he backed out the door.

Misty passed him by on her way back in, eyeing him hard. Looking downright concerned as she came through the door. "Who was that?"

"Just some customer." It wasn't often Misty seemed to be caught off guard, but she definitely was then. "Why? What's up, foxy?"

She shrugged, still looking unsettled. "I couldn't get a read on him."

A read. As in what breed of shifter he was. Huh, I hadn't thought about that possibility. "Maybe he's human."

"Humans don't look that good at his age. No offense."

She wasn't wrong. "None taken."

"Be careful with that one, at least until I can figure out what he is."

"You don't have to worry about that. I'm not interested in any more interactions with that jerk."

That jerk…who I couldn't keep my eyes off of.

That jerk…who had left me feeling completely unbalanced.

That jerk…who I'd be looking to come back to the bakery tomorrow.

Yeah. That one. Crap.

2

GINGER

I had cupcakes on the brain.

It was well past the bakery's closing time, I'd been home for hours, and yet I couldn't get desserts off my mind. After a group call with my sisters so we could go over what needed to be done tomorrow—and discuss Coco's very sudden and exciting love life with handsome Magnus—I'd sat down to figure out what I needed to try next. Specifically, how to meld flavors to come up with amazing, irresistible treats for the Cake-ily Ever After customers. Treats I hadn't made before. Something new and exciting. But no matter how long I sat on my couch with my favorite brain-dump notebook and my thinking playlist on, my focus seemed to be running on empty. At least, in relation to baking.

Other things, I couldn't *not* focus on. Like cinnamon. And jerks.

It didn't help that the jerk who'd called me Sparky at the bakery that day seemed to be the biggest distraction I'd ever encountered. That graying hair and those blue eyes danced through my head whenever I tried to buckle down and think, and the whole irritation at him calling me whatever he wanted to instead of asking my name like a gentleman really threw me for a loop. Especially since I didn't know *his* name.

93

Maybe I'd assign him one the way he'd assigned Sparky to me. Mr.-Name-Wronger.

No.

Mr. Nickname-Maker-Upper.

Even more no.

Namey McNamerson, Mayor of Namington.

Yeah, that didn't even work in my head.

Whatever I finally decided to call him, he'd gotten under my skin enough to take up space in my head. No man did that—when I was work, I was *all* work. When I was learning a new skill, I concentrated on every detail and kept side projects away. Whatever I did, I did with my full attention and focus. Until him.

Not that I was doing him.

Oh god, the idea of *doing* him…right there in my living room…on my floor. Yeah, that'd be the situation for sure. With all the heat behind his eyes? He'd be too intense to wait for the bedroom, too demanding to let me escape to someplace soft and private. He'd take me as soon as the door closed—throw me on the floor, rip off my panties, and thrust inside without preamble. Comfort be damned. I could practically see him there; practically feel his eyes on me. Almost taste…

"Fuck." I tossed the notepad aside. This night was not going to go the way I'd wanted it to. A drink. I definitely needed to get out of the house and find myself a drink. And maybe someone who actually had the decency to ask my name to distract me. To take my mind off of Mr. I-Like-Cinnamon.

That name still didn't work. I'd noodle on it for a bit.

Thirty minutes of prep and a ten-minute drive later, I walked into my least favorite bar in the cove. It was a total tourist place, one the locals rarely spent time in. Perfect for what I needed tonight—fresh meat. People who didn't know me, whom I didn't already have a history with. I needed strangers, and the whole damn town was filled with visitors coming in for Nico and Fiona's wedding. The bar seemed perfect.

"A mojito, please," I called to the bartender as soon as he walked up. Johnny was his name. Human, moved to the cove a few years back, already knowing way more about shifters and the paranormal world than most people, and tended to keep to himself. He was cute in a bad boy sort of way—a little rough around the edges, a little on the dangerous side if you didn't know him. A little hot. He looked like a man who'd spank your ass all Saturday night then rotate your tires without you asking him to because they were looking a little worn on Sunday. He was a bit older as well—he had some salt and pepper going on around his temples. Just like the guy from the bakery that morning. The one who'd called me Sparky.

Bastard.

"Here you go, Ginger. Let me know if you need anything else." Johnny shot me a wink and headed down the bar, answering calls for drinks. I watched him walk away—because how could you not when the guy had a perfect ass cupped in worn denim?—before scoping out the scene. Looking for someone to talk with. Someone to give my attention to. Someone like the dark-haired guy staring back at me from the other end of the bar. No girl on his arm, watching me as if he liked what he saw, and totally not a resident of Kinship Cove. Or, at least, not one I recognized. Jackpot.

Ready to play, I shot him *the look*. You know the one—slight smile, coquettish angle to the head, definite eye contact as I gave just the slightest nod. The *you might have a shot at getting into my panties if you play your cards right* look. Not that I was searching for all that—I just needed a few drinks, some good conversation, and a way to forget my day. If I needed to use a little sex appeal to get all that, so be it.

My target accepted the look, pushing off the bar and heading my way. He wore a cocky smirk on his face—definite turn-off—and took long, slow steps. Sort of…slow motion almost.

Oh fuck, if he was a sloth shifter, I was going to lose my mind.

"Hi," he said when he finally—and I do mean *finally*—ended up beside me.

"Hi yourself." I looked him up and down, taking it all in. Dark jeans, tight button-up shirt, rolled sleeves to attract the gaze to his impressive forearms, and that smirk. It really wasn't working for me, but I wasn't ready to cut my losses yet. "In town for the wedding?"

"Yeah. My band did some work for the bride's clan leader."

Growing up in a town filled with shifters, words meant different things to me than to the general population. He'd said band, and though he technically could have meant a literal musical band, my guess was he meant a band of gorillas. That made more sense in a town like Kinship Cove. Also, the bride's clan leader? Fiona was a wolf of the pack variety. By saying clan leader, he meant the bear who ran the town. Jericho, the man also known as the town mayor. A bear shifter my sisters and I often called Uncle simply because he'd been such good friends with our dad. Gorilla shifter who had dealings with the head bear shifter in charge…the HBIC. I could work with this.

"So you know Jericho, then."

"I do, though I'd rather get to know you better. What's your name, princess?"

Christ, could men quit with the nicknames already? "Ginger. And you are?"

"Luca. So what is it you do, Ginger? Other than stand around busy bars showing up all the other women in the place."

I'd like to say I took his compliment in stride, but I didn't. In fact, I'm pretty sure I scowled. I also took a step back, which opened up a line of view I hadn't been able to access before. A line that stretched across the bar and gave me the perfect shot of exactly the person I didn't want to see.

Mr. *You Smell Like Cinnamon*

And he wasn't alone.

"Where'd you go?"

I snapped my attention back to Lucas. Luke. Lucaphobia. What was his name again? "Oh, sorry. I run the bakery in town with my sisters."

"A bakery? How quaint."

My head cocked of its own accord, and the ice in my voice was something I couldn't defrost as I repeated, "Quaint."

"Sure. You know…chicks baking stuff. That whole barefoot in the kitchen thing. Quaint."

I could have killed him. Well, not really, but I could have eviscerated him with my words. I chose not to because, at that moment, Sparky-

Caller caught my eye. He'd leaned down a little so the blonde practically hanging off his arm could whisper in his ear, but his attention stayed locked on me. And I had the urge to take advantage of that.

So I laughed, and I grabbed L-name-dude's arm and moved a little closer. And I gave the gorilla shifter my biggest, flirtiest smile while I tried not to hate him for thinking my owning a thriving business that fed people in town was *quaint*.

"Barefoot? That would break an awful lot of health codes, I'm sure. I'd hate to have to close because I can't keep my shoes on—we're quite popular, you know."

"Well, if you're the one working the counter, I would bet you are. How could anyone say no to such a smile?" He pulled me closer, hovering on that line between intimate and creepy. Sort of laying a toe over it, to be honest. "So does that mean you'll make me breakfast in the morning, my little baker?"

I shot a glance down the bar to find Sparky-Caller no longer looking at me. In fact, he was no longer anywhere that I could see him. Perhaps he'd left…with the blonde.

Not that I cared.

At all.

Damn it. Sparky-Caller had turned me into a liar and a player, because there was no way Gorilla-guy had a shot. Time to change plans.

I set my nearly full drink on the counter and fanned my face. "Woo-hoo. It's warm in here. Isn't it warm?"

"Uh, not really. No."

"Yeah, it seems too warm. What's the rule? Beer to liquor, you'll never be sicker? Maybe I shouldn't have gone for a rum drink after the beers I had with my dinner." I forced a gag, bringing my hand up to my mouth and staring at him with wide eyes. "I'm going to head to the ladies' real quick."

Gorilla-guy looked suitably horrified. "Yeah. Sure. I'll, uh, be right here."

Of course he would.

I rushed across the bar, slipping through the crowd at a speed slightly below actually needing to vomit. No need to make a scene or anything. I turned just before the hallway leading to the restrooms and headed for the patio instead. Fresh air. I needed some fresh air to clear my head of all the drama and bad juju of the day.

Sadly, it seemed my juju could only get worse. The second I stepped outside, all the drama I needed to blow off my mind surrounded me instead.

"Not looking so sparky, Sparky."

Fuck my life. "My name isn't Sparky."

"But it fits you." Name-Caller—seriously, it had been the best I could come up with, and now it was stuck in my head—slipped out of the shadows, almost as if he was made from the darkness. Or maybe that was just a glimpse of his soul. And no, I didn't think I was being overdramatic at all. "I'm surprised to see you here tonight."

"Not sure why. I do live in this town, you know."

"This isn't the bar townies go to, though."

No, it wasn't. But visitors didn't usually know that. "So you're more familiar with Kinship Cove than a regular tourist."

"I've been here a few times over the years."

"Must have been more than a few times to learn the local secrets." I stepped toward him, unable not to. Drawn to that devilish grin and those blue eyes. To the air of danger and darkness that seemed to surround him. To the tingle his very presence brought to my skin. "Why do you hang around so much?"

"Something here has always called to me." He slithered closer, bringing the heat of his body with him. Warming me almost from the inside out. "I've come back here for years, trying to figure out why. Wondering what could possibly be so important as to hold my attention for so long."

My lord, his cold eyes were almost hypnotizing. Almost. "Must be a lot of patience," I said, stealing a glance at the gray hair along his temples. Trying really damn hard not to lick my lips. "You're not exactly a spring chicken."

His grin turned positively deadly...to my panties. "No, I'm not. I'm quite a bit older than you in fact."

I didn't inch closer. Nope. I totally didn't. And I was a lying liar who lied.

"How do you know how old I am?"

In a deep, rumbling voice, he murmured, "You're not the only one with friends in town."

"You asked about me?" The threat of that, the overstep, should have fired up my temper. Maybe. Coulda, woulda, shoulda, and all that. Instead, I felt even more drawn to him. Found myself practically pressed against him—chest-to-chest. Well, chest-to-breasts. I'd much rather have been hand-to-breast, to be honest. A little nipple tweak would really help a girl out right then. Not that I'd ever ask him for such a thing. Christ, if he ever purposely touched me, I might explode. Death by spontaneous orgasm. It could happen.

Sadly, he didn't grab my breast or my hip or my ass or anything fun. He didn't push me over that orgasmic cliff with his touch like I sorta wanted him to—and by sorta, I absolutely meant totally. Nope, no touchy-feely for me. He spoke again instead, using that mouth and those plush, pink lips in a way that could only be seen as a waste. By me.

"I said I've been waiting patiently to see what's been snagging my attention here. I've come to the conclusion that you play into it."

My doubt became a rocket ready to take off for the moon, it was so powerful. "So I play into something that calls to you, yet you're out tonight with someone else? Seems contradictory."

The way his grin turned wicked gave me about one-point-two seconds to accept the fact that I'd screwed up by mentioning the blonde.

"Does seeing me with someone else piss you off?"

Yup. Screwed up. Now I looked jealous. Walked right into that one. "No. Of course not. Why should it?" My defense sounded petulant and untrue even to *my own* ears. He knew it, too—and Name-Caller didn't seem to be the type of man to miss an opportunity.

He herded me backward, brushing my arm with his as he angled himself closer. Pinning me in place against the wall with that ice-blue gaze. And his muscles. Oh my, his muscles. We met hips to shoulders this time. So many muscles in all those inches. So much tingling going on in my naughty bits.

"You didn't look too happy inside yourself, Sparky. Perhaps your date should try harder."

Breathe, Ginger. Breathe. "He's not my date."

"Good."

Something in that word, in the force behind it, had me squinting a little as I looked him over. As I asked with every bit of sass the good lord had given me, "Did *me* being here with him piss *you* off?"

"Yes."

Simple. Direct. And utterly confusing. "So you can date someone else, and I can't?"

"I'm not here on a date."

"Then who was the blonde?"

"Someone not at all interesting." Closer yet, his lips practically brushed my cheek as he whispered, "So you did notice me."

"How could I not?" I bit my lip and shrugged a shoulder as his icy eyes held mine. And then I grinned, "You were quite likely the oldest man in the bar. You stood out from the crowd with your gray hair. Hell, I should call you daddy."

That was...one hell of a slip of the tongue.

A low growl rumbled through his chest, something deep and almost feral. Animalistic. I hadn't taken him for a shifter, but that didn't mean he wasn't one. That growl sounded too rough, too strong to be human. Shifters had two sides to them—two beings in one body. And right then, I was pretty sure I'd upset the beast within him. Whatever kind it was.

He caged me in against the wall with his arms, rocking his hips into mine. Letting me feel where he was so hard and long and thick for me. "You call me daddy, and I just might keep you."

Words were hard to grasp. Too hard to put together into any sort of response. I wanted to kiss him. Wanted to weave my fingers through that wavy gray hair and tug him closer. Wanted to wrap my body around his bigger one. Death. This was death. Or it would be. This man, those eyes, that grin—death to my single life forever. He was a keeper, but I wasn't one to be kept. Normally. For him? Oh hell, maybe.

So I inched forward, letting our bodies touch all the way to the knees. Letting us feel. The spicy scent of his aftershave almost had me drooling, and the heat rolling off his body set mine on fire. Or maybe that was simply him being his sexy, infuriating, good-smelling self.

Did I mention he smelled amazing? Because I really need to make that point stick. Ah-may-zing.

I licked my lips, nuzzling his neck and breathing in through my mouth so I could bring the flavor of him inside of me. Unable to resist it. "You smell like…"

"Cinnamon?"

Oh my, his growl sent a shiver up my spine. "Sort of, but spicier."

"I know." He nuzzled my neck right back, tugging me into his chest with one hand on my hip as I bent my head back. Waiting and wanting and needing so much more from him. So close to coming right there on the patio with him doing nothing more than cuddling that I almost felt bad about it. Almost.

He didn't seem to feel bad at all. "You should kiss me, Sparky. I'd really like for you to."

"Not going to happen, old man."

"Why not?"

Because I was an idiot. Because I wouldn't be able to stop at just one kiss. Because if I fucked him on the patio of this bar, people might talk. More. They might talk more. Because I'd never get enough with just one night. Shit. "Because you should make the first move."

"I can't do that."

He doesn't want to kiss me.

Ice water flashed through my veins, cooling my blood in a heartbeat. Shame and embarrassment cleared my head faster than anything else could have, pulling me out of whatever trance he'd put me under. No way was he human. He had to be a shifter of some sort. No regular man had ever been able to take over my senses like that. Had made me want and need and crave as much as this guy did. He had to be some sort of magical creature with powers of seduction. A male succubus or something.

Which would be an incubus.

Come on, brain. Keep up.

Without a word, I forced my feet to move, my hands to push against him and shove him back. I ignored the way my fingers tingled as I touched his chest, the way they wanted to curl into his shirt and tug instead of push. No good could come from that tingling. That tingling was a sign of danger, and I fully intended to listen to the warning. So I pushed him, and I slipped to the side to move around him. To leave before he unsettled me even more than he already had. Damn Name-Caller wasn't not playing the game the same way I did, wasn't turning into putty for me to mold and bend to my will. Instead, he had somehow begun running the show. Forcing me to abide by his rules and trying hard to make me the one who bent. That had never happened.

And I wasn't in the mood to learn a new trick right then.

"I think it's time for me to head home. I've had enough of you for one day."

"Me and enough in the same sentence. I doubt that will ever happen again."

Seriously, I had no response to that. None. No words for the arrogance of his. Okay, fine—I rolled my eyes a little. I mean, that was over the top even for a man like him. So instead of speaking, I locked my eyes on the door leading into the bar and strode in that direction. Escape in my grasp.

He didn't try to stop me, though he did run his fingers along my arm as I moved past him. He also seduced me with a single sentence. Or tried to. "I like you jealous, Sparky."

Okay, yeah. Seduced. Totally. Such a jerk.

"I don't like you at all," I said, even as my entire body burned from such a simple touch. Hormones were a bitch and all that.

"You'll change your mind soon enough."

But as I hit the door, as something in my gut tugged and made me want to go back, I turned. His rakish smirk and casual lean against the wall only confirmed my opinion—the man was dangerous in a way that I needed to avoid. So I pulled on my inner Wonder Woman, threw up my invisible shield, and tossed my hair over my shoulder. Badass woman. That's what I needed to be. And I knew how.

I posed in the stance that showed off the s-curve of my body— breasts out, hips slightly turned, booty on display—so he could get one last good look at what he'd missed out on. I pursed my lips just enough to hopefully make him think of kisses and blowies—things he'd never get from me—and I raised a single eyebrow in a move that'd taken me months in front of the mirror to perfect and was worth every single second for moments just like this one.

Badass woman definitely activated. "Not in this lifetime. Don't come back to the bakery. We don't need your business."

And then I left. Hoping and praying I could make it out to my car without him chasing me down.

Badass or not, I doubted I'd be able to resist him a second time.

3

KINGSTON

The city of Kinship Cove sat nestled between a wall of rock and an ocean, the location providing spectacular wind patterns that were much too fun not to ride along. Especially during the dark of night when the human world went quiet and still. Most certainly on the nights after I'd finally—too many centuries past my birth to even count —met my fated mate.

Thinking of the spitfire with the sparks in her eyes, I swooped toward the ground, following my instincts as I stretched my wings. My inner dragon had been screaming to be released all day, ever since the moment he'd basically dragged me into the little bakery in town and I'd seen her. The one who would be mine. Dragons didn't do the whole immediate fated mate thing like some shifters. We had more choice in the matter, but something about Kinship Cove had drawn me to it for decades. Something had led me to the perfect place at just the right time. A feeling on the air. A vibration through the fates. A scent on the breeze.

Cinnamon.

Of course she smelled like cinnamon. Like a dragon in heat—all fiery and strong, sweet in the right amount but hard to handle in large doses.

My Sparky—Ginger, as I'd learned—had been offered up on a platter for me right there in her bakery, and I refused to turn her away.

With a quiet roar toward the rocky coast, I spun in midair and headed back toward the steep mountainside. I'd already found her address—it didn't take much digging for that. Seemed everyone in town knew the three girls who ran the bakery. The men especially seemed to know my mate, a fact that both frustrated me and brought pride to my inner beast. Our woman was wanted, desired by all, yet no one had been able to catch her. To snag her attention for long. That was fine by me—she'd played with the boys. I'd show her how good a real man—a dragon shifter mate—could be. I'd make her forget every other male in town and only turn that bright, flirty smile my way.

Once I convinced her to make the first move.

Spotting an old friend sitting on a ridge of stone, I dove lower, landing in a swirl of magic and fabric as all my parts, pieces, and clothes reformed from the scales of my dragon side.

"I've always envied you that trick." Jericho—bear clan leader and mayor of Kinship Cove—didn't even look my way as he asked, "What's got you flying so high tonight, friend?"

Friend. I didn't have many of those anymore. Too many years alone had left me slightly cranky, and even the calmest of my dragon brethren seemed to end up making me want to fight them to the death with their inane chatter and constant noise. Jericho, though, was different. His thoughtful nature soothed the anger constantly coursing through me. Something I'd never expected from a bear shifter.

"I've met my mate." Simple. Honest. To the point. So unlike me.

Jericho sighed, his brow furrowing. "Here? In town?"

"Indeed. You know her, from what I understand."

"Let me guess—one of the Chance sisters who owns the bakery."

I couldn't have been more shocked. "How did you guess?"

The look in his eye as he glanced my way seemed angry and hard, wary in a way. "Seems to be their season. Which one is yours?"

"Ginger."

His robust laugh broke the silence of the night. "Ah, you're in for one hell of a ride, my friend."

Something I'd already guessed. "What about you? I assumed you'd have settled down with a nice sow by now, popped out a few cubs. All that…domestic shit."

"The fates haven't given me a sow."

His tone seemed final, as if he didn't want to speak more on the topic. But I'd been around a long time—longer than my bear friend, for sure—and I could tell a side step when I saw one. The fates may not have given him a female bear, but they'd given him something. He wasn't happy about it, though.

And it wasn't my place to push. "Well, old friend, I do believe I shall hit the skies again. Perhaps ride the air to the north side of town."

"Ginger lives on the north side of town."

"I'm aware."

He stopped me with a growl and a glare. "I understand dragons have different rules for—well, everything. But that girl is like family to me. Don't fuck around."

Oh, I was going to fuck. Around, below, on top, from the side, upside down…however she let me inside what I knew would be the sweetest pussy the fates had ever created, I'd happily take it. And I'd give her everything I had to make sure she walked away satisfied, if she could walk at all.

He didn't need to know that, though. "Of course. She's my mate—I'll cherish her for the rest of my days."

He grunted. "Good. Go on, then. I can't wait to watch this one play out."

I had my scales on and the wind beneath my wings seconds later, having jumped right off the cliff in my human form and shifted in midair. That always garnered a reaction from the mammals I left on the ground. Jericho merely chuckled. Not what I'd been expecting. The man seemed lost, something I'd never sensed with him before. Whatever was going on, whatever he felt was missing in his life, I could only hope the fates gave him the opportunity to fix it. Time grew lonely after a century or so.

Refocusing on the new woman in my life, I swept through the night air on my way to the north. To the group of houses that hugged the edge of town with their backs to the forest. Ginger lived there—close enough to walk to work but just far enough away from the bars not to have them be a nuisance. Smart location—and perfectly her. She may have shown up at a bar that night, she may have even frequented them often, but she wouldn't want them interrupting her evenings or causing issues near her home. She had a den of sorts. A quiet, private residence where she could hole up and be herself. Be truly comfortable. I liked that about her.

It took me three loops around the house to finally spot her—she'd apparently taken to her tub for an evening wash. The idea of all that wet skin—of how warm and fragrant she would be in that steamy room—made my cock leak with need. But I was a gentleman—sometimes—and a dragon shifter who followed the rules laid out by the royal dragon clan. I'd not yet received permission from Ginger to do anything with her or to her—something I needed before I could act. Something only she could give me—no coercion allowed.

So instead of creeping outside her window and getting a good eyeful of all that human flesh, I flew up onto the roof and perched carefully along the ridgeline. And I watched the world pass by. Rigid and ready for battle.

My mate deserved a guardian, and I would be that for her. Even if it was all she ever wanted from me.

As the sun rose over the mountains to the east, Ginger made her way to work along the quiet Kinship Cove streets. I followed behind her, in the air. Watching over her still. I hadn't slept the night before, hadn't closed my eyes for a moment. The idea of losing my mate before I truly had her had settled into my head and gut like a stone, so I'd stayed awake to keep her safe. But I'd grown weary of the distance and wanted to see her face up close, wanted to hear her voice and smell that spicy cinnamon scent on the air.

Thankfully, the bakery would be open soon, and I could make a legitimate visit. I waited outside for the girl behind the counter—not

Ginger this time—to turn the sign to Open, then waited a few minutes more. A man walked through the door looking positively frantic. A wolf shifter, if my guess was right—and it usually was. He left soon after without a thing in his hands and an angry sort of glare on his face. Odd…and possibly dangerous. Eight minutes was way more than enough to have my mate out of my sights. I rushed across the street, slowing only when I reached the door with the little bell overhead and pushed through it.

But it wasn't Ginger behind the counter.

"Welcome to Cake—" The girl's eyes went big as she saw me, her nose practically twitching. Shifter—Vulpes genus, if the scent didn't lie. Fox shifters weren't as prevalent as wolves or bears, but I'd run into a handful over the years. Eaten a few as well, to be honest. I doubted I could say the same for her and dragons—the meeting or eating. This could be fun.

"Good morning," I said, trying my hardest to keep any sort of growl from my voice.

"Who are you, and what are you doing here?"

No pleasantries. All righty. "I'm Kingston, and I'd—"

"I don't need your name. What sort of shifter are you, and why can't I smell you?"

Ah. That was easy. "I'm a dragon shifter, fox. You can't smell me because I choose not to telegraph my species."

"Dragon. Huh…hadn't thought of that."

Of course not—we weren't exactly your garden-variety predator. But her lack of knowledge on my breed did little to assuage the deep need within me to check on my mate. "Yes, well…that's what I am. Now, I don't want to be a bother, but I was hoping to see Ginger."

"No."

I…hadn't expected that. "Excuse me."

"I said no. You can*not* see Ginger." The fox shook her head and dropped her towel onto the counter. "What does some dragon want with Ginger, anyway?"

The word dragon dripped with disdain, a fact that had my inner beast snarling and ready to fight. Not that I could let him. So I reined him in, and I did my best not to let the little snack get a glimpse of the claws pushing through my fingers.

"I believe that's between me—" I paused, making sure to put enough weight behind my words so as to make my point clear "—and my mate."

She didn't even blink. "Bullshit. Dragons don't mate for life like the rest of us. They pick their partners and form a breakable bond."

Ignorance and the secrets of my breed would be the death of me. From boredom. "Not all dragons mate, no. But some do. Including me—my bond to Ginger isn't the breakable sort."

The girl shook her head, looking far more irritated than I would have expected. "First the wolves come after Coco, and now a dragon's set his sights on Ginger. These girls are dangerous." She looked up and caught my eye once more. "If you're fucking around with her, you'll have to deal with me."

"Am I supposed to be afraid of a fox?"

"Maybe. Maybe not. But my family skulk will hunt you down and tear you to pieces if you mess with that girl. Starting with all your favorite bits, you get me? She's important to us."

She was important to me, too. And I could do nothing but respect the zeal this little creature used to protect her. I would make sure not to eat any of the local foxes for snacks, after all. "Understood. There will be no fucking around…without express consent from Ginger herself."

"Yeah, I've heard about your rules of consent when picking a partner. You need her to make the first move, right?"

Unfortunately. "Right."

"Good luck with that. I'm Misty, by the way. I have a feeling you should know that sooner rather than later."

Suddenly Ginger appeared, carrying a tray weighted down by huge cupcakes covered in frosting of various pastel shades. "I swear, if Coco is getting banged like a screen door in a hurricane by Mr. Hot Silver Fox instead of being on time to work, I'm going to lose my shit."

"Pretty sure she's not the one getting banged," Misty said, tossing a wink in my direction. "Magnus just left—he said he's looking for Coco."

Ginger frowned, having not noticed me yet. "But…Coco's not here. She's always here on time—early, even. The brat makes us all look like slackers." She grabbed her phone from her back pocket, still not looking up as she tapped and scrolled. "The chicken shit sent a text. She says she's not coming in this morning but will be here after we close to finish the macarons."

"Sounds like she's sick."

"No, it sounds like she's hiding. I swear, I tell my sister to fuck her ex-boyfriend's dad one time, and the world goes to hell."

Misty's grin grew wide and...mocking. "It does—it really, really does. We'll deal with that in a second, though. You've got a visitor."

Ginger's head snapped up, and she followed Misty's nod in my direction. A delightful flush rose along her neck and over her cheeks as her eyes met mine. One I could practically taste. By the fates, she was stunning. Hair up, eyes bright, skin delightfully pink. I wanted to pin her against the glass display case and kiss her delicate throat, wanted to slide my hand up under that white shirt she wore and tweak her nipples until she begged for more. I wanted so much...but I couldn't take from her. I had to wait to be offered.

But my mate's mind wasn't focused on me and all the things I could do for her. At least, not yet.

"Tell Madeleine we've got an errand to run," she said to Misty before turning my way and cocking her head at me—the breadth of her attitude on full display. "I have a feeling Coco's dealing with bad-date fallout, and no man is worth a Chance woman's tears."

"If a male makes his woman cry, he's no man," I replied, giving her what I could only hope was a sincere smile. It didn't appear to help my case at all. Oh sure, Ginger set her tray down and came around the counter toward me, but she didn't look open or giving. In fact, she looked like a damned challenge. One I'd happily accept. "Good morning, Sparky."

"What are you doing here?"

"I was hoping for a little something for breakfast. Perhaps a cinnamon muffin."

Her adorable scowl made an appearance on those lips I longed to taste. "We don't have cinnamon. How about chocolate?"

"I'm not a fan of chocolate. My tongue likes something with a bit more bite." I grinned as her flush darkened her cheeks again. "How about one of those cupcakes? They look delicious."

"It's a bit early, don't you think?"

"It's never too early for me, Sparky. Not for anything."

She rolled her eyes but couldn't hide the barest hint of a smile that softened her already pretty face. Ginger moved as if to leave, as if to escape back behind the counter, but I couldn't let her go. I grabbed her arm—gently, not forcing her to stay, but imploring—and waited for her to meet my stare again. Waited to look into the eyes of my fated mate. And when she did, I lost my breath.

The beauty and depth of her dark eyes—the glimpse of her soul those windows offered me—would be branded on my heart for eternity. Mine. All mine—I just had to win her.

"Yes?" she asked, seeming almost as breathless as I felt.

I couldn't hold back another second. Couldn't miss an opportunity. Dragon mating customs said she had to make the first move, but I could make sure we were at least in the same room when she decided to do something. And I could use any and all of my skills to get her there. "I'd like for the two of us to have dinner together."

"Oh, you would?"

"Yes."

"Well, I think you should learn to ask nicely."

"I did."

"No, you demanded."

My spitfire tried to leave, to turn and pull away from me, but I held strong. Still not forcing the issue—something that could anger the dragon rulers if they found out and bring trouble raining down upon me. No, I didn't force. I simply requested. Physically.

"Ginger," I murmured, dropping my voice lower, teasing her with the power behind my inner dragon.

Her pupils dilated, and her jaw dropped a little, parting those soft, plush, pink lips of hers. "You're not being nice."

"Oh, I can be nice, my girl. I can be very, very nice."

She shook her head a little, as if trying to clear her head. "I can't... I don't even know your name."

"It's Kingston, and I'll do my best to charm you tonight so you'll be screaming it later."

Spell broken, she jerked back, a storm brewing behind her eyes. "You're an asshole."

"And deep down, you like me that way. Now, about dinner tonight—I'll pick you up at five."

"I don't think—"

"Don't forget you have to deliver the groom's cake for the rehearsal dinner," Misty—my intrepid little fox shifter who had apparently been hiding in a corner—said, completely derailing whatever argument Ginger might have had. Helpful fox, indeed.

Ginger didn't seem to think the same if her little scowl was any indication. "I won't."

I couldn't pass by an opening. "I'll help you," I said, smiling when Ginger's surprised eyes met mine again. "Then we can go to dinner."

Arms crossed, hip cocked, looking far too sexy in her fury, my mate said, "I don't remember saying yes."

"I never heard you say no, either. Dragons like specificity, love." I tapped the tip of her nose and turned to leave, knowing my time was up. "See you tonight."

She could have said no, could have told me to kiss off, could have done a hundred different things to make her displeasure at the idea of spending time with me known.

She did nothing but allow me to walk away.

I took that as a resounding yes to my offer.

Now, to get to the winning her over...for real, this time.

4

GINGER

You really should be making bread."

I looked up at my youngest sister, frowning when I met Madeleine's concerned stare. "Huh?"

She nodded toward the table where I'd been folding the cupcake batter together. Though folding was a bit of a stretch at that point. "You're beating the hell out of that batter. You'd be better off making bread if you're so worked up."

"I'm not worked up."

Her eyebrows practically jumped off her forehead. If eyebrows could move autonomously. And off the body part they grew out of. "So are we lying to ourselves, or simply too blinded to see what's going on? Because I have to tell you, the timing is horrible."

"Yeah. Horrible timing." What with rehearsal dinner cookies and cakes due, my cupcakes for the parties before the wedding, and the actual wedding cake. The three of us were all equally slammed. But Coco...well, she'd been dealt the worst hand.

I flicked a glance at my other sister. The poor thing seemed to be in her own world, one filled with sadness and tears. One that existed in the arid desert that was heartbreak. Seeing the girl so shattered, so completely lost inside her own pain, ripped out my heart and tap-danced across it. Coco's latest crush—a wolf shifter named Magnus—seemed to have gone off the rails. She'd been so happy just the day before, laughing and joking and excited for dinner out with her man. This morning, though, she'd failed to come to work, so we'd been forced to basically drag her out of bed and into the shop. And now? She was the Kinship Cove spokesperson for how depression hurts.

I wouldn't follow in her footsteps.

No way, no how, no flipping chance. I wasn't about to let anyone get that close to me, wasn't going to open myself up for such pain. Not unless they were the *right* someone. And by right, I meant perfect—everything I could ever want. The dream guy I'd been chasing since I got my first Ken doll. Since I began planning weddings with my already suitably prepared—and gloriously independent—Barbies. Ken had been perfect, though. Mr. Right versus Mr. Right Now. I refused to settle for less.

"Welp, these ears are about as pointy as they're going to ever be. I thought the cake was done before, but that little extra swirl of gray really does make it perfect. Right?" Madeleine stepped back from the groom's cake—a ridiculously large three-dimensional wolf sitting and howling, because what else would a wolf shifter want?—and nodded once. "Yep, perfect. You're delivering this tonight, remember?"

As if I could forget. Between Madeleine and Misty, they'd reminded me eight-hundred times already. I'd never forgotten to make a delivery before.

Except that one time with the cookies for an otter shifter's baptism.

Oh, and the muffins for Jericho's meeting with the mountain goat shifters.

And okay, the bagels for the alligator consortium had been a little late, but that really hadn't been my fault.

Damn it, I was totally going to forget the cake.

"I won't forget."

Madeleine looked skeptical but didn't say another word, instead sliding the cake onto one of the rolling carts we used for heavy or fragile items and wheeling it into the walk-in refrigerator. I was pretty sure there'd be bright-colored signs all over the kitchen by the end of the day, all with the same message in capital letters.

DON'T FORGET TO DELIVER THE CAKE.

I would not forget.

Hopefully.

Back to the cupcakes. I poured the overworked batter into a cupcake tin and set them in the oven to cook. I doubted they'd come out the right texture, but I had to try. As the best—albeit, only—bakery in town, we'd won the contract for all the desserts at the biggest wedding of the year. Madeleine had made the groom's cake and was working away on a ridiculously huge wedding cake with more decorations than I'd ever seen, and Coco had been making her famous macaron cookies for days for the rehearsal dinner. Meanwhile, I was in charge of the desserts for the bachelor and bachelorette parties. What goes better with a night on the town than booze? Nothing. Hence why, as soon as I had my next batch of cupcakes in the oven, I grabbed a bag of pale green buttercream and began frosting my tequila-soaked cakes. Everyone liked a margarita, right?

Right.

My boozy cakes had gotten us a lot of attention when I'd started adding them to the rotation last year. From whiskey to vodka, margarita to cosmopolitan, I had a cupcake for whatever your favorite alcoholic beverage happened to be. Fiona, the bride in the upcoming wedding, had basically demanded dozens of the liquored-up cupcakes for her last night as a single woman, and how could I possibly refuse her? I liked the wolf shifter. I wouldn't tell Coco that, seeing as how the woman was the mate of her ex-boyfriend, though that wasn't Fiona's fault. Fate was a tricky mistress—something I'd learned well growing up in Kinship Cove.

Thankfully, my friendship with Fiona had garnered me an invitation to the bachelorette shindig, which had somehow become one of the most-anticipated events in Kinship Cove history. I'd be out on the town tomorrow night with a gaggle of girls—not literally, they weren't all geese shifters—and a hell of a lot of opportunity for trouble. It sounded perfect, exactly what I needed to unwind.

Unlike dinner with that man—Kingston.

The second his name crossed through my mind, the man himself appeared. He walked through the back entrance to the shop as if he owned the place, looking...

Okay, fine, he looked like sex on legs. All debonair and stylish with those ice-blue eyes locked on me and a sexy-as-fuck smirk on his face. I hated him. I also wanted to ride his face. Totally normal, right?

"I'm not ready to go yet," I said, tearing my eyes away from him—damn, those dark jeans hugged him in all the right places—to work on my cupcakes.

"I'll wait."

Of course he would. "What if I said I didn't want to go?"

"I'd wait longer until you came to your senses."

"You're arrogant."

"It comes with the breed."

That caught my attention. "The breed?"

"Dragon. I'm a shifter, Sparky."

The man was a beast...quite literally. "You're a dragon."

"Yes."

"A real dragon."

The slow roll of his shoulder into a shrug only made him appear that much more refined somehow. "Last time I checked, yes."

"Huh."

"Just huh?"

It was my turn to shrug. "I've never met a dragon."

But I knew about them—players, non-maters, they tended to stay isolated from other shifters and never really pair up. They also tended to take what they wanted no matter what it was—money, treasures, women. Thieves, pirates, and plunderers, the lot of them. At least, that's what I'd been told. Thinking back over how he'd acted around me—about the blonde at the bar—he certainly seemed to fit the mold.

He also had a wicked smile that melted my panties right off my body. "You *have* met a dragon. Me."

Smartass. "No. I mean, I've lived in shifter town all my life. I thought I'd met every kind of shifter out there. A dragon is new."

"We're rare."

"How rare?"

"Rare enough that you've never met one."

"Not helpful."

"Not trying to be."

I huffed, and he smirked. That was fine—two could play at this game. And by two, I meant me because he might as well raise the white flag. I'd win. Starting with a hit no guy wanted to take.

"Why are dragons so rare anyway? Are there…known issues with—" I motioned toward his little dragon "—the equipment?"

He looked ready to roast me with his flame breath…if he could actually do that. "No issues, no."

"Oh, because I once met a cheetah shifter, and she went on and on about the male cheetah's low sperm viability. It's a thing for them."

"I'm not a cheetah shifter."

"Hmmm. Long gestational periods like elephants?"

"No, not elephant-like either."

If his scowl got any deeper, his face might crack. Perfect.

I tapped my chin, pretending to think…or not pretending. I needed one more dig. I found life in general to be far more balanced in groups of threes. Either that or I really just wanted to see how low that scowl would hang out on his handsome face before he blew up. Could go either way.

"So, no erectile dysfunction—that you'll admit to"—I shot him a wink—"and no excessively long gestational periods. I've seen you move, so you're not simply too slow and sloth-like. Seriously, Kingston—why so rare?"

He huffed, sounding so long-suffering I almost felt sorry for him.

Nope, that was a lie. I wasn't even close to that point yet.

"We don't mate the same way as other shifters."

"Oh, so…there's positioning issues? What…do you just squirt the sperm at an egg or something? I'm pretty sure there was a—"

"Damn it, woman, no. We don't squirt sperm."

"Pity. That might be fun to watch."

"I don't know what I did to deserve such a creature," he said, looking way more cross than he had been when he walked in. I was on a roll. "We have rules of engagement when it comes to these things, and we tend to find our partners very late in life, so we don't reproduce as quickly as say...a rabbit shifter."

Partners, not mates. And the whole rabbit thing...yeah. Hump like bunnies meant something completely different in Kinship Cove. No, wait, scratch that. It meant the same thing all over. Universal excessive-humping term. "No joke there. I went to high school with a girl—" I gaped at him, the perfect dig hitting me so hard I almost gasped. "Hey, is that why you're so old?"

Kingston jerked as if I'd slapped him, and I had to bite back my smile. "Excuse me?"

"Well, I mean...you've got the gray hair going on. Not that it's a bad thing—you're rocking the silver fox look."

"Silver. Fox. Look."

The amount of disdain in his voice reached epic proportions. I was talking full-out Professor Snape on a bad day quantities. I considered that winning.

"Silver fox—older man, you know? You fit the part. I assumed you were trying to be a sugar daddy or something, what with the age difference between us." I frowned, pulling my lips down hard, making sure to exaggerate the move. "You know, I might be too much for you. Maybe we shouldn't go to dinner. I'd hate to keep you out too late."

Kingston-of-the-bad-nicknames did *not* seem amused. "You think I'm too old to keep up with you."

Not a question. Not a tough statement to answer, either. "Maybe."

He stepped closer, crowding me. Taking up all the space in my world and filling my vision with only him. "Don't push me, little girl."

"Why not, old man?"

His hands landed on my hips, and I gasped, the rush of arousal that simple touch caused almost bringing me to my knees. I caught a glimpse of something dark and shiny as I practically fell into his grasp, but then we were airborne. I don't know how he slipped through the doorway of the bakery, never saw him truly shift, but there was no denying the fact that I'd just been kidnapped by a dragon.

And I was pretty sure I liked it.

As I saw Kinship Cove from an entirely new angle—looking down on it—I tried to control the pounding rhythm of my heart. So high, so fast—Kingston flew us across town and toward the mountains. His claws rested curled against my stomach, long and sharp and dangerous-looking but tucked carefully away. I wasn't scared, and he wasn't trying to hurt me. I had a feeling he was likely trying to make a point, one I'd concede eventually because I didn't want him to drop me. Seemed reasonable, right?

Kingston flew us all the way to a deep ledge about halfway up the ridge to the west of town. Forested on one side with an obvious path, it didn't feel like the sort of place a serial killer would take their next victim. Lucky for me.

When Kingston set me down, he flew to the other side of the ledge, landing so very carefully. And then he waited—watching me. Letting me look him over. Taller than I'd expected—bigger, too—he stood in all his dragon glory. Black scales with a sort of iridescent quality to them that brought out blues, greens, and purples, huge blue eyes with football-shaped pupils, and wings. Big, leathery wings sprouting from behind his shoulders and sitting higher than his head.

Dragon.

Yep.

He was a dragon.

And I had no idea what to do with my attraction to him.

"Please shift back," I whispered, shaking with the need to touch, the desire coursing through me. Something about having been touched by him, overpowered by his strength and speed, had lit a fire inside of me. And I wanted to watch it burn.

With a rush of air that felt soft against my skin and something close to the smell of ozone before a storm, Kingston swirled and shifted shapes, appearing in his human form within a second. Still watching me with those cold blue eyes.

And...dressed?

"Are dragons the only shifters who shift with their clothes intact?" Because I'd seen far too many naked shifters in human forms after they'd shifted and didn't have spare clothes stashed somewhere. The streets of Kinship Cove were filled with bare asses on the regular.

"I believe so, yes. Our magic is much older than most other shifters, though. Why?" He cocked his head and stepped closer, looking far too arrogant to take seriously. "Were you looking forward to seeing me bare?"

Yes. Definitely yes. "Of course not."

"You're lying."

I totally was. "Am not."

He grabbed my hand, tugging me against his chest and nuzzling my neck. Making me tremble. "I can smell it on you, Sparky."

"Oh god," I said as his hands began to roam and his lips brushed my skin. So hot, his touch. So blissfully hot and strong and perfect. I wanted more. Needed it. Had to have it. And yet… "Please don't ruin this with that annoying nickname."

"Ruin what?" he asked as his teeth skimmed over my neck.

I squeezed his biceps, trapping him against me. Unsure if I wanted to tell him to bite me or not. Knowing it was time to get a little daring with him. So I laid my cards on the table…or boulder, seeing as we were on a mountain. "Our first kiss."

"Are you going to kiss me, Sparky?"

"Not if you keep calling me that name."

"But I like it. It suits you."

He would never give up the name, and I was tired of focusing on it. "Hey, Kingston?"

"Yeah, Sparky?"

Jerk. I rose onto the balls of my feet. "Shut up."

And then I kissed him. Deep and hard and groaning softly as flesh met flesh and tongues tangled, I kissed him with everything I had and everything I'd ever hoped for. I kissed him for seconds, minutes, and hours, kissed him in every way I could think of. I planted my lips on his and refused to remove them as the wind blew past us and the scent of cinnamon practically bathed the area. Now *that* was a kiss—every sense involved, every touch magnified by the energy between us. A kiss to end on, to replace the memories of all others. An absolutely perfect last first kiss.

As Kingston's tongue tangled with mine and his growl became the only sound I could hear, everything I'd ever thought I knew about kissing and attraction and life in general exploded around me and resettled into a new sort of truth I hadn't known existed. This man, I could focus on. This man, I could give all of my attention to. If I'd been a shifter and he'd been anything other than a dragon, I'd have said that the fates had thrown us together intentionally.

But I was human.

And his breed didn't have fated mates.

Which meant, even before I took a ride on Kingston's little dragon, I was utterly and completely screwed.

Here's to hoping he was worth it.

5

GINGER

Dragon shifters tasted sweet and spicy like cinnamon candies.

I should know. I'd likely been kissing Kingston for hours—standing up, sitting on his lap, lying in the grass. The kisses had grown passionate and rough then settled down into soft pecks and smooth brushes of tongue and back again. They'd been deep, and they'd been barely more than our lips brushing. Kissing Kingston had become my life, my world, my only pleasure. Not his hands as they roamed slowly over my body and the way he rocked his hips into mine in a telling rhythm. No…just kissing. I couldn't get enough. And that flavor of hot cinnamon candy certainly added to the moment.

Yet, knowing what Kingston tasted like didn't explain my obsession. Not completely. As much as I loved kissing him—and let's be honest, no one would want to spend hours engaging in mouth foreplay unless they truly adored every second of it—I had to stop. I needed to catch my breath and think, but when I pulled my lips from his, Kingston simply moved on to other parts of my body. Naughty dragon.

"Oh, my sweet Ginger," he murmured as he left a trail of tingles down my neck. I groaned and tilted my head back, giving him room. Shivering as he flicked his tongue against my skin. I had a feeling he had more dexterity in that particular appendage than a human male. I also had a feeling I was really going to like it if he kept moving down my body.

Maybe stopping wasn't such a good idea, after all.

"Kingston," I gasped as he laid me back against the rocky ground before biting my collarbone and hovering over me.

"I'm right here, beautiful. Right here."

And he was…right there. And I mean *right there*. I didn't know how he'd slipped between my thighs—damn dragon magic—but he had. I could feel him. Feel his little dragon, which obviously wasn't so little. Could feel how much he wanted me. And I liked it. I was ready for more than just kissing. So ready

Kingston licked his way down my neck, hissing and growling with every taste. Biting softly as he rocked against me. So good. Everything he did felt so good, every sound he made ramped up the heat within me. I was burning alive for him, a sensation I'd never experienced. One I wanted to drown in. One I—

He bit my nipple.

Over my shirt, no warning, no gentleness to it. He bit my nipple hard, making me gasp and arch off the ground. Driving my body up and into his.

Later. I could drown in experiences later.

"Someone likes a little rough play," Kingston murmured, breathing hot and hard over my nipple as if to exacerbate the sting of what he'd done. "Don't worry, Sparky. I'll learn your wants. I'll give you exactly what you need."

Right at that moment, what I needed was more of him. Everywhere. I gripped Kingston's hair and tugged him back up my body, needing his taste on my tongue again. Wanting to have my lips on his as I ground against him. As we teased each other with the writhing motion of our bodies. The flavor of his tongue, the pressure of his mouth on mine, was a drug I couldn't have stopped craving. One I'd never quit…unless he took it away from me. A sobering thought, and one I shoved to the back of my mind. Screw the train wreck headed my way. This would be worth it. Kingston would be worth it. I could already tell.

"Want you," I gasped, giving myself over to the desire swirling within me. I never made the first move, but Kingston brought out that side of me. From the kiss to this—I was taking charge. I tugged him closer, using his body heat to burn through any distracting thoughts. To lose myself in his body. He rocked his hips at the perfect speed to send shivers of desire up my spine, making it pretty easy to stop thinking altogether. "I want you now, Kingston. Please."

His growl shook me down to my toes. "Is that consent, my beautiful girl? Because I need that from you. I can't coerce you into anything."

"You looking the way you do is coercion enough." I grinned as he chuckled, enjoying the buildup between us. The way we fit. The comfort he gave me. This was real. So very real.

"You have to be sure. My dragon magic can lead you down a path you don't mean to follow, which is why I need..." Kingston stopped moving, stopped kissing and licking and writhing to stare down at me with the most intense expression on his face that I'd ever experienced. I could *feel* the weight of his gaze, the lust in his eyes. I felt everything between us, and the heft of it—the solidness—stole my breath.

"What do you need?" I asked, my voice low and breathy. A whisper of sound so as not to break the spell of the moment. "Anything, just tell me. I'll give it to you."

His lips kicked up a tick. "I need you. This. My cock inside you. Your body wrapped around mine. Your taste on my tongue and your thighs pinned against my ears as I eat your sweet cunt. I need to bury myself in your heat and come inside you. I need to hear you scream my name as you milk me dry. I need it all, Sparky. But what I need doesn't matter— what you *want* does. Give me your consent to all of that or just some, to kisses and petting or full-out fucking. Whatever you want, I'll provide. Whatever you don't want will be withheld."

My choice. My decision. My words could end this or take me right over the edge. Drop me on the hard ground below and shatter everything inside of me when he left me behind. My words could be a shield to hide behind or a key to set myself free, even if only for a moment.

I would always choose my freedom. "You. I want all of you."

"Is that consent, beautiful?" Kingston asked, his entire body rigid over mine, a deep rumble to his words. "I'll give you every part of me without blinking, but will you reciprocate? Are you telling me I get all of you?"

All of me. Every inch. Every piece…even the ones I worried he'd break. Just for one night, I'd give myself to someone else. Just one. "Yes. All of me."

"Thank the fates." Kingston lunged, taking my mouth in a kiss so hot and strong and powerful, I practically came from that act alone. But he wasn't finished with me—not by a long shot. Without words, he tore himself away and dove down the length of my body, teasing my hip bones as he yanked my skirt down my legs, rumbling against my pussy as he spread my legs wide with his shoulders.

"Wanted to taste you since I first saw you in the bakery. Wanted your flavor to coat my tongue as I licked your perfect pussy."

But he didn't. He waited, staring down at me with a rapt expression on his face, looking so lost in thought that I worried he'd leave me hanging. That he'd distracted himself enough to stop. Not happening.

"So…go ahead."

"You're catching on to this consent thing," he said, and then he stopped talking and started licking. Sucking. Flicking his tongue against me. Wrapping his lips around my clit and making me arch against his body as fire blazed under my skin. The man was good—really, really good. He had me rocking against his face and riding his fingers in no time, had me crying out for more and hanging on to his hair for leverage, too. A girl could get used to being worshiped that way.

She shouldn't. But she could.

Banishing thoughts of non-matings and partners and things ending eventually, I let my body take over. Let the pleasure ratcheting me higher build and grow and throw me right over the edge. Let it crest within me as every muscle clenched and shook. As I came. Kingston didn't stop, though. Oh no. He slowed a little, humming softly against my skin like some sort of human-dragon-vibrator combo. He kept his hand teasing through my slit and his breath against my clit until I calmed enough to moan his name, and then he started all over again. It didn't take long for me to come again, to yelp and clench and try to pull the man inside of me as my body demanded to be filled. Demanded we move on to the next level. The one that involved his cock inside of me.

"Enough," I said, tugging Kingston back up my body again. Wrapping my legs around his hips when I finally had him on top of me. "More. I need more."

"More what, my beautiful girl?" Kingston kissed me softly, sharing my taste. Moaning softly before saying, "Tell me what you consent to, and I'll do it. Anything."

Consent. Again. He gave me the power to say what we were going to do. I hadn't expected that. Not from a dragon especially. But I liked it. A lot.

"What if I said I wanted you to take off all your clothes?"

"Is that what you want?"

Duh. "Yes."

The man rose to his feet, all animal grace and danger, before stripping out of his clothes. Naked. He looked so damn good naked.

"Now what?"

It took me way too long to answer, seeing as how I was distracted by all the naked. "Come back down here."

He laid his body on mine, both of us sighing when the warmth of our skin coming together grew. "I'm down here. What is it you want me to do?"

Oh, he was going to make me ask for it. Not yet, though. I liked the idea of teasing him too much. "Kiss me."

I didn't even have the words out before his lips were on mine, his tongue caressing my own. Kingston knew how to kiss for sure. No overly wet or rough movements—just the silky glide of his lips on mine, the deep pressure of a man who wanted to be kissed, and the delicious taste of cinnamon. Always.

"Now what?" he asked when he finally pulled away, breathing harder than usual.

I wasn't faring much better. "My breasts. I want to feel your hands on my breasts."

"Just my hands?" He grabbed one breast, kneading softly as he watched his own actions. "Be specific, Sparky. Will your nipples be satisfied with just a tweak from my fingers?"

He tweaked.

I nearly arched right off the ground. "Your mouth. Please."

"My pleasure."

Lies. The pleasure was all mine. His soft lips surrounded the tip of my breast. His tongue—wet and hot and so very dexterous—flicked my nipple as he sucked. So much, and yet it wasn't enough. My pussy clenched on air, wanting more. Needing to be filled. And as much as I liked teasing him, dragging this out and making him wait to get his, I was beginning to think the person suffering was really me.

Even though I'd already gotten off.

Twice.

Whatever. I was greedy.

"Kingston," I gasped as he bit—actually *bit*—down on my nipple. "Now. More…now."

"More what? I need the words, Sparky."

I'd love to have said that his use of my nickname brought me to my senses and made me stop. That would be a lie, though. It did nothing of the sort. In fact, I sort of liked it.

Dragon magic was no joke.

"Come on, my sweet girl." Kingston rocked his hips against mine, teasing me with his hard cock between my thighs. Rubbing against where I was so wet for him, so swollen and needy. "Tell me, and it's yours. You don't even have to ask. Just say it. Consent for me, and I'll give you everything."

Why would I say no? "I want you inside me."

"What part of me?" Kingston slipped a hand between us, circling my clit with his finger before sliding it back. Teasing my entrance instead. "My finger? My hand? Or my cock?"

"Kingston," I whined, trying so hard to rub myself against his evil hand.

"This is fun, my love. Making you ask for what you want, gaining your consent at every step along the way. Fun and necessary. So tell me what you want. What part of me do you want inside this perfectly pink pussy? My finger?" He dragged a knuckle along my clit, the evil dragon. "My hand?" He pulled away from me just a moment before his palm came down harder than I'd expected, making contact with my most sensitive area from top to bottom. Smacking it and giving me another small orgasm with his forcefulness. "Oh, you like that one. But there's another option. If you ask for it, I can give you all of me. My cock buried so deep inside of you, filling you up the way you crave." He dragged the head of his cock along my slit, soaking it, teasing my entrance with the tip. "Which part of me do you want?"

As if I could think with him *right there*. "All of the above?"

He chuckled. "Greedy girl."

Told ya so.

"Let's save something for later. Right now, I want this." I reached between us to grab hold of his little dragon, squeezing and running my fist up and down his length. "Can I have this, please?"

"Such a good girl." He brushed my hand aside, angling his body to drag the head of his cock over my clit. "I'll absolutely give you what you want, especially since you asked so nicely."

"What if I hadn't?"

He paused, his brow furrowing. "Hadn't what?"

"Asked nicely. Would you still give me what I wanted?"

"Yes." He slipped inside, giving me more than just the tip this time but still holding back. "But I would have made you work a little harder for it."

I gripped his shoulders as he pressed deeper, filling me slowly. So very slowly. "Then I guess it's a good thing I know how to say please."

"Give me a few minutes, and I'll teach you how to scream it."

Thankfully, the man lived up to his promise. Within seconds—not minutes—he had thrust deep, stretching me around his considerable girth and filling my pussy in a way that had me moaning like a porn star. Or so I assumed. It wasn't like I watched porn on the regular.

Okay, fine. I did. And I liked it. But I liked the real thing better, especially with Kingston. The man knew exactly what to say to rev my engine.

"Fuck, Sparky. You feel so good wrapped around my cock. So perfect and hot."

See?

Kingston pounded home so deep and hard that I slid across the rocky ground, hanging on to his shoulders and speaking partial words and nonsensical syllables with every thrust. Clinging to him as I crested again, as he made me come harder than I ever had before. As he groaned and arched and pressed deep, coming inside me. Bare. Raw. Unprotected.

Not the smartest thing I'd ever done, but too good to stop.

And afterward, as we lay in the shadows wrapped around one another, as he drifted off to sleep in my arms, I basked in the warmth of staying the night with a man. Falling asleep with one. Something I'd never done before. Something that could possibly change the way I looked at relationships forever.

Something that made me hunger for long term and potential and matings and things I'd never wanted.

Until him.

6

KINGSTON

The night of no sleep must have caught up with me, because I couldn't remember saying even a word after I'd finally come inside my mate. Not one. Nothing sweet or loving to soothe her. Nothing to pontificate on the gloriousness of our coupling. Nothing to explain who I was or how our mating would work. I went from the perfect heat of her body to the blackness of sleep like some sort of human male.

What woke me up from my much-needed slumber was a vibration against my hips and the feeling of something hot running along my cock. Something wet like a—

"Fuck, Sparky." I grabbed her head and arched back as she took me into her mouth. *All* the damn way into her mouth. So deep, so hot and wet and fucking perfect. No way was I going to last. Which only meant I got to taste her sweet pussy that much sooner. "Ah, yeah. That's it. Suck me harder."

She did, groaning softly as she bobbed over me. Fuck sleep. Who needed it when I had a gorgeous, sexy girl doing such naughty things? Not me. Or, at least, I'd convince myself of that, no matter how heavy my eyelids grew or how slow my brain felt. I could stay awake for this. Definitely.

Fighting hard not to ruin the moment by falling asleep and missing it, I rocked my hips slowly, forcing myself a little deeper as Ginger hollowed her cheeks and sucked me like her life depended on it. By the fates, the woman gave good head. Not too wet, not too sloppy, and a fuckton of pressure drawing me into her throat. I could live forever in that heat. Could die inside her mouth with no regrets. Save one.

"Get up here," I said, tugging on her shoulders. She popped off my cock and licked her lips, almost making me come right there.

"But I was just getting started."

Yeah, she was. The pretty pout on her lips almost made me acquiesce to her wants. I needed more than her mouth, though. I craved a taste of her. "It's my turn."

Her smile nearly gutted me, and the slinky way she crawled up my body had every inch of me sitting up to take notice. By the fates, she was sexy.

"What did you have in mind?"

"I want you on my face." As soon as I could reach, I grabbed her by the hips. Tugging her up my body. Past my chest. Positioning her thighs on either side of my head. Her soft giggle sounded more nervous than I would have liked, though. "Are you still consenting?"

"Sure. I mean…I'll try anything once."

I froze, my hands wrapped around her soft thighs, the scent of her pussy making my voice more growl than it should have been. Or perhaps it was the neglect she'd suffered from her previous partners. "You've never ridden a partner's face?"

"That's a little personal."

"Amuse me."

"Okay." She looked down at me, her dark hair falling forward. Her hazel eyes locked on mine even as a flush bloomed on her chest and neck. Nervous. She was nervous. "I've had guys go down on me, just not —" she waved a hand toward where her hips met my head "—like this."

"I get to be first."

Her head cock and eyebrow raise shouted louder than she ever would. "If that's what you want."

It was. It very much was. I didn't care about her past—was actually thrilled she could be an active, vocal lover so I could make sure to please her—but to give her something new felt like a gift. An opportunity to prove my worth. And I would.

"I won't pass up the chance to give you new experiences, Sparky." I lifted my head, seeking her out. Needing her taste on my throat. "Shuffle a little closer. I want your pussy all over me."

She shuffled, that delicious flush growing darker. "This is seriously awkward."

"Why? Because you could smother me with your pussy if you wanted to?"

"Keep calling me Sparky, and I might think about it."

"Please do. It would be a noble way to die."

"Oh please. As if—"

Her words died with a strangled sort of sound as I licked her from one end of her pussy to the other. No sucking, no fingers, nothing penetrating—just my tongue on her heated flesh. Tasting. And if I purposefully added a little pressure and flick as I finally reached her clit, then so be it. She deserved it.

"Still consenting, my beautiful girl?"

Her thighs trembled. "Yeah. Still in."

"Good." I licked her again, adding more pressure. More flicks. More of everything. Teeth and lips joined my tongue as she began to lose herself to the experience. As she grabbed my hair and rocked her hips, riding my face the way I'd wanted. Needed. Craved.

I worked her good, and when she came, when she cried my name and arched her back as she coated my chin in her arousal, pride stronger than any other filled me. I'd done it—pleased my mate with a new experience. Something other males hadn't given her. I'd succeeded.

"Oh, Kingston. How do you do this to me?" she whispered, running her fingers through my hair as I lay beneath her, my belly wet from where I'd come right along with her. No stimulation needed other than her scent, her taste, and the sound of my name on her lips. Bliss. And I was the lucky bastard who would get to have this woman forever.

I wanted to tell her so much, to give her my past and my plans, my breed heritage and how it would work with hers. I wanted to hold her and talk as the night passed, but I only got one. I managed to pull her into my arms and roll over her. To wrap my arms around her and hold her close before sleep became too hard to resist and I fell into a deep slumber. My mate by my side. Where she belonged.

We could talk in the morning.

GINGER

Sleeping outside with the bugs and the noises and all the things that could go wrong wasn't usually my thing, but with Kingston, I slept hard. I dreamed hard, too. Vivid, swirling dreams of animals running through forests and splashing through streams. Of wolves hunting together in the early evening light. Of a lone animal sitting in a clearing and howling toward the moon, his pointy ears up and his fur swirled and sweet. Tasty, really. All the animals would want a bite of him. They'd want to lick the frosting from—

"Shit." I sat straight up just as the sun peeked over the mountaintop, coming awake from a dead sleep with only one thought in my mind. "I forgot to deliver the cake."

Thankfully, Kingston didn't wake up at my outburst. Just what I needed him to do. Sure, it would have been easier to shake him until his eyes came open then ask him to bring me back home. He'd probably have kissed me, shifted forms, and flown me all the way down the side of the mountain. But the idea of how this would end—of the awkwardness of goodbye after such an amazing night—made me avoid that option. It would be better for both of us for me to walk away. No scenes, no excuses. Dragons didn't take mates like other shifters, so this was just a one-night thing. One glorious, beautiful night that I'd remember long after Kingston had left the cove.

Maybe forever.

And wasn't he a jerk for making me want more of him?

I couldn't be that clingy girl, though. That woman who refused to let go when the man made it clear he didn't want more. I had my pride to protect and my rules to follow—one and done. No commitments, no long term, no complications. My head knew better than to get tangled up in some fantasy of happily ever after just because the dick was good.

My heart...well, I was pretty sure I'd already fucked that all up by spending any time with the naked dragon wrapped around me. He'd pulverized it with his devilish grins and sweet words, with his sexy ice-blue eyes and the way he sought my consent for every move. He'd destroyed me in the best way with far more than just good sex. I liked his attitude and irritating ways. Wanted to hear him call me Sparky even though it drove me insane. I wanted...lots of things I simply couldn't have.

I gave myself to the count of twenty to take advantage of our positions. Running my fingers through his salt-and-pepper hair, brushing my hands down his muscled shoulders and arms. Absorbing his heat and his cinnamon smell. Saying goodbye to the way he made my heart thump so hard. Cementing him into my memory for those nights when I was alone and wishing for something I simply wasn't ever going to have.

Eighteen—nineteen—twenty. Time to go.

Kingston slept through me extracting myself from his hold. Slept through me stumbling around to find my clothes. Even slept right on through me cursing his name as I sought a way off the cliff—thank goodness for the hiking trails my sisters and I had explored on a daily basis as kids—and made my way back to town. The man didn't even stir as I left him on that cliff.

Which was likely a good thing.

I could avoid the awkwardness of the end of the one-night stand and all. No "I'll call you"s or "We'll get together soon"s, no simple lies meant to make the other person feel better. Just me slipping through the shadows and doing my best not to think about the possibilities of a life where the fates didn't control men like Kingston. Where maybe—just maybe—I could let my guard down and allow myself to have more than one night.

I walked away from Kingston before he could walk away from me, leaving a little piece of my heart on that cliff with the dragon who'd rocked my world.

Damn him.

7

KINGSTON

There were three things a dragon never wanted to experience.

The first was to be trapped on the ground by some sort of damage to their wings. We were flight animals; we danced on air streams and currents.

Second was to be cold. As cold-blooded animals, we tended to seek warmth from external sources. Sunshine was good, hot water better, but the friction of two bodies coming together was the best. A lack of that… well, it made us cranky.

But the third, the one that was every dragon's greatest fear, was to be rejected by their mate. It took us so long to find one, and we had so many hoops to jump through to confirm their active and enthusiastic consent along the way, that losing them before we could finalize the mating seemed almost horrific. At least, that's what I'd always assumed, listening to the other dragons tell stories and legends. I couldn't really say, seeing as how I'd never found my fated mate.

Until Ginger.

I'd thought locating her, being with her, convincing her to give me a chance to please her, would be the start of something between us. Would open up the door to a true mating. But when I woke up alone on the cliff—cold and mateless under a sun far too high to be in a morning sky—I experienced two of the three things dragons never wanted to at once.

Thankfully, I could still fly.

As soon as I realized my mate was well and truly gone and had been for hours, I yanked on my clothes and shifted forms, flying hard and fast toward the other end of town. I never slept deep like I had the night before, never let myself rest heavy enough for anyone to sneak up—or out—on me. Apparently, showering my mate with orgasms and finding my own release inside of her had worn me out. Or perhaps not sleeping the night before to guard her home had caught up with me. Either way, my timing was shit. I would have liked to have woken her up with my mouth on her sweet cunt again, but she'd left. Left... for reasons I couldn't possibly fathom. Something that needed rectifying. I hadn't explained our mating yet, hadn't bitten her and claimed her as mine. I needed to find her and convince her to be with me. Always.

And then I'd spank her pert little ass nice and hard for leaving me alone without a word of goodbye.

I headed to her home first, shifting as I landed and rushing onto the porch.

"Ginger." I pounded on the door, yelling her name multiple times. A waste of time, it seemed. No answer. Nothing inside to indicate she was home either. I pounded louder and longer, though. Just in case.

"Yo," a man said, walking out the door of the house next door and glaring my way. "What's the problem?"

I had no time for such small talk. "Do you know Ginger Chance? I'm looking for her."

"Yeah, I know her. Are you sure you do?"

Protective. That was the only way to describe the man's stance and tone. He was protecting Ginger from me, a comical thought. Being that I was her mate, she was safest with me. But this guy—this lion shifter by the scent of him—apparently thought he knew best what she needed. Cute.

And irritating. "I'm pretty sure I know her better than most considering I'm her mate. Have you seen her today or not?"

"You got Ginger for a mate?" He laughed. "What did you do so wrong as to piss off the fates that bad?"

My growl silenced his chuckle. "Have you seen my mate?"

"Nah, man. Not today. You might want to try the bakery where she works."

Of course. "Thank you."

I shifted on the spot and shot into the air, ignoring the lion's startled gasp. *That's right, fucker. Ginger has a dragon for a mate.*

But only if she accepted me as such.

I flew toward the bakery, passing over the building and dropping down behind it. I didn't sense Ginger, didn't catch her spicy scent on the air, but that didn't stop me from rushing for the door. What did was a woman. A small, quiet woman I recognized as one of Ginger's sisters, walking out of the building I was attempting to enter.

Convenient. "Where is she?"

The woman—Madeleine, if I remembered right—yelped and spun, practically falling back against the dumpster. Before I could offer her my hand to help her regain her footing, the back door burst open and a man rushed between us. A man I recognized.

"Jericho—"

"Get the fuck away from her."

I froze, glancing from Madeleine to Jericho and back again. Figuring out things faster than he likely had. His snarl and protective stance told me everything I needed to know—he'd found his mate all right. And it definitely wasn't another bear.

But that was his business—I had my own battle to wage with the fates. So I put my hands up, and I took a step away from Madeleine. "I wasn't trying to hurt your mate. I was simply trying to find mine."

"I'm not his mate," Madeleine said, sounding much angrier than I would have expected. And so very wrong as well.

Jericho huffed, a miserable sort of sound if I'd ever heard one. "What is it you need, Kingston?"

"Ginger. Where is she?"

"Why?" Madeleine asked.

Honesty seemed like the right strategy with the girl. "She's my mate."

Her face fell, her entire countenance crumpling before my eyes. "Oh."

That was it. Nothing more. And yet, she'd just painted me a picture of complete and utter devastation. Never had a single syllable carried so much pain. "I'm sorry. I don't know—"

"She's fine," Jericho said, moving between me and the girl again. "Ginger's not here, though. You should be on your way."

"Not without something. I want to know where my mate is. I need to know that she's okay."

Jericho twitched his nose, an odd motion from such a big man, and glanced down at Madeleine. "What do you think?"

Madeleine huffed a sarcastic-sounding laugh before looking up at Jericho with the saddest eyes known to man...or beast. "So, when it's about Ginger, you care what I think?"

"Mad—"

"Ginger's not here and not coming in," she said, completely overstepping the bear shifter before her. "I don't know where she is, but she and Coco both skipped out of work for the day. I do know that she's going to be at the party tonight, though. Fiona's bachelorette. It's at the Metro Club."

A party. She'd slipped away from me without saying goodbye and was going to *a party* at the Metro Club—a place where singles drank and danced all over one another. Where sex happened in the bathrooms, in the dark corners, and on the dance floor. And Ginger would be there tonight. Without me by her side.

I wanted to be pissed at her, to roar my hurt feelings all over the town and burn things down with my rage, but I couldn't. I hadn't been clear, hadn't given her enough reasons to stay with me. Hadn't spoiled her enough to win her over. I'd gotten her consent for sex but not for a true mating with me.

I would change all that.

Tonight.

Decision made, I nodded once at Ginger's sister. "Thank you."

Madeleine shrugged. "My sister deserves happiness."

"As do you."

That sad sort of smile returned. "I do. And I plan to stop letting things hold me back so I can find it." She pushed past Jericho and me, heading for a small red car at the back of the lot. "Have fun, boys. I've got business to do."

We watched her drive off. Me, worried and anxious to leave but somehow unable to; Jericho, tense and looking ready to fight.

"What kind of business do you think she meant?" he finally asked, still not looking away from where her car had disappeared around the building.

"Perhaps her mate should already know that."

"I'm not her mate."

Lies. "Could have fooled me."

He sighed, finally meeting my gaze. Looking pensive and wary. "I've known her since she was in diapers."

Such a silly thing to worry about. "She's not in diapers anymore."

"Don't you think I know that?" he asked with a growl, running his hand through his hair as he began to pace. "I fucking know she's not in diapers anymore. I've known it since before she graduated high school when I felt like a lecherous old man for even glancing her way." He sighed again. "I still feel like a lecherous old man."

"I'm likely hundreds of years older than my mate, and you're the one feeling like a dirty old man for the gift the fates have given you." I patted him on his big shoulder. "I'd love to stay and make you see how stupid you're being, but I have a mate to track down."

"How'd you lose her, anyway?"

"Fell asleep."

He grunted. "Sleep is good."

"Mates are better." I shifted and took off before he could answer, launching myself straight up into the skies over Kinship Cove to keep watch for my mate in case she decided to show herself.

And if not, I'd be heading to the Metro Club tonight.

8

GINGER

Get your grumpy ass in this car," Fiona yelled as she popped her head through the open sunroof of the limousine.

"Yeah, yeah. I'm coming." I set the last of the cupcake trays in the trunk and shut the lid before running to lock the back door of the bakery. The sun was well past the beginning-to-set phase, and the shop had likely been closed for a couple of hours already. Coco and Madeleine were probably each at home. I'd missed my sisters while I'd played hooky from the bakery. Had needed to talk to them about Kingston and what had happened last night. About all the reasons why my chest had felt so tight all day.

But I'd texted them that I wouldn't be in and had instead spent the day with Fiona and her friends at the hotel, thinking a change of scenery would clear my head a little.

It did not. If anything, my mind was far more jumbled than it had been all day. Stupid brain. Stupid heart. Stupid me letting one overrule the other.

"Move it, human. We've got men to grind on."

Stupid idea thinking a bachelorette party was what I needed after having the best sex of my life then basically ghosting the guy I'd had it with. Lord, give me the strength not to smack someone tonight.

"Done," I said as I slipped into the back seat once more, pasting on a smile to hide my foul mood. "Boozy cupcakes acquired."

"What were the ones you made at the hotel?" Fiona asked, knocking on the window to tell the driver we were ready to roll again. "I thought those were the boozy ones?"

If I could have, I would have blushed. Not because I'd been stress baking—I'd spent a large chunk of my day hiding out in the basement kitchen of the hotel baking. And thinking. And pretty much hiding from my life. No, that wasn't what made the heat rise in my cheeks. It was *what* I'd been baking. And why.

"No booze—just spice. Cinnamon, mostly. They were cinnamon and ginger cake with an apple puree filling and caramel buttercream frosting."

Fiona stared at me for a solid ten seconds before cursing softly. "Those sound amazing."

Yeah. They did. And I'd likely never be able to eat or drink that spicy flavor again without a yawning pit of despair opening up in my gut. Thanks, Kingston.

I shrugged, not wanting to admit my ridiculous obsession with cinnamon that had finally driven away the distractions and given me something new and exciting to add to the bakery menu. Or my obsession with the man behind the inspiration. "Cupcakes are good, but liquor is better. Let's hit the club."

"Perfect," Cleo, one of Fiona's friends, practically purred. The girl had that sexy, big cat shifter thing down pat. Hell, she might have been a tiger shifter for all I knew. "I can't wait to hit the dance floor."

Fiona and the rest of the girls—all six of them—agreed and began talking over what songs they wanted to hear and how much they wanted to shake their asses. Me? I kept my sad sack self in the corner. If I hadn't promised Fiona I'd go with her to her party—and if I hadn't used her as an excuse to hide from dealing with my feelings for Kingston all day—I'd simply head home. I didn't want to dance or drink, I wanted to wallow.

I'd spent my day with these girls—getting my hair and makeup done and drinking mimosas until my tongue hurt from all the acid. The only breaks I'd taken from their company were those moments in the basement kitchen baking feverishly to try to capture the perfect flavor profile—to distract myself from all the thoughts and feelings running through me. All the things about Kingston that wouldn't let me go. His sweetness, his dirty mouth, the demanding way he took me, how he didn't make a move without my consent. The way he tasted like a cinnamon candy, burning his essence into my body. All of it—I loved all of it.

But love wasn't my thing. It wasn't what I wanted or needed. Especially not with a dragon shifter. They didn't stay true to anyone. That's what I'd always heard. The one shifter breed that didn't take a true mate, or didn't stick to just one. None of that should have bothered me. I, myself, liked to make my relationships last just one night. Maybe two if the chemistry was right. I was more of a hit it and quit it girl than the long-haul sort.

But Kingston had me thinking long haul, which couldn't happen because he wasn't down for that.

And wasn't that something like karma coming to bite me in the ass? The player being played. Well done, fates. Well done.

Feeling ridiculously lost and off-balance, I pulled out my phone and texted the one person I figured would understand.

Me: How's the wolf?

Coco: Sweaty

Me: Do I want to know?

Coco: Yes, but I'm not going to tell you.

Coco: What's wrong?

Me: Why does anything have to be wrong?

Coco: Because you're texting me. And you forgot to deliver the groom's cake. Thanks for that, by the way.

Me: Yeah, sorry. I had man issues.

Coco: Man or dragon?

How the hell did she know already?

Coco: Misty ratted you out, in case you were wondering how I knew.

And now she was psychic. Wonderful.

Me: You two conspiring against me?

Coco: Of course. You okay?

Me: Yeah. Just heading out for the night and feeling a bit wobbly.

Coco: Call your dragon.

Me: Not happening.

Coco: Misty thinks he's your mate.

Me: Dragons don't do the whole fated mates thing.

Coco: That could be a rumor. Like how we all thought bear shifters hibernated all winter.

Me: Uncle Jericho sleeps for like twenty hours a day in the winter.

Coco: True, but that's not like hibernation. That's just...seasonal affective disorder or something.

Me: Not sure there's a real difference there.

Coco: Fine. Bad example. Why not find out what your dragon wants before writing him off? Ask him.

As if.

Me: I think I'd rather masturbate my way to happiness, thank you very much.

Coco: Graphic.

Me: Yup.

Coco: Fine. Do nothing. See if I care.

She cared. Otherwise, she wouldn't have said that.

Me: Love you, sis. I really am sorry I forgot to deliver the cake. Everything go okay?

Coco: In the end, yes. Dropping off the cake? Not so much.

Me: Sorry. I got swept away...literally.

Coco: Sounds fun. I'm going to need you to tell me all about it.

Me: Dinner this week? All three of us. It's been a while.

Coco: I'm in. I'll set it up with Maddie.

Ever the responsible sister.

Me: Sounds good. Pulling up at the club—gotta go.

Coco: Be safe

Me: Mind your wolf.

Coco: I would if you'd quit interrupting us.

Me: Brat.

Coco: Nag.

Coco: Now quit texting me. I'm busy being naked.

*Me: Thanks for the visual. I'll be dancing my frustrations away.
Clothed.*

Coco: Where's the fun in that?

"You ready?"

I looked up from my phone, meeting Fiona's worried gaze. That wouldn't do. The bride shouldn't be worried about me or my nonexistent love life. It was time to paste a smile on my face, pull up my big-girl panties, and shake my ass across the dance floor. Even if my heart did feel as if it had been shredded into ribbons. That's what you called taking one for the team. The team being a very sexy, very successful wolf shifter with a new mate who totally didn't deserve her.

"Absolutely," I said, using every ounce of giddy I could drum up from within me to keep my smile bright and my energy excited. "Let's go celebrate your last night being a single woman."

"That ship has sailed, my friend. The second the fates put us together, I was a goner."

And…smile, gone. Thankfully, Fiona didn't notice. She headed inside with Cleo and a few others, leaving me and a couple of girls to deal with the cupcakes. I didn't even try to buoy my mood. Fates and mates and shifters…oh my. The paranormal creatures around me had flipped my world upside down, and I didn't like it.

"Come on, ladies," I said, refusing to let my crappy mood ruin anyone's good time. "Let's get these trays inside. The first round of margarita cupcakes is on me."

151

9

GINGER

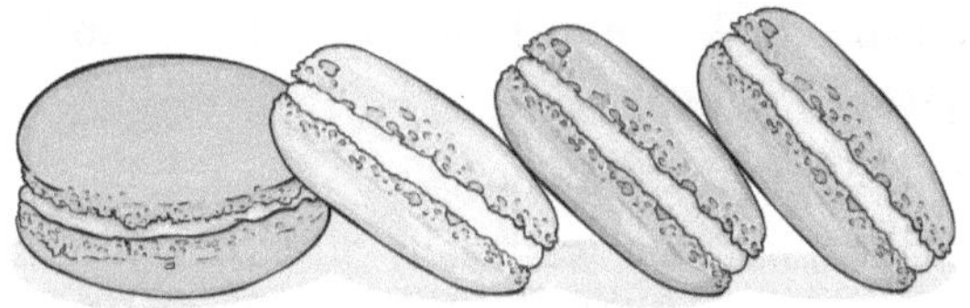

Want to know what the worst idea in the history of the world was?

Me thinking hanging out with a bunch of drunken shifters was a good plan.

Past-Ginger was an idiot of epic proportions.

"Drink, Ginger. You need to loosen up."

If Fiona hadn't been the one getting married in the morning, I might have smacked her. Instead, I pasted on a goofy grin. "I've had like six cupcakes. I'm totally buzzing already."

I wasn't, but no way was I telling her that. Sometimes it was easier—and more polite—to lie. I mean, no one wanted to hear that the party in their honor made a guest want to poke her eyes out with a dirty spork. I was blunt…I wasn't a bitch. Most days.

Fiona left me to hit the dance floor with the other girls. A good thing because my mood was likely to spread like a disease through this place. Best to leave me to my cranky, lonely self. Unfortunately, a single girl sitting in a club all alone was the target for more attention than I would have liked and opened me up to attacks of the less feminine and much less wanted variety.

"Feeling better tonight?" A guy sat next to me, one who looked a little familiar. One with an arrogant sort of smirk that pinged at something in my head. Something I couldn't quite grab hold of.

"Do I know you?"

"I can't believe you don't remember." He laughed like some douchebag on TV—head back, hand on his chest, totally exaggerated and way too loud. Not at all creepy.

Totally creepy. "I guess I don't. Maybe I should—"

His hand on my thigh stopped me from rising. And speaking. And thinking. Who was this guy?

"We met the other night. I'm Luca."

I think I blinked, but that was really all I could do. Luca? No clue. And also, that hand needed to be gone. Immediately. I shoved it off my leg and inched back, cursing myself for sitting in the corner and trapping myself.

He must have caught on to my utter lack of knowledge of his existence. "At the bar. We were talking, but you said it was warm and ran for the bathroom."

Oh hell. Luca—L-Name guy, gorilla shifter, had done dealings with Jericho. Thought my owning a bakery was quaint.

I was still mad about that.

"Right. Sorry. It's dark in here." *And you're totally forgettable.*

"Sure thing. I get it, but now you know who I am. I was hoping to run into you again." He leaned closer, looking at me in a way that... well... You know that feeling? That tingle on the back of your neck that tells you—the prey animal—to get the hell away from something scary? Yeah. I had it. He was looking at me with far more interest than I wanted.

Time to skedaddle. "Well, Lu—" Lucas? Luke? Ludacris? Shit, his name never quite stuck. I coughed to cover up my fumble. "Excuse me. Must be my allergies. So yeah, it was good to see you again, but I think I'm going to go join my friends on the dance floor."

"I'll come with you."

So...he was a guy who couldn't take a hint. Shocking. I didn't want to make a scene, though, plus I had a gaggle of female shifters who could back me up. So I kept my mouth shut and made my way through the crowd. Luca followed—a little too closely for my comfort, to be honest.

"Oh, looks like Ginger got herself a live one," Cora—bear shifter—said. I tried to shake my head, to give her the "this guy needs to go away" look, but she was too far into her tray of cupcakes to pick up what I was putting down. Figured.

"Aren't you two cute together?" Fiona said, literally shoving me back toward Luca. "You should totally dance."

"Yeah, I don't think—"

"We should." Gorilla-guy grabbed me by the hips and yanked me against him as the girls tittered and giggled and basically acted like drunken matchmakers. I rocked side to side, trying hard to keep my composure—and plan my escape—as Luca bumped against me. Seriously, who thought dry-humping a girl's ass was hot? When had this become a thing? I didn't need some stranger's half-hard dick pressed against me. I didn't know where that thing had been. Besides…my mind was still stuck on a certain dragon shifter who could probably mop the floor with this gorilla. He had the only dick I was interested in. Not that I was going to have it again. No dick for me. No dragon shifter, either. Kingston—totally unforgettable name—would likely leave town soon enough, taking a piece of my heart with him.

And now I'd be singing that old Janis Joplin song the rest of the night. The one about taking another little piece of my heart. The one I only knew about fifteen words of. Wonderful.

Trying to focus on the here and now, I danced away from L-Name and his half-hard dick to a more open area on the floor. Arms up, eyes open, watching as Fiona and Cora and the rest of the girls laughed and moved, I gave myself over to the music. Throwing myself into the moves as the music blared and the bass pumped through the space. It was loud, hot, a little wild…and not at all what I needed right then. But I tried. At least until I noticed the girls had moved themselves farther away from me than I'd like. Never leave your pack, and all that. I moved as if to head for them, but Luca grabbed my arm and pulled me back against him.

"Where are you going, Ging?"

Two soft Gs, of course. As if the final "er" was just too much to say. What was with men not using my name lately? And why did Ging bug me way more than Sparky?

I really needed to go home. "This was fun, but I want to join my friends."

"You don't need them. I'm right here." And that, my friends, was when he grabbed me. Not like Kingston had the night before—not gently guiding me where he wanted me to go. Nope. Gorilla-guy grabbed my arm hard, almost making me flinch, and he pulled me against him. Tugged, yanked, jerked, snatched—whatever verb fit the vision of a huge man dragging a not-so-huge girl against his chest, that was it. And I was done.

"That's really not how this works." I tried to extricate myself from his gorilla grip, but he only tugged harder, rubbing himself against me. Again with the grinding. This wasn't my thing. Usually dancing with a hot guy was fun, usually watching a couple basically have sex not fifteen feet in front of me was a riot, usually I got into the sensuality of the club and let my hair down.

Tonight wasn't a usual night.

And this guy wasn't playing by my rules.

"Hey," I said, once again trying to pull away from the hands that kept clinging to me. "I think it's time for me to go."

"What? The night's just getting started."

Jesus, the man should have been an octopus instead of a gorilla. Who knew giant apes were so handsy?

"Yeah, but it's been a long day, and I'm not feeling up to this."

His face turned hard, his lips tight. "You're not leaving me again."

"Excuse me?" If there was any more sarcasm and disbelief available in my tone, I couldn't find it. Every bit of force went into the "scuse" of excuse, every ounce of independent "don't you dare tell me what to do"-ness backing up those words. I wasn't being polite with that question, in case that wasn't clear. "I'm not interested in dancing with you, so I'm leaving."

I made it three steps, three short, clipped steps, before a big hand landed on my shoulder and I was spinning. Not in a good way.

Not good at all.

KINGSTON

The Metro Lounge sat at the edge of town in what had likely been an industrial area of the city. Well, as industrial as Kinship Cove got. Still, the street seemed dark and deserted, the club situated in a big warehouse-looking building, and the music loud enough to hear three blocks away.

I was going to hate this place.

But, if Ginger was in there, I had to go. I needed to find her, to make sure she was okay. To spank that pert ass of hers for leaving me so stealthily. Never again. If I couldn't allow myself to sleep another night for the rest of my life just to keep her with me, I'd do it. She was worth sleepless nights and always being on guard.

That didn't mean I still wouldn't spank her later. I'd bet she'd like that.

The club was about as dark and loud and hyped-up as I'd expected. Human and shifter alike crowded into every available space, talking too loud, drinking too much, and basically getting in my way. But even over all that, over the liquor and the perfume and the sex—because, by the fates, did the place smell like sex—I caught a whiff of exactly what I'd been looking for. Cinnamon.

Ginger. I released my dragon enough to hunt for my mate, pushing past people unapologetically as I tracked my girl. Let everyone be pissed that I'd shoved them out of my way. I gave no fucks about their hurt feelings. All I cared about, all I needed in that moment, was my mate.

Whom I finally spotted out on the dance floor.

With the guy from the bar the other night.

And she was kissing him.

My dragon roared in my head, and my gut filled with hot lead. Or, at least, it felt that way. My mate had her lips on another man's. Had her hands gripping his arms and pulling him tighter. Had her—

Wait.

I allowed my dragon to come even closer to the surface, gave him a bit more rein to use his senses. Something looked off about the picture before me. More off than just Ginger in another man's arms. She wasn't pulling him closer; she was pushing against him. And she definitely wasn't kissing him back.

A whiff of cinnamon pulsed by me again, my dragon picking it out of the rest of the scents with ease. But this time, there was an acrid sort of tinge to it. An added odor that told me exactly how Ginger was feeling.

Scared. That scent meant fear. My mate felt *fear*.

With a roar that sent other shifters skittering away, I raced across the dance floor, unable to control the beast within, knowing my scales would be showing and my eyes would be changed into my beast's. Not caring at all if I scared the people on the floor. Hoping like hell that I terrified the man who'd dared to put his hands where they didn't belong. Where they weren't wanted. Where he didn't have consent to touch.

Ginger finally pulled herself away from the man just as I reached them. The glare she shot him looked mean enough to peel paint. Cute, but not enough. A man like him wouldn't respond to a look. That was okay—I'd give him what he'd understand.

Edging past Ginger, I grabbed his shoulder. One tug spun him around, and then I pushed. Hard. Perhaps a little too hard.

Back in the fifties, I'd become interested in a sport called bowling. Throwing a ball down a lane toward ten pins all lined up and ready to fall. Well, the man—a gorilla shifter, by the scent of him—wasn't truly a ball, and all the people dancing in the way of my throw weren't pins, but the visual worked. Bowling for humans. Oddly satisfying.

"What the fuck?" Gorilla-man said as he scrambled to stand. From twenty feet away. If I'd been in my dragon form, I would have swished my tail in glee. Not too bad of a throw considering I hadn't bowled in a number of decades. Some things you never forgot, apparently.

Like the fact that this fucker had been pawing all over *my* girl. "She didn't ask you to kiss her, did she?"

The shock on his face told me enough, even though he opened his mouth to let his stupidity shine. "She's a tease. She fucking wanted it but was playing it off like she didn't."

"Oh no," Ginger said, moving beside me. "There was no playing. I didn't want it."

Gorilla-boy pouted. And by pouted, I mean, glowered in our direction. "This is bullshit."

"No, it's dragon shit," I said, making sure to let my throaty rumble roll through my words. "And if you want to keep all of your appendages —especially the ones I'm sure you're just so proud of—you'd better keep your hands off my mate."

His eyes grew wide, and his face paled. Yes, sometimes reminding people you were an ancient beast bred to hunt and kill really could be fun. For me.

"Yeah, well…"

I raised an eyebrow and crossed my arms over my chest, waiting. Hoping he'd say something just as ignorant as before so I could smack him down again. Physically, this time. It'd been a stressful day—I could use a little release.

Fortunately for him, Gorilla-guy took off across the floor instead of standing his ground. Figured. I huffed, watching him leave, fighting the urge to follow him. To rip him to pieces with my bare hands. To shoot fireballs at him. Being a gentleman and trying to rebuild the reputations of dragon shifters everywhere really was a pain in the ass at times.

"Mate?"

Speaking of pains in my ass… I turned slowly, meeting Ginger's surprised stare. Unable to speak for a long second as I got lost in her hazel eyes. By the fates, she was beautiful.

"Yes. Mate, as in mine. Now, do you mind telling me why you disappeared last night, girl?"

"I didn't disappear, I left."

"Same thing."

"Two totally different things."

My mate was a brat. "I swear to the fates, girl—"

"Quit calling me girl."

"Quit behaving like one."

That glare I'd seen pointed at Gorilla-man turned on me, but it didn't even slow me down. Neither did the sight of a group of women headed my way. Likely friends of Ginger's coming to her rescue. Too bad they hadn't noticed the guy assaulting her on the dance floor. Didn't matter, though, because I had. I'd protected her as a mate should. And I was done with the noise and the stench of this place.

"We need to have a conversation," I said, trying hard to keep my dragon contained.

Ginger, on the other hand, seemed ready to rile him up. "You want to talk? Fine. Go ahead."

As in, right there in the melee, with her friends looking on. Not happening. "I'd prefer a little privacy."

"I'd prefer not to be manhandled."

"Then don't come to a club without someone to keep an eye on you."

"I can take care of myself."

"I can do it better."

"You're an asshole."

"No, I'm a dragon shifter who's found his reason for being. Now, are you willing to come talk to me somewhere other than this den of iniquity or not, mate?"

The word *mate* seemed to get her attention. She gasped softly, her eyes widening. Her arms crossing as she seemed to hold herself together. "Fine. Whatever you want."

"You're lucky I'm not going to take you at your word."

"You mean we're not going to talk?"

"Oh, we totally are. I mean taking whatever I want. Because right now, I want to spank that ass of yours until you come to your senses. But I'll settle for this."

I picked her up around the waist and rushed for the door, leaving behind yells and cries of people who had no true idea what was going on. I was sure her friends were worried about her, but I no longer cared. They'd failed her, and I wouldn't do the same.

Not that she would ever make it easy on me. "Put me down."

"No."

"You don't get to order me around and just...take me."

I gave that perfect ass one hard spank, just to prove a point. "Technically, I do. You said, whatever I want. That's part of being a mate. I get to order you around, and you get to order *me* around. Especially in the bedroom. I'm taking you at your word."

"The bedroom? As if." She grunted as I tossed her up and over my shoulder. "You're an asshole, and I am so not fucking you again."

With her head by my ass and her feet dangling over the front of my shoulder, I didn't have it in me to argue that point. I had control over her for now. So I pinned her to me as I shifted forms in the alley, and I took off. Flying through the skies and heading back to the scene of the crime. To the mountains. To our cliff.

To a quiet place where I could be alone with my mate and try to convince her that I was worthy of her attention.

And then spank her ass some more.

GINGER

I am a strong, independent woman who doesn't need a man to sweep me off my feet. I am a strong...

The mantra repeated in my head as a man—one who drove me crazy —quite literally swept me off my feet. And off the ground. Kinship Cove was really pretty from the sky at night. The lights of the actual town stood in stark contrast to the blanket of black below me, and the houses spreading out toward the mountains glowed softly. Kingston flew above the treetops, giving me a wonderful view of the cove and the mountains ringing our little town. Gorgeous, romantic, and—if I hadn't been kidnapped by someone with scales—a fabulous date sort of thing.

But Kingston was in his dragon form. And he'd snatched me away from my friends. Those two things didn't equate to fabulous, and they sort of negated my mantra. Strong, independent...but at the mercy of a mythical beast. Like some sort of fairy-tale princess. With a dirty mouth.

"You're a real asshole, you know that?"

I wasn't sure if a dragon could laugh, but if he could, Kingston was. At me. Asshole was too nice of a word for him. Still, I held tight to his arms and rested in his clawed grip, watching the town pass by below me. But inside? I was a mess of nerves. I'd never gotten motion sick in the past, but the way my stomach churned seemed about right for how that should feel. Nauseated. Pukey. Vomitus. About to blow chunks. They all worked. But it wasn't the flying that got to me. In fact, I felt quite secure in Kingston's grip.

What I didn't feel secure in was my own ability to resist him. He'd called me his mate. *Mate.* Even though dragons didn't take fated mates like other shifters. Or so I'd thought. The possibility that I could have been wrong—that there might be more to us than a single night—didn't help the feeling of needing to lose my lunch. Or dinner. Or…whatever.

Eventually, Kingston descended to a large overlook on the side of the mountain. A cliff I recognized well. One I'd had to hike down from just that morning. Pretty sure I still had a little grit lodged in my butt cheek from what we'd done on that cliff the night before. Good times.

Ones not to be repeated, though. Nope. No way.

Yet.

"Don't you dare think of leaving me up here," I said, shooting that big, scary beast with my harshest glare. Trust me on that—I'd practiced it almost as much as my favorite smile. "You brought me here, you can bring me home. That walk down is a bit treacherous, and these heels are definitely not meant for hiking."

Gold. Four-inch stilettos. Strappy as all get-out. They were my favorites. No way was I ruining them.

Kingston shifted to his human form—something I'd never seen up close with any shifter. I stared as he went from a huge, black beast to a swirl of smoke and scales and skin and cloth. Seconds. He did all that changing in seconds. I couldn't even change my shoes that fast.

He stood in human form, spearing me with a glare that sent a shiver up my spine.

"Those shoes are meant to be digging into my ass as I fuck you, but we'll get there."

Oh god, I hoped so. Sort of. "Not happening."

His smirk didn't do anything to reassure me. "We'll see, Sparky."

"So we're back to the nicknames?"

"Would you rather I call you girl?"

"Never."

"How about *mate?*"

Oh my. That word sent not ice but heat, and not up my spine but down deep in my gut. Lower, even. All the way between my legs.

I would not let him seduce me with a word. "I thought dragons didn't take mates."

"We don't."

I...what? "But you called me your mate."

"I know what I said, and you are."

"I'm confused."

"We don't *take* mates. We...ask them to join us," he said, an almost embarrassed sort of growl in his voice.

"You...ask?"

"Yes."

"I'm going to need an explanation."

He sighed, all long and loud and frustrated. "We're not like other shifters."

"I swear to god, if you give me some 'and you're not like other girls' line, I will cut you."

"Nothing can cut through my scales."

"Nothing?"

"Nothing."

"Well, that's not helpful."

"Not to you. It's quite lovely for me." He shrugged. "I sort of like not being killed."

"I can understand that."

"May I continue now?"

I settled in on a rock and waved my hand in a circle. "Sure. Why the hell not?"

He might have rolled his eyes. I couldn't say that I would have blamed him.

"Dragons aren't like other shifters—" he held a finger up when I opened my mouth "—because we don't fall into the insta-love matings. Our dragons take their time in choosing their soul mate, and once we do, we work to prove ourselves as a good match. There's nothing forced or inevitable about it."

"So…no wacky *'Mine'* stuff?"

"Oh no. You're mine, Sparky. But instead of the fates taking away your free will, you have a choice. If I prove myself to be a good mate for you, we can be together. If I don't…" He shrugged. "Well, it happens."

No loss of agency. No forced togetherness. No getting trapped with a douchecanoe like Nico. This wasn't sounding too bad. It also shed light on a few things. "That's why you wouldn't kiss me."

"You have to make the first move."

Huh. "So when I said you could do whatever you wanted—"

"My dragon was exceptionally happy." He grinned, a fire burning in his eyes. "But I reined him in."

"Why?"

"Because you didn't mean that the way we took it, and I won't trick you into being with me."

"No?"

"No. I'll fight for you, though. I'll prove myself to be a good mate."

"What if I don't want a mate?"

He blinked. Silent. Still. "I'd never force you."

No, he wouldn't. I knew that like I knew my own name…which wasn't Sparky. But sometimes you had to bend a little. And me? I was ready to get bendy.

I rose to my feet, frowning his way. Approaching him slowly. Making the first move in a physical sense. "And if I choose you?"

"Then I would spend the rest of my days making sure you were the happiest woman in all of Kinship Cove."

"Yeah?"

"Yeah." He stalked closer, never releasing me from his gaze. Locking me in place with a look. One filled with heat and need, with lust and desire. With everything. "I'm yours, Ginger. I always will be, though that doesn't mean you have to be mine. But if you choose to be, I'll work hard to keep that beautiful smile on your face." He brushed my hair over my shoulder, so close I could smell him. So handsome it hurt. "I'll make sure no one ever lays a hand on you without your permission, including me. It's always your call."

Those words warmed me in ways nothing else could have. This was my decision. Not fate's, not his, not anyone else's. All mine. I could have more than a night with him, could have days and weeks and months and…more. Just more. We didn't need to say the F-word tonight, didn't need to make promises that would outlast both of us. We could simply belong to each other, take care of each other, and be together. All I had to do was choose.

And in my heart, my choice was easy.

"Do I get to call you daddy?"

His growl broke the quiet of the evening. "You can call me whatever you like so long as you first call me yours."

"Yours?"

"Mine," he growled, his entire body stiff with what I could only guess was anticipation. "I need to hear it, Sparky."

Yeah, so…we could work on that. Later.

I gave him a cheeky sort of smile and grabbed his arms, unable not to touch him as I whispered, "Mine."

Without visible movement, Kingston had me on the ground. One second, I stood on my feet; the next, I was lying on my back with him hovering over me. His growl had grown longer and louder than before, becoming a continuous rumble that vibrated against my chest as he used frantic hands to strip me. I felt just as crazed, yanking and tugging on his clothes until they gave way. Until we lay naked and together under a starry sky on top of a cliff. One I could guarantee I wasn't leaving without him.

"I don't want to walk home tonight."

"I have no intention of letting you." He nudged his way against me, slipping inside with just the tip of himself. Staring down at me with a look of complete concentration. "Say it."

"Say what?"

"Tell me you're mine and that I'm yours. Give me consent, Sparky."

Oh, that name again. He almost didn't deserve my immediate compliance. Almost. But if I had to wait a moment more for him to be inside me, I might die.

Death by lack of sex.

It could be a thing.

"You're mine," I said, not whispering. Making sure he and the fates above heard me. Just in case. "And I'm yours. Now fuck me, Daddy. I think it's time to be mates."

"It's always time to be mates." He pushed his way inside me, stretching me. Filling me to the point of almost too full. Just before the point of pain. So good, this man. So strong and big.

And mine.

As he took me on that cliff under the open sky, as he bit my neck and whispered filthy words in my ear and made me come again and again… and again…I knew I'd made the right decision. My body loved this man, but so did the rest of me. His demanding nature was the ultimate compliment to me—the salty to my sweet. Or sweet to my salty…that descriptor really depended on my mood. But I digress.

At some point, Kingston flipped me onto my knees and spent a good few minutes spanking my ass as I laughed and tried to crawl away from his hand. He simply held me tighter and growled my name as he listed all the things I'd supposedly done to deserve his smacks. Things like making him drool over cinnamon cupcakes and requiring him to take longer showers because he needed to jack off to thoughts of me just like this. He made me laugh as he pretended to punish me, and that was something I looked forward to repeating for the foreseeable future.

This man, this dragon, was all mine. And though I'd never expected anything to last more than one night, I looked forward to what was to come with us. I'd never be bored, that was for sure.

I'd also need to find new ways to drive him crazy so he could spank me again.

And so I could call him daddy.

EPILOGUE

GINGER

"Get down from there, girl."

Lord, Kingston truly liked living on the edge. And by edge, I meant the edge of my temper.

I stretched a little farther, biting my tongue as I reached for the little silver shape that seemed to be hiding from me. "Never. I need to find the next hook in line."

"You know, if you'd planned to start hooking, you could have told me. I'd happily pay for your services."

Ah, sex-worker jokes. Always fun. "You keep me in good wine and ice cream. My services are on the house."

"Good to know. Now would you like to tell me why you're in such a precarious position, or should I guess?"

By precarious, he meant up on a ladder in front of the bakery, stretching to the right as far as my body would let me. I mean, I wasn't high enough to die if I fell, but...it wasn't the safest thing I'd ever done. Not that I'd admit that to him.

"I wanted to get the string lights up before the first snow."

"Hi. My name is Kingston, and I'll be the creature with wings in your life. You could have asked me for help."

I stuck out my tongue at him, fighting back a smile as he grinned my way. "Some things I like to do myself."

"Like put yourself in a position where you could break a few bones? We need to change that mind-set, Sparky. Put safety first and all that."

"Maybe tomorrow." I stretched a little farther, fumbling for the hook. "Got it!"

I snagged the wire over the hook just as I lost my balance. The ladder seemed to slip out from under my feet, and the ground moved toward me at an alarming rate of speed. I never hit the pavement, though. I mean, I hit what felt like a brick wall, but it had arms that slowed my fall and a scent that soothed the panic inside of me.

A wall of dragon.

My dragon.

And boy was he cranky.

"By the fates, girl. I'm never leaving you alone again," he said, growling deep and long and not at all sexy-like. Yup. Still a lying liar.

"Sometimes you must. How was work?"

Kingston had moved to Kinship Cove for the opportunity to expand his client base. At least, that's what I told myself—we both knew he'd moved to be closer to me. Lying liars, remember? He consulted with local fisherman on how to better distribute their products. Dragon couriers were a thing, apparently, and he had a network of friends who could cart the fish from Kinship Cove all the way across the mountains and to the next shifter town. For a fee, of course.

"Work was fine. How about you? Any new treats I need to try?"

I grinned up at him as he carried me inside the bakery. "You have developed quite the sweet tooth."

"Only for your sweets," he said just before he finally kissed me. "Mmm, spicy."

"More."

He came in for another kiss, shifting me in his arms so I could wrap my legs around his waist as he held me up by my ass. As he teased me with squeezes and rubs. As he pinned me against the wall and growled deep in his chest, pressing his cock against me.

"We should go home." I wiggled against him, making sure he knew what I wanted. Not that I ever had a problem with that. The man was insatiable and absolutely obsessed with pleasing me. Our orgasm division was split at a five-to-one ratio in my favor. Not that I was complaining.

"We should. I'd hate to spank this pert little ass where everyone could see."

He gave me a pinch to make his point. I jumped. You would have too. "Not sure why I deserve a spanking. I was just doing my job."

"Danger is not in your job description. Neither is electrical work."

"I'm an owner. Everything is in my job description."

"Well, let's put that in mine instead."

"You don't work here."

"I can. And I will for that sort of stuff." He kissed me again, letting me drop to my feet. "Ask me to help you, Sparky. I'll happily do whatever you need."

"Fine." I flipped the sign in the window to Closed and hurried to the door, locking it before I turned to wag a finger at the man who drove me absolutely crazy...in the best way possible. "But no ladders for you."

"No?"

"No. You could fall."

"I wouldn't fall."

"You might. And you're older than me. You might not bounce back as quickly." I dragged him into the kitchen, biting back my grin as he scowled. Oh, this man was so much fun.

"I bounce back just fine."

"You could break a hip. And then what would you do? How would you keep me all safe and happy if you were immobilized, Daddy?"

That did it. He growled deep and snatched me right off the ground, shoving me against the back door as he practically panted. His pupils had turned catlike, his skin growing darker as his scales peeked through. I loved bringing forth his dragon. Loved the animalistic side of him.

Especially when we were at home and I could get him naked.

Because naked in the bakery was no longer allowed.

Don't ask.

"Home," I said, wanting so much more than I could take in the place where I worked. "Right now."

"Are you demanding something, mate?"

"Yes."

"Well, okay then."

And then we were flying. And I was laughing the whole way.

Being mated to a dragon shifter was the best thing ever, especially for commuting.

Not that I'd ever tell him that particular fact about our relationship.

Okay, fine…I might. But only if it meant he'd fly faster. I needed his hands on me, not his claws. Needed his body weight on me, not lifting me up. I needed him.

Every day.

Always.

And maybe…just maybe…forever.

Eventually.

HONEY BEAR

KINSHIP COVE: MATES & MACARONS

Sometimes the happy in happily ever after is relative. Or related. Sort of. The third slice of sweetness from the Cake-ily Ever After bakery in Kinship Cove will definitely satisfy your sweet tooth.

I'm supposed to be the nice sister. The good one. The girl everyone can count on and who rallies the troops whenever one of us needs a little boost. I'm not supposed to be anything other than sweet. I'm not the one secretly pining for a man twice my age. A man who shifts into a bear at whim and runs the whole darn town with a calm sort of confidence never before seen in Kinship Cove. But I do pine. I pine hard.

And when I make bad decisions because of that, I become the sister with a burden bigger than she can carry.

And a secret.

What would you do if you needed money fast? What wouldn't you do?

I won't sell my body. So instead, I'll sell the closest thing I can—to whoever has the right amount of cash.

And I'll cross my fingers and hope the bear shifter who refuses to see me as anything other than *sweet* never finds out.

1

MADELEINE

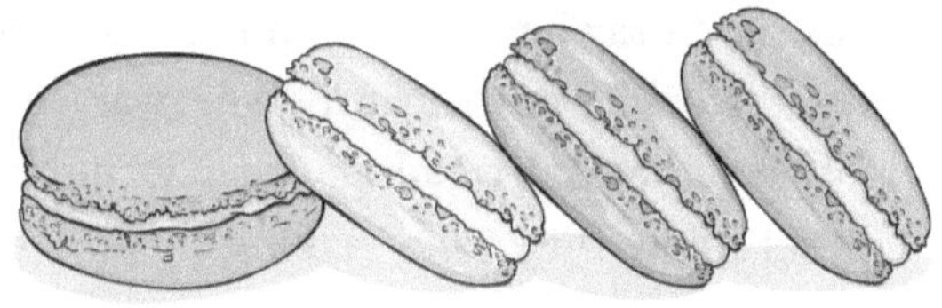

People will buy absolutely anything. I should know, I'd bought a dilapidated house that tried to kill me occasionally, and I was selling things most people would never share with the world. Or maybe they would if they knew there was a market for such things. If they knew what assumedly desperate men would pay to get their hands on them.

Maybe.

Okay, probably not.

That was the thought running through my head as I dragged buttercream frosting into fur-like swirls. Not that I could concentrate on the morality of commerce or the cake that needed to be finished. My phone had been pinging all afternoon, alerting me to new bids on my latest auction. Bids that meant this would be a very profitable day for me. Every extra dollar made the tightness around my chest ease, made the panic I'd been living with in my heart for the last six months calm a little more. A couple of sales like this every week, and I'd be able to breathe normally again within a matter of months. So long as I could come to grips with…selling *stuff*.

Buying and selling made the world turn, and I'd found a particular niche that paid well for what I deemed a small amount of my time and energy. But it wasn't the cakes and cookies my sisters and I made at the Cake-ily Ever After bakery. Nope. I mean, those sold just fine, but small businesses were expensive, and there were three of us running this one. If I needed real cash—and I did, a lot of it—I had to strike out on my own. So I had. With raging success. Not that I could tell my sisters what I was doing.

Speaking of sisters, something was up with mine. Coco…well, she'd gotten her heart broken that morning. Ginger and I had been forced to show up at her house and drag her butt out of bed, but that didn't mean she wanted to be at work. The macarons she was making for the rehearsal dinner of an important wedding order would be finished on time, but she was definitely miserable making them. Or being in the kitchen. Or…existing. Poor girl.

In stark contrast, Ginger didn't seem unhappy in the least. More irritated and almost nervous. Ginger never seemed nervous, so that definitely struck me as odd. Though Coco never looked like a zombie while making cookies either. They were both definitely off their game. And me?

I was trying to hold everyone together as I sold stuff online that I still couldn't believe people wanted to buy. But they did, bless them.

Me: Two minutes and the auction closes. Who will be the winner?

A flurry of bids appeared, people upping one another in one- and five-dollar increments. Meanwhile, I sculpted with buttercream frosting and calculated how far I was from getting what I needed.

The $3,500 for the roof repair that would hopefully keep wet plaster from falling on my head in the upstairs hallway.

Then the $7,000 for the new front window so birds stopped joining me for coffee in the morning.

Plus the $20,000 to replumb the house so I could actually take a *hot* shower instead of daily cold ones.

That…was a lot of money. Much more than I'd make in a single auction. But with everything I sold, every little bid that raised the price of my items, I chipped away at that ridiculous total. Someday, this would all be worth it. I hoped.

The timer on my phone sounded, indicating the auction had run its course. I checked the screen, nearly dancing in place with joy. Four figures. Not a mid or high four figures, but four figures. Chip, chip, chip.

Me: Auction officially closed. Thank you, everyone, for participating—please look for another sale in the next day or so.

I pulled up the profile of the winner—a man from the next town over who'd been a previous and consistent customer of mine since I'd started this crazy business experiment. He'd want to do an in-person pickup. Usually, I preferred to ship my goods—way less creepy—but this guy...I made exceptions for him. He'd been one of my very first customers and never balked at a price. He'd practically paid for the new breaker box I'd installed a few months back after an electrical fire had broken out in my home. Who knew old houses weren't set up to run a coffee maker and charge my phone all at once? Thank goodness I didn't do something wild like turn on every light in the house at once.

The horror.

I might have been a little bitter about all the trouble the house had been giving me since I'd signed over a ridiculous amount of money to buy it. The place had become the bane of my existence, the excess I never should have signed up for. The one thing I couldn't have walked away from because of what it represented, and at the same time, the noose around my neck.

Fires, broken pipes, a roof that simply would *not* stop leaking... If something could go wrong, it did. I called the house Matilda, and she quite obviously hated my guts.

My phone lit up with an alert from the site I used to host my sales.

Buyer: Do you have time now for an exchange? I know it's last-minute, but I'm already on my way. I'll chip in an extra $100 for speedy turnaround.

I stole a look in Coco's direction. She might as well have been in her own world for all the attention she paid to the rest of us. And Ginger? She was still terrorizing a batch of cupcakes that would likely end up too chewy to eat, what with the way she'd beaten that batter half to death. Neither would notice if I turned and walked out the back door. Time to make a little extra cash.

"Welp, these ears are about as pointy as they're going to ever be. I thought the cake was done before, but that little extra swirl of gray really does make it perfect. Right?" I stepped back from the groom's cake—a huge, three-dimensional wolf sitting and howling—and nodded once. "Yep, perfect. You're delivering this tonight, remember?"

Ginger's face was far too expressive. I saw every single look, knew all the thoughts floating through her pretty head. Irritation, likely at being reminded. Again. Thoughtfulness as she probably remembered all the times she actually *had* forgotten such a simple task. Then resignation. She'd forget. I knew it; she knew it. If Coco had been more aware, she'd have known it. But Ginger never was one to admit defeat.

"I won't forget."

Lie. One I didn't have time to argue over. I gave Ginger a "sure you won't" look before rolling the cart the wolf cake sat on into the walk-in refrigerator. The darn thing would be much too heavy to move any other way. To be honest, I worried about how Ginger would even get it to the rehearsal dinner that night, but not enough to stop me from making my sale. An extra hundred for quick delivery! I needed the money, and my customer needed my goods.

Commerce was a glorious thing.

As soon as I had the cake secured, I slipped through the kitchen and onto the sales floor. Today was our late weekday, the only night of the workweek we stayed open until dinnertime. We didn't need to—very few people came in after one. We had extended store hours on the weekends for the tourists, but we started so early on the weekdays to deal with the coffee and breakfast crowd that closing early made sense. Thursdays we stayed open late enough to snag the business commuters coming back from work on their way home.

A man crossed my path at the swinging doors, beelining his way toward Ginger. Older, handsome, lean but muscled—he could likely stop traffic if the drivers were all straight women looking for a silver fox to play with. A perfect fit for my wilder sister. I preferred my men a little...bulkier. A little more aggressive in their look.

A little more like the man talking to our customer service clerk.

Jericho.

A.K.A. Mayor of Kinship Cove.

A.K.A. my uncle, though only in some sort of nonfamilial way that made him decidedly desirable and yet frustratingly off-limits.

"No, no, three's more than enough. My runs through the woods are getting longer every day because of these things." He patted his impressively ribbed stomach, making my brain go wonky at the thought of what all that delicious muscle would feel like under my fingertips and against my lips. "Why do you have to make such amazing honey buns?"

As if he couldn't turn them down. The man was made of control. Every aspect of his life, every part of his personality. I should know—I'd tried to break that control and failed miserably.

Misty shot me a smile, one that showed far too many of her sharp, fox-shifter teeth for my liking. One I didn't trust for a second. "Madeleine makes them *special* every morning just for you."

Yup. Totally not trustworthy. She knew all about my crush on the mayor, as well as his adamant shutdown of anything more than friendship between the two of us. Yet she never let up on trying to play some sort of subtle matchmaker. If it had ever worked, I would have called her an evil genius. Since it never did, I considered her a sadist.

Jericho looked my way, locking his amber eyes on mine. My entire world went fuzzy around the edges. Why? Why did my brain and heart and soul have to choose *him* as the ideal man for me? Why, when I knew I couldn't have him? Knew he didn't want me? He'd never see me as a woman—just little Maddy, the sweetest of the Chance sisters. The quiet one. Downright virginal. Yeah, that's what my sisters thought. Jericho probably did too. I was too young for him, too innocent.

If only they knew me.

"You make these?" Jericho asked, his voice a touch lower than before. A tiny bit rougher. Or maybe I just hoped it was. Fantasies were hard to let go of.

"I do," I said, trying my hardest to keep from moving closer to him. "I make them every morning because I know they're your favorite."

"Well then, I'll take the six." He grinned, pulling a matching smile from me as he said, "I can't let my Maddy work so hard for nothing."

Smile…gone. Maddy. I hated that nickname almost as much as I hated the stupid ribbed abs and sculptured chest his shirt clung to. And his broad shoulders. And oh, those thick forearms. Seriously, the man was pure muscle. Lickable in so many ways. And I hated all of them.

"Great," I said a little too brightly before directing my attention back to Misty. "I know we have another twenty minutes until we close, but I have to go."

"Go?" she asked, looking completely surprised. "Go where?"

"I have an errand to run."

"So you're not going to help Ginger deliver the cake to the rehearsal dinner?"

"She won't forget."

If the look Misty shot me had words attached to it, they'd be *You're an idiot if you believe that.* And she wasn't wrong.

"Just…remind her."

"Yeah, right. That'll work." Misty handed Jericho a bag filled with the treats I'd spent months developing for him. "Here you go, Mayor. Enjoy them."

"Thanks. An errand?" His brow dropped, and he stared at me with those golden-brown eyes I'd always found so fascinating. "Is there something I could help you with? I'm happy to do whatever to make sure you girls have what you need."

His words gutted me because he'd made it clear what I needed didn't matter to him not all that long ago. I'd been drunk when I'd thrown myself at him one evening after what I now called "the night the roof came crashing down...literally," but I remembered his brush-off. His perfectly effective physical and verbal shutdown.

His rejection.

I remembered, and I still ached from the humiliation of it. "This isn't something you can help with, but thank you. Enjoy your honey buns."

But when I spun to leave, Jericho called, "Maddy, wait."

I closed my eyes and took a deep breath, needing to escape. Needing to curl into the grumble of his voice and live there. Needing...so much more than he would ever be willing to give me. "Yeah?"

"Is everything okay with the house?" He coughed, which covered the gasp I released perfectly. "I mean...I worry about you in the big old house all alone."

His family's house. The one his great-aunt had lived in when she'd taken in my sisters and me after our parents had died. The one he would have let be torn down had I not stepped in to buy it.

The house that hated me for some unknown reason.

I huffed a laugh, still not turning around. Unable to look him in the face as I said, "Matilda's fine. We're fine. Everything is fine."

Everything was about as far from fine as possible, but no way was I going to tell him that.

"Good. Okay, well...if you need help—"

"I don't, but thanks." And with that, I rushed back into the kitchen and away from the man who'd haunted my every waking thought—and even my sleeping ones—for years. No one else had ever compared to him; no one had mattered as much to me. I doubted anyone ever would. But Jericho had laid down the law the one time I'd tried to tell him what I wanted. He'd cut me off mid-sentence to remind me how he'd always be there for me...and my sisters. How he'd always be Uncle Jericho.

I hadn't wanted him as an uncle then, and I didn't now.

But that day, that horrible, humiliating day, he'd told me something else. He'd reminded me that I needed to be careful in a town full of shifters. That men would come sniffing around someday, and I was sweet enough to be irresistible to some. I'd taken that literally. And when those men *had* come sniffing around? I'd figured out a way to capitalize on their attraction and earn more money than I'd ever been able to make in the bakery business.

I grabbed my purse out of the office and hurried to my car in the back. My sisters would likely be shocked if they knew what I was about to do, and Jericho—well, he'd hate it. He'd probably think it was too dangerous and uncouth. Too gritty for sweet little Maddy and her innocent mind.

He was wrong, and that was too damn bad. I had a house to fix up, one I'd only bought because of the link it held to the man himself, and a point to make clear. Jericho had told me men would come sniffing around, and they did. But instead of dating them, I sold them what they wanted.

What they drooled over.

All because Matilda needed to be made whole again.

Once in the car, I pulled out my phone and finally returned the text to my client.

Me: I'm on my way to the pickup point now.

Buyer: And you're still wearing them?

Deep breaths. It's just business. Don't think about why that matters.

Me: Of course.

Buyer: See you in fifteen.

I slipped on my sunglasses and tossed my phone into the console. Fifteen minutes to drive across town. Another three to deal with the buyer and hand over the product. Ten more until I made it home. Half an hour, and I could be in my house and ready for a bath. A lukewarm one, but that was par for the course with Matilda. Didn't really matter anyway—I'd need some way to relax after the havoc of the last few days.

But first, I needed to meet my client. No way would I disappoint him by being late. I had my professional reputation to uphold.

Selling the panties I'd worn all day was serious business, and the money I made would hopefully save me from the wrath of Matilda. Someday. But in the meantime, I needed to keep this entire enterprise a secret—from my sisters, from the customers at the bakery, and from Jericho.

Especially from Jericho.

2

MADELEINE

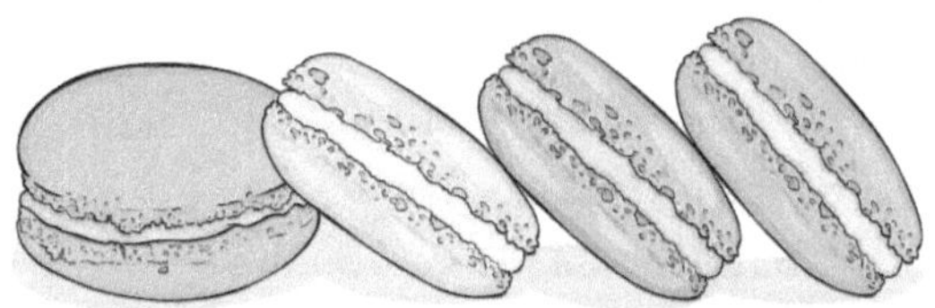

On the far side of town, just before the industrial district that ended at the wharf where the fishing boats bobbed in the water, sat a little bookstore with the most perfect golden glow shining through the front windows. I'd spent much of my childhood in the store, many days through my teenaged years too. It was practically a third home to me after Matilda and the bakery. I knew every inch, every nook and shadowy corner. I knew the old lady behind the counter and the young girl running the stand that sold teas from around the world and our baked goods. I knew every inch of the place, which was why I'd always picked it to meet this particular client.

Selling my worn panties had come up in the strangest of ways. I'd been stalking Jericho's profile on Facebook—something I still did, unfortunately, even though there was nothing personal posted—when a small ad on the right-hand side had caught my attention. Something about work from home opportunities. I'd just found another leak in Matilda's roof and still hadn't replaced the boiler that had broken right at the end of winter. I'd been desperate for money, so I'd clicked on the ad. Three hours and one hell of a rabbit hole later, I'd registered myself on a website where I could sell worn panties or lingerie, uploaded what I'd considered was an innocently sexy picture of myself looking as virginal as possible, and written a bio that I hoped would attract plenty of customers. Everyone always thought I was sweet—might as well play off that assumption.

It took three days for me to realize just how much men went for that whole sweet thing. Three days to make my first sale, shattering all my expectations for what the market would tolerate in terms of price. Everything snowballed from there. My marketing skills had been successful, and my side business had taken off in a way I'd never thought possible.

Praise be to the makers of lace and satin.

Usually, I mailed the *product* to customers all across the country, but someone local had found me on the site. Someone who paid a premium to make sure the panties had been worn and to have me hand-deliver them. Someone who pulled into the spot two down from me just as I stepped out of my car.

"Hey, Franny."

Because him knowing my real name was way too personal and dangerous. "Ryder."

There was no way that was his real name. Who named their kid Ryder, unless their last name was Flynn? But even then, Eugene would have been more appropriate.

He was no Ryder, no Eugene either. But then again, I was no Rapunzel.

Ryder-not-really-Ryder followed me into the bookstore, up the stairs, and toward the back corner, chatting easily about his day and the drive over the mountain. He wasn't from Kinship Cove, and according to what I'd told him, neither was I. This just happened to be a midpoint for the two of us. I'd never mentioned the exact town where I did live just in case. Living a double life meant keeping track of the details so they didn't trip you up. No specifics meant no mistakes later.

"So," he said as soon as we reached the shadowy back corner where we always conducted our transactions. "You've been wearing them all day?"

I nearly rolled my eyes. Always so needy. "Since last night—like the auction said, I slept in them and everything."

He may have moaned, and I might have shuddered a little at that sound, though I did my best to hold it in. Trying not to show him how weird this all seemed. Whatever—he had cash in his hand, and I had a window that needed replacing. And a sucktastic roof that continued to leak even after I'd paid to have it replaced. And plumbing issues. Matilda was drowning me in debt, and Ryder-not-really-Ryder was the life preserver I needed. So I tucked myself into the corner and reached under my skirt, keeping my eyes on Ryder's chin the entire time as I pulled off my underwear and handed them to him.

Almost done.

Ryder gripped the pink cotton in his fist. "Seriously, I don't know what it is about you that makes my senses go so haywire. You have no idea how much this—"

"I don't want to know." I held out my hand. "The auction site has already sent me the payment for the product, but you said an extra hundred for quick turnaround?"

He shook his head but reached into his pocket, pulling a crisp hundred-dollar bill from his wallet and handing it to me without argument.

Once I had the extra money secured, I pushed past him, needing to escape. Job done. Day over. Time to get back to Matilda and make sure she hadn't disintegrated in the hours I'd been outside of her walls. "Have a safe drive home, Ryder."

"Yeah. You too, Franny. See you soon, I'm sure."

I nearly stumbled at the reminder that I'd repeat this same thing at some point. A week...maybe two at most if Ryder-not-really-Ryder's purchasing pattern continued. Maybe by then, I'd have sold enough through the mail that I could stop meeting him in person. Mailing the panties didn't bother me nearly as much. In person, knowing he was watching me, having to hear the sound of his enjoyment...that made me feel a little skeevy.

Not that selling dirty underwear wasn't skeevy no matter the delivery method.

Ugh. I needed a bath.

Sadly, that thought got put on hold the second I stepped outside and saw a very grumpy-looking bear shifter sitting on the hood of my car. A bear shifter I thought I'd left at the bakery. A bear shifter in a suit that made him look even more intimidating than he usually did. Farkity fark.

I nearly stumbled. "Jericho."

"Maddy." Jericho rose to his feet, his heavy brow pulled tight and a questioning expression on his handsome face. "You ran off so fast, I was a little worried. Is everything okay?"

Nope. Not even a little bit. "It's fine. Everything's fine. I have to get home, though."

"Home."

"Yeah, you know. To your house. I mean, their house. I mean…the house I bought."

He nodded slowly. "The one you bought from my great-aunt."

"Exactly."

"I will never understand what attracted you to that old place. She hadn't put any work into it for years."

Tell me about it. "I like old homes."

Another lie. Sort of. I liked old homes with character—Matilda had far more attitude than character. Everything that could go wrong did, and every repair cost three times as much as normal because the repair people had never seen anything like however the place was built.

But Jericho had grown up there. And I'd first realized my feelings for him were much more than they should have been in that home. I'd been drawn to its curving archways and window nooks my whole life, and his link to the house only cemented my desire to own it. The idea of losing that side of myself, of giving up that connection to the only man I'd ever truly seen as more than a friend, had nearly killed me. So I'd jumped in headfirst and bought the place when his great-aunt had moved away.

And I'd been struggling financially ever since.

"So, you're good?" he asked, looking me up and down. "Everything's okay at the house?"

I could have laughed, but then he'd figure out how far over my head I was. "Everything's fine. Great. The house is—" *falling down around me* "—perfect."

His frown deepened. "If you're sure—"

And that was the moment Ryder-really-not-Ryder walked out of the bookstore and came to a jerky stop as he took in what had to be a fascinating scene. I mean, he'd just bought the panties I'd been wearing —likely still had them in his pocket—and there I was chatting up a huge man with arms as big as branches and a neck like a tree trunk. There was no doubting the alphaness of Jericho and no getting past the point that he had turned his steely gaze on the man behind me. Who, again, probably had my underwear…

In

His

Pocket

"So, I'm going to go," I said, inching past a very stiff and growly Jericho. "You should too. Nothing to see here. No issues. Everything is absolutely—"

"Fine," he said, his voice like a rumble of thunder in the summer. "Yeah, I keep hearing you say that."

Ryder took a step back and hurried toward his car but not before reaching into his pocket. Jericho sniffed, and his growl grew louder, more aggressive. I'd never seen him lose a single ounce of that legendary control, never witnessed him being anything other than perfectly polished and presentable. Until then. There had to be a reason. Something that was making his nostrils flare and his growl deepen, something he could sense on the wind that—

Oh no.

I was an idiot.

Scent.

Shifters had strong olfactory senses.

Jericho could probably *smell* me on Ryder.

This would not end well if I didn't do something drastic.

"Hey," I said, jumping in front of Jericho and placing a hand on his chest. His very hard, muscled chest. *Focus.* "Quit growling at strangers."

"You know that guy?"

To lie, or not to lie. That was the question. I chose a wobbly sort of answer. "Not really. Seriously, though—no growling. You'll scare people."

Jericho straightened a little, still breathing hard but cutting off the rumbling sound. Taking a moment to close his eyes before refocusing that laser-like attention on me. "What's going on with you, Madeleine?"

He never used my full name. Never. Hearing it from his lips, the way his tongue worked from the d to the l, made my skin positively tingle.

But he looked away from me, back to where Ryder was pulling out of his spot, and the entirety of my world crashing down on top of me became real.

He could not learn my secret.

"Nothing's going on," I said, leaning closer and rising up on the balls of my feet. "Go home, Jericho. I'm fine."

And then, to prove my point and hopefully to make him forget all about the man who had my panties in his pocket, I kissed Jericho's cheek. Sort of. More like the corner of his mouth. Eyes closed, his warm, spicy scent surrounding me, I pressed my lips as close to his as I could without crossing the lines he'd cemented into place and topped with barbed wire. So warm and soft and tingle-inducing. So perfect.

I might have sighed. I also might have broken my own heart, knowing he didn't feel the same way about that kiss. That he was likely standing there trying to be polite as I basically assaulted the corner of his mouth. Even when his hand landed on my hip, seeming to pull me closer instead of pushing me away, and his chest rumbled against mine. I kissed him, and he let me. Or maybe that was just my imagination.

I was a true masochist—I couldn't get enough of him. I kept my lips pressed to his cheek for far too long. Kept my body pressed against his in a way that was purely non-friend-like. I gave myself over to the quiet calm of my flesh on his for several moments longer than would be considered polite. Long enough for him to moan softly and tug me in tighter. Long enough for the world to stop spinning then speed back up.

Long enough to remember that he didn't want me.

Long enough to soar high into the skies and crash to the ground right there with my body crushed against his and my lips on his cheek as his hand held me in place.

Thankfully, I was pretty darn good at picking up the pieces and putting myself back together.

"Have a good night," I whispered before dropping back down and pulling away from him. Ripping the two of us apart in a way that hurt so much more than I wanted it to. I hated it—hated him for making me feel this way. Hated fate for throwing us together and not giving him to me as a mate or a boyfriend or…anything. In that moment—with his scent still clouding my mind and the taste of his skin on my lips—I hated the world for ever putting this man in my path. Life would have been easier had I never met him.

Or at least, I told myself that.

Jericho's hand seemed to clutch my hip that much tighter, but then he stepped away. Not looking at me. That perfect control snapping back into place. "Yeah. You too, Maddy."

One word pulverized what was left of my heart. Jericho had used the nickname, of course. I should have known. He always called me Maddy —that single Madeleine had been a fluke. A mistake. A stumble from the man who never stumbled. I shouldn't have hoped it meant anything more.

I shook my head and turned my back on Jericho just like at the bakery. Just like I'd been doing for days, weeks, and months. Turning away and trying my hardest to leave him behind, not that it ever worked.

Maybe someday, I could extricate my heart from his hold. Maybe I'd figure out how to disentangle my life from his. Maybe I'd find someone else to obsess over.

It could happen.

Maybe.

3

JERICHO

Sweet blessings of the fates, my nose was going to be the death of me. Specifically, my nose when Madeleine Chance stood anywhere near me. I'd been fighting a losing battle against that girl since the day she'd come of age, since she'd crossed my path as an adult instead of a child and my bear had roared inside of me, demanding I stake my claim on her. Since I'd finally realized she was my true and only mate.

And there was nothing that upset my bear more than the smell of his mate without his scent woven through it.

The scent of a woman tended to concentrate in one particular area—that heavenly slit between her legs where the proof of her hidden desires was revealed. The place men lost their damn minds to gain access to. I'd never gotten close enough to Madeleine to experience that essence as intimately as I wanted to—couldn't even think about that without losing control of my inner bear—but I still knew it. Could identify her in a lineup blindfolded and without hearing her voice, from a single whiff.

As I stood outside the little bookstore on the edge of town, the scent of Madeleine had nearly overpowered me. I could detect it without trying to, could practically taste the sweet honey of her femininity on the air around us. But not directly from her. No, instead, I'd scented her on the stranger who'd walked out of the bookstore after her. The man who'd looked terrified to see me.

As he should have been, because if he was fucking around with my Madeleine, he had a short life-span left.

Not that I had any right to be mad.

Or upset.

Or motherfucking heartbroken and ready to rage against the world at the very thought of their scents mingling for reasons other than casual contact. Which likely wasn't the case—Madeleine usually ran toward me. But not today. Today, she'd kept her distance at the bakery, fleeing at the first chance she could. I'd followed her because the move had seemed so out of character for her, but she was doing it again. Running away from me and forcing my attention away from that other man. Making my chest tighten up at the thought of somehow losing the only woman I would ever want, the one I'd never had. Making my inner bear want to give chase yet again.

I watched Madeleine's retreat without saying a word. No *Wait* or *Stop* or *Don't walk away*. No *Please* or *Mine* or *Mate* either. Just like every other time we ended up alone together, I watched instead of acted. I couldn't help but watch her. My bear, the beast inside of me who ruled half my psyche, had been in love with her since she'd come of age. Had known she was his fated mate since before that. The man…well, I was in love with her too. Not just for being the woman the fates divined as the perfect match for me, but because of her sweetness. Her kindness. The slight crookedness to her smile and the way her eyes lit up with excitement when she talked. The sway of her hips and the curve of her ass helped too. How her waist clipped in and gave her one of those hourglass figures that would feel really damn good under my hands. Or lips.

"Fucking perv," I said under my breath as her little car disappeared over the hill on its way back toward downtown. Yes, Madeleine was my mate. Yes, she was way more than old enough to take a mate, or a lover, as humans did. And yes, I struggled with both of those things. I'd known the three sisters since they'd been in diapers, had been good friends with their parents before their untimely death. Had been there when my great-aunt had stepped in and brought the girls home with her so they could stay in Kinship Cove after being orphaned. She'd finished raising them in the very house Madeleine now owned, one where I'd spent a fuckton of time because my bear had always wanted to be there.

As soon as Madeleine had matured and I'd seen her as our fated mate, I'd finally understood why.

And realized there was no way I could have her.

I had a legacy to uphold—a town that had been managed by someone in my family for centuries to give my attention to. Politics was a hard business filled with lies and betrayal and people shining a spotlight on every fault and flaw you had. Life as a politician's partner meant forgotten dinners and broken promises, meant smiling in front of the cameras when you wanted to cry, and never letting a single crack show in the armor you placed around yourself. Madeleine was so soft and sweet, my adversaries would eat her alive. She and her sisters would be put in a position they'd never asked to be in, would be scrutinized under the worst kind of microscope. I couldn't force them into that sort of life simply because taking care of Kinship Cove was my family's duty to uphold. I couldn't ask the woman my heart belonged to to endure that sort of torture until someone else in my family could step up to the plate and take their turn under the harsh glare of public life.

I couldn't, but I wanted to. I wanted to make Madeleine mine all the damn time.

And I'd been close to doing so. So close. My bear had worn me down over the years, making me crave her more and more. Keeping me awake at night with thoughts of her warm, soft body curled against mine. So tiny, my Madeleine. Her feet would likely not reach past my thighs when we would lie together. An image that made my bear practically stand up and roar his frustration to the world at not knowing how that felt. I'd been ready to give in to my needs and simply take her as mine after so many years of resisting.

But then a fucking lion shifter named Spencer had challenged me in the next election, and he'd come for my good-guy reputation. He'd twisted the image I'd made sure to cultivate for years in the public eye—not soft, but fair. Honest. Hard-working. Spencer had called my acts of kindness weak, my lack of a mate a failure of my beast to attract one. He'd tried to attack my every move and motive with little success. Me taking on a young human woman as my fated mate—one raised at least partially in my family's home? He'd sink his teeth deep into that. I'd be painted as a filthy old man with no morals. And my Madeleine? Her reputation would be dragged through the mud. Her every clothing choice and action called into question and scrutinized. I knew how men like Spencer worked—how little respect they paid to the women in their lives. He'd crush my girl to get to me. No way could I do that to her. Ever.

Between their dad trusting me, my great-aunt's sweetness toward them, and the fact that my political adversary was looking for anything to undermine my clean-cut image in town and would completely use her as ammunition, there was simply no way I could risk claiming her as mine yet.

Just a little longer, I told my inner bear. *Maybe after the election.*

Yeah, he wasn't any happier about that thought than I was.

After a groan and an adjustment to my wickedly hard cock, I trudged to my truck. The scent of Madeleine clung to me, though, so retreating inside the vehicle did nothing but concentrate it. Didn't help that I had a sweater of hers in my glove box, like some sort of creeper. I mean, I wouldn't have kept it forever—just until her scent faded enough that I could stop wanting to rub the damn thing all over my body.

Which I'd done.

More than I cared to admit.

Jacking off with a girl's sweater definitely put me in creeper territory, especially since she didn't know I'd kept it. Not like I stole the damn thing, though—not really. She'd left it with me a couple of weeks ago after I'd given her a ride home from a birthday party that had gotten a little out of hand. It'd been the first time I'd seen her drunk and…well, horny. She'd flirted and giggled and pawed at me. I'd loved every second, too. But I'd been forced to reject her advances. I'd done my best to be smooth about it, but the way her face had fallen that night—how hurt and pained she'd looked—had haunted me ever since. As had the idea that I finally could have claimed her as my mate but hadn't.

Turning Madeleine down had been the hardest decision of my life and one I regretted more and more as the days passed.

I didn't know if I could hold out much longer.

I didn't know if she would even give me a chance once she knew what a life dealing with men like Spencer would entail.

I didn't know shit.

The trip back across town to the rehearsal dinner of a business associate's daughter seemed to take hours instead of minutes, mostly because my thoughts kept circling the completely screwed-up reality I'd found myself in. It wasn't until my phone rang that I realized I'd been driving in a similar shape—circles upon circles upon circles. And I was exceptionally late. *Shit.*

"Jericho here," I said as soon as I clicked the button for the Bluetooth to connect to the speaker system of my car.

"You do realize these wolves are major donors to your campaign fund, right?" Parker—my sister, full-time campaign manager, and part-time ballbuster—didn't pull any punches. Not that I expected her to.

"I'll be there in ten."

"You'd better." The call ended there. No goodbye or see you soon, not that I expected one. I didn't pay her to coddle me. I paid her to kick my ass when I needed it, and right then, I needed it. I had an election coming up, and my spot as mayor was being challenged hard by a lion shifter with deep pockets. I needed to build up my war chest and make sure the town saw me in the light they always had—the strong, powerful leader who put the town first and never let my adversaries get under my skin. If they only knew there was a human girl rocking my world on a daily basis—that I wanted to punch the guy running against me in the nose every time he showed his wrinkled face—I'd likely lose my election, my job, and my chance to leave my family's legacy to Kinship Cove intact.

Control. Kinship Cove expected their mayor to stay in control.

Every man in my family had run the town at some point, and every one had made it better during their tenure as mayor. I hadn't been in the position long enough to have enacted any real changes yet, but I had plans. Big ones. Plans that would raise the entire town up a level and give every resident a more stable foundation. I had to focus on that goal, that ending.

And once I was in a spot where I could hand the town over to someone else in my family, I could have my mate.

Maybe.

If she could ever want me.

My sister met me at the front door of the banquet hall, a stiff smile on her face. "You're late."

"I told you I'd be here in ten. It's only been—" I checked my phone screen "—nine minutes."

"Yes, but that ten was already twenty past your scheduled time to arrive. Where have you been?"

No way was I telling her about following Madeleine to the bookstore. She already thought I was insane for avoiding my mate and trying to loosen the hold of fate even temporarily. My bad for telling her about my draw to the human girl one night when I'd had too much to drink and had gone too many days without seeing the smile on my mate's face.

No way could I deal with her mocking me right then.

"I needed to take some time to think."

"About Madeleine."

Damn her. "Hush."

"No, I won't hush. You'd better figure out what you're going to do about that whole situation and soon. If you're not ahead of this, and Spencer gets a hold of the information, he'll spin it to make you look like a perv. Or worse, weak."

It was a damned battle not to allow my face to twist into an expression of disgust or rage. One I won, though just barely. Spencer had already attempted to dig up dirt on me. So far, he'd been unsuccessful, but I had no doubt he'd get something to stick. It could *not* be my mating with Madeleine. I refused to ruin that girl's reputation for my political gain.

But I wasn't oblivious to how these things worked. "He'll twist whatever he can get his hands on, no matter what it is. Especially anything about Madeleine."

"Because she's human."

My chest burned at the thought of what a man like Spencer would say to that fact. "Yeah."

"That guy is the *worst* sort of shifter."

"And he riles up some of the old guard who like the idea of us versus them. Shifter versus human."

Parker nodded. "Yup. The worst."

"So I wait until after the election."

"Yeah, good luck with that. Every day, you look more and more like a man about to explode." Parker tugged on my sleeves and adjusted my tie before smacking me on the shoulder. Hard. "Mate up, brother."

I sighed as the leader of the local wolf pack made eye contact before heading my way. "It's not that easy."

"Seems easy enough to me. Tell her what might come her way so she can be prepared, claim her like you know you want to, and she's yours forever. The alternative is you miserable, and I'm not down with putting up with that sort of shit," she muttered before turning on her megawatt smile and directing it at the incoming wolf. "Flannigan! How are you this evening?"

And just like that, the show was on. Parker led the way, making sure to say each guest's name so I didn't call them by a wrong one, and directing the conversations down a path that kept the tone lively and smooth—no drama, no political wrangling, and no fun. Especially since Madeleine wasn't attending the rehearsal dinner for Nico and Fiona's wedding. Not that I'd expected her to or would have been able to act on any sort of need to touch or taste her. Oh no, that would cause gossip. Would give Spencer a rock to turn over. I refused to give that man anything, especially in regard to Madeleine.

Still, it would have been nice to have at least seen her throughout the evening. To know that she was safe. To be in the same room as her for a few hours and calm my inner beast.

"You look like someone took away your favorite toy." Misty, the fox shifter who worked at the bakery with my mate and whose family owned the diner in Kinship Cove, sidled up beside me as I waited for the bartender to pour me a drink. I needed one badly, no matter how many dirty looks Parker might throw my way.

I tugged at my tie and sighed. "It's been a long day."

"For everyone. I mean, my bosses were all in odd moods today."

Her bosses, which included Madeleine, who had seemed off. "What do you mean by odd?"

"Well Coco's a zombie—there's some serious drama there with a wolf shifter who might have broken her heart."

"Still hung up on Nico, is she?"

"No. His dad." Misty shook her head and waved me off when I jerked around to face her. "Long story and definitely not one for here. Though if you see a cranky, miserable wolf shifter with salt-and-pepper hair, you'll know who I'm talking about. So, Coco's a mess, and Ginger disappeared with a dragon this afternoon, which meant she forgot to deliver the cake that Madeleine made for this event—"

"What can I do to help?" Just knowing something was wrong in my mate's world sent my mind into overdrive. I needed tasks, details, plans —I needed to do what I could to ease the strain on her.

But again, Misty just waved me off. "You're sweet, but I've got things covered. Or most things. The Coco and Ginger problems are close to being settled. There's just one thread left untied by the way I see it."

I swear, the fox talked in riddles sometimes. "And what thread are you going on about?"

"Madeleine. With her sisters mated off, she's going to be alone."

My heart crashed into the floor and rebounded back up into my chest, drying out my mouth in the process. Fuck, those words hurt. Something I couldn't show in a roomful of people, so I grabbed my drink from the bartender instead as I snapped, "So?"

One word—a challenge, really. As if there was any doubt the sneaky fox didn't know about my link to Madeleine. She could probably sense the fates trying to pull us together—could likely sniff out the trails of destiny around us.

She could also probably bite my hand clear off my wrist with the teeth she bared as she pushed me behind a huge fake plant and leaned in close. "So? Is that the best you got, bear? Because it's not good enough.

You're not good enough right now for that girl. In fact, instead of trying to help the fates along, perhaps it's time for me to break that connection."

"Don't threaten me, fox."

"I'll do whatever I need to do to secure that girl's future. Madeleine needs to find a man—a real one, not someone who will keep her at arm's length for reasons that make no sense to anyone else. The girl needs a life, needs to find someone. She needs to start *dating*. All she does is work and fix up that old house your family conned her into buying."

"We didn't con her—"

"Yeah, yeah. I know. She just *had* to buy that house." She tapped her chin, looking far too curious for my liking. "I wonder why that is. I mean, the place is a dump, and she's not really the handiest woman on the planet. What made her jump into fixing the place up?"

A question I'd asked myself a number of times. "She said she always liked being there when she was a child."

"Yeah, but she's not a child anymore, and that house was a money pit. Still is."

True, which was why I hadn't wanted it. But this whole conversation wasn't about an old house—I knew it, and Misty knew it. "Get to the point, fox."

She gave me a hard look. "You want directness? Cool—here you go. I'm saying shit or get off the pot, bear. The girl needs someone to be her partner, and if you're not going to fill that role, step out of her way so I can get her paired off. You're not the only one trying to fulfill a promise to their parents."

My growl slipped out of its own accord, my bear ready to battle the little fox. Misty just grinned.

"Yeah. That's what I figured. You'd better take care of your mate and soon, Mayor. If you don't, I will. She's a hot commodity and deserves so much better than you're giving her."

I took a sip of my drink and whispered, "Don't I know it."

"Then do better. She needs help, and you're failing her. That's not how a mating should be." And with that, she turned and flounced—

literally flounced—as if we'd been talking about the weather instead of my mate. But before I could do anything like recover from her words or follow her or sneak out and go chase down Madeleine so I could beg her to be mine, Nico—the groom—appeared with a beaming Fiona on his arm. I pasted on a smile and got back to work, greeting the happy couple with congratulations, knowing this was the wrong place to be. These were the wrong people to be talking to. The wrong room to spend my time in.

I was duty-bound to stay even though everything about the situation was wrong.

And I didn't know how to right any of it.

4

MADELEINE

My sisters didn't come into work on Friday morning. Misty did, thank the stars, or I'd have been both baking and running the front all by myself. Something we'd all done before, but I especially never wanted to do again. I couldn't even be mad at the two for not showing up, though. Coco had her breakup with the silver-haired wolf shifter, and Ginger had gotten carried away by a dragon. Literally.

Living in Kinship Cove had always been a little odd, but lately, things had gotten downright weird.

Still, it sucked to be all alone in the kitchen, and there was always so much to do. Cleaning, prepping, baking…cookies! So many darn cookies to be made and decorated. They were the bread and butter—no pun intended—of our operation. Everyone loved cookies. We could barely get through a transaction without selling half a dozen of them. Cookies were what kept the lights on at the bakery. Cookies should have outweighed the drama in their lives. They took priority in mine.

Cookies were my complete and utter focus.

Which was a sad, sad fact I didn't want to think about.

Thankfully, Misty burst through the kitchen door at that exact moment, looking all sorts of frustrated. "What are you doing?"

I had a piping bag filled with bright pink icing in my hand and was leaning over a tray of half-decorated cookies, so of course, I said, "Ironing my socks. You?"

Her eye roll was a thing of beauty. "You're supposed to be the sweet, nice one. Why so much snark?"

Sweet...again. Coco was the friendly one. Ginger the sexy, funny one. I got sweet and nice, as if I were some sort of child or doll or... whatever else might be sweet and nice. It shouldn't have rankled as much as it did. "It was a long night."

"House fall down around your head?"

"No," I snapped, glaring her way even as the latest issues with my financial sinkhole of a house danced through my head. Matilda was certainly giving me a run for my money. Or she was simply taking it. Either way.

Still, my answer didn't seem to satisfy Misty. Have you ever seen a fox on the hunt? The way their heads drop and their gaze completely locks on their prey? Yeah. That was Misty as she said, "But something's wrong with the house."

Always. "Not really *wrong*."

"You're lying."

"Am not."

"Are so. You always get these little pink blotches on your neck when you lie."

Damn pale skin. "It's the light reflecting off the cookies."

"It's your body saying 'Stop lying to your friend, bitch.' So, what gives? What's wrong this time?"

Ugh. What *wasn't* wrong? In my head, I tossed the current list of issues up in the air and snagged just one to talk about. "There's a leak in the roof."

"I thought you'd already replaced the roof."

"I did."

"But it's leaking."

"Yeah."

"Did you call the roofer back to fix it?"

I would have done anything to be able to decorate the darn cookies in peace at that point. This wasn't going to end well, but I'd committed. I had to follow through with this conversation. "I did."

"And what did he say?"

My mouth went dry as a bone. "It will cost another $3,500 for the repairs."

"On the roof he replaced."

Yeah. I could practically *feel* her disbelief at that one. "It's not his fault. The house is—"

"In need of demolition."

"Stop it."

Misty came up beside me, soft and quiet in a way she never was around the other girls. Around anyone but me. Misty Version 2.0—the one with a heart. "You know the house isn't him, right?"

And just like that, my face grew hot and my chest tightened, making it harder to breathe. "It's not about him."

Her voice dropped even lower, her words still hitting hard with every syllable. "Everything you do is about him."

I couldn't even argue with her about that. So instead, I went back to the cookies. Pink icing on a soft sugar cookie base—perfectly adorable and sweet.

Sort of like how people saw me.

Like how that roofer probably saw me. I'd thought before that I'd been taken advantage of. I had no idea what went into repairing or replacing a roof, but I'd always fallen back on the fact that Ralph the roofer was licensed through the city and seemed like a nice guy. Plus, the house really was such a mess. Maybe he was in the right, and the extra repairs weren't his fault. Maybe Matilda was just that far gone that she needed the roof repaired two times in a year.

Or maybe I was a sucker who refused to stand up for herself, and everyone in town knew it.

The bell over the front door rang, and Misty gave me a sad smile before heading for the counter. Good thing, because I couldn't have argued with her, couldn't have spent another second wondering if I was such a failure at basic communication that I'd walked right into a con. I couldn't have done anything but put more sweet, pink icing on those soft sugar cookies because at least they made sense.

Baked goods had always made sense, though that fact only made me feel like even more of a dolt.

When Coco had come back from pastry school overseas, she'd wanted to open a bakery or a restaurant. I'd convinced her to go the bakery route, knowing Jericho loved his pastries and sweets too much to resist. I'd developed a lot of the menu, spent my time working out just the right blend of sweet and savory to tempt him into needing our goods daily. And then his family home had come up for sale, so I'd bought it, desperate to hold on to that connection to him. That feeling of completeness when I was around him.

I'd started selling my panties online to pay for all the repairs on the neglected old house even Jericho hadn't thought could be saved, all for a man who didn't want me.

I had done everything for him—and gotten nothing in return. I was a total idiot.

The pinging of my phone had me dropping a dollop of icing right where it shouldn't have been. Typical. As was the message on the screen.

Ryder: Got something for me? I don't want to wait or go the auction route.

And just like that, the day seemed a little brighter.

Me: I have what I'm wearing, though I didn't sleep in them.

Ryder: That's okay. I need another hit to make it through this weekend.

Hit. Like a drug. That wasn't creepy *at all*.

Me: Then they're yours. If the price is right.

Ryder: $750 and in-person exchange.

It wasn't as much as I could make in an auction, but it was a good chunk of change. And I needed the money.

Me: Deal. And the exchange?

Ryder: Usual place, but can we make it early? I've got plans tonight that can't be broken.

Meanwhile, I had a bakery to shut down for the day and a dilapidated old house to go home to. Alone. I was completely flexible—not that I was telling him that.

Me: Of course. Just tell me when.

Ryder: You're the best. Let's say meet up in an hour.

Me: Got it.

"One more sale, that much closer to those roof repairs." I tucked my phone away and carried the tray of cookies into the walk-in refrigerator. The icing needed to set up before we delivered them tomorrow, which gave me the perfect excuse to cut the day short.

"Hey, Misty," I said as I pushed through the doors into the front of the bakery. "I'm done here. Why don't we call it a day so you can—"

My words caught in my throat as I looked up…and straight into the eyes of Jericho.

"Closing early?" The deep bass of his voice caused a shimmy inside of me, one I was so used to and yet never prepared for.

I could fake it, though. Just like always when he came around. Pretend he didn't affect me the way he did. "Don't worry, Mayor. Main Street will survive without us."

As would he. As would this town. They would survive losing all three of us sisters—or just me. I could walk away tomorrow, and I doubted anyone would miss me except Coco, Ginger, and Misty. A heartbreaking thought that didn't help my desolate mood.

Jericho must have noticed something in my expression because he frowned. "I didn't mean anything by that, Maddy. I just—"

Maddy. Again with the childlike name. Damn him.

"It's fine. Misty, can you empty the cases, please, and box up what's left for the food pantry?"

"Yeah. Okay." Misty got to work, her movements quick and efficient. Trained. Practiced. More in control than I could be at that moment.

I breezed past Jericho, trying hard to control my breathing. To hide every feeling beating me over the head about that man. "Here. Have a honey bun. I know they're your favorite."

Jericho stayed silent for a beat before grunting a soft, irritated sound. "I shouldn't."

It had taken me close to eight months to perfect the recipe for the buns. Countless hours of researching various techniques and baking hundreds upon hundreds of samples. Butter cold or softened, sugar refined, natural, or confectioners. Maple syrup or cinnamon or both to add that little extra something. Hours of my life…lost to making the absolutely most perfect sticky bun in the history of sticky buns just so this man would notice something about me.

And he didn't want it. "There's only one left, and I can't send just one to the food pantry. I'm going to throw it away if you don't want it, so, please. Take it. Give it away if you must."

Jericho stared at me for a long moment, that sticky bun between us in my outstretched hand. Was it a metaphor of sorts? Like, if he chose to eat the sticky bun, would he someday choose to be with me? What a silly, childish idea. And yet my heart stuttered when he reached for it.

"Thank you." Two simple words simply given. His fingers brushed mine through the waxed paper I held the bun with. A touch and yet not. Hope and yet hopeless. A life…and yet not.

And I needed to go meet a customer.

"Go on home, Misty," I said, not even looking to where she stood silent and still. Likely watching my interaction with Jericho. Likely seeing every emotion I was struggling so hard to disguise. "I'll finish up here."

"Whatever you say, boss." She left out the back without another word as I quickly wiped down the counters.

Jericho waited until he heard the back door close before taking a bite of his treat. His groan nearly knocked me to my knees.

"I love these."

"I know."

"They're my favorite of all the things you three make."

"I know that too."

"Sweet." He sighed, his voice dropping into a lower, growly tone as he murmured, "Just like you."

There was that word again—sweet. Like a child. I was so sick of everyone thinking I was *sweet*. My eyes burned with unshed tears I refused to let fall as I stalked closer. As I invaded his space and looked him dead in the eye. I'd show him sweet.

"I'm not sweet, you know." I moved even closer, rising onto the balls of my feet—my god, did he smell amazing—to whisper in his ear. "I'm not innocent either."

For one glorious moment, his amber eyes met mine, his gaze burning into me and making my knees wobble. The smell of him, the heat, that look—I couldn't breathe. Couldn't dare a single move that might break the spell. I couldn't—

He looked down and took a step away from me. Another. Putting space between us even as his hands clenched and the low rumble of his growl vibrated through the air.

"Maddy, I can't—"

Can't. Won't. Don't want to. All the same thing.

"Yeah, well…neither can I." I turned abruptly and headed for the register, yanking out the till as the tears began to sting even more. "I've got this, you know. I can close this place down by myself. There's no reason—" *none at all, apparently* "—for you to stick around."

He paused, his growl quieting. "I'll walk you to your car."

"It's daylight outside. I'll be fine." I headed for the kitchen, running away. Needing an escape Jericho wasn't about to give me.

"Maybe I won't."

As if someone would ever even think to take on a man the size of him.

"Whatever works for you." I shrugged and tucked the money into the small safe that sat in the kitchen office. Coco would rail at me for the mess I was leaving behind, but I couldn't stand another minute alone with Jericho. And I had panties to sell. A fact that made me feel oddly powerful in that moment.

"Allow me." Jericho held the door for me as I walked out, not that I got very far.

"Wait," I said as I took one last look behind me. "I left the office light on."

"I'll get it."

"Thanks." I stepped outside, distracted by my inability to find my keys in my bag. Wallet, lip gloss, spare panties in case a sale came up— because that was a thing in my life—and sunglasses all practically leaped into my hands. Keys? Not so much. I reached deeper, my face almost buried in the bag as the door closed behind me. My fingers brushed metal, and I grinned as I clasped the jagged—

"Where is she?"

I yelped and spun, practically falling back against the dumpster, dropping my keys back into the bottomless pit that my purse had somehow become. Which really wasn't what I should have been focusing on, but seriously—they'd taken an age to find.

Scary man voice, Madeleine. Scary. Man. Voice.

Right. That seemed more important. Before I could regain my footing or even get a solid glimpse of whoever had taken up residence behind the bakery, the back door burst open and Jericho rushed between me and the man.

A man I suddenly recognized. "Jericho—"

"Get the fuck away from her."

Kingston—the dragon shifter I was pretty sure was dating my sister Ginger—looked from me to Jericho and back again. As if putting pieces of something together. Some sort of puzzle. One only he could see. Slowly, he raised his hands and took a large and purposeful step away from me. "I wasn't trying to hurt your mate. I was simply trying to find mine."

Mate. As if. I'd been wishing so hard for some trick of fate to tie me to the man I'd been obsessed with almost my entire life that I didn't think there were any wishes left for me. No room for more. I'd asked for too much.

And gotten nothing.

"I'm not his mate," I said, suddenly angry at the world for my lot in life and at myself for putting up with as much as I had.

Jericho huffed from behind me. "What is it you need, Kingston?"

"Ginger. Where is she?"

I gave Kingston a harder once-over—disheveled clothes, messy hair, and a look of pure panic in his eyes. This was not the confident man who'd swept in and stolen Ginger away. This was a man who'd had everything he wanted taken from him. I knew that look, so I asked, "Why?"

He looked me square in the eye. "She's my mate."

Such conviction. Such honesty behind those words. A declaration of a connection he refused to deny. Something I would never get. "Oh."

Kingston inched forward as if to reach for me. "I'm sorry. I don't know—"

"She's fine," Jericho said, moving between us again. "Ginger's not here, though. You should be on your way."

"Not without something. I want to know where my mate is. I need to know that she's okay."

Jericho glanced down at me. "What do you think?"

I huffed a laugh—couldn't help myself. This entire situation was so far out of the realm of normal. "So, when it's about Ginger, you care what I think?"

"Mad—"

"Ginger's not here and not coming in," I said, completely overstepping the bear shifter before me. "I don't know where she is, but she and Coco both skipped out of work for the day. I do know that Ginger's going to be at the party tonight, though. Fiona's bachelorette. It's at the Metro Club."

Kingston nodded slightly, his eyes already darting to the sky as if wanting to take off in flight. He was a dragon shifter, after all. "Thank you."

A polite one, apparently. Ginger could have done a lot worse. "My sister deserves happiness."

"As do you."

But my happiness would only come after I stopped chasing things I'd never catch. Letting go of my obsession with Jericho would be like breaking my own heart, but it needed to be done. Starting right then. "I do. And I plan to stop letting things hold me back so I can find it. Have fun, boys. I've got business to do." I pushed past both men, heading for my personal escape plan as visions of dinners and movies and date nights with another person—not Jericho—danced through my mind. I would embrace those, strive for them, even if they made my stomach clench in the most horrible way. And I'd do it with a smile pasted on my face.

Strong. I needed to be strong. To move my future in a solid direction and not allow myself to stay tangled up with a man who didn't need or want me. But my actions had to be drastic—a sledgehammer, not a scalpel. I'd put in my time. Struggled and wished and fought for something I couldn't have for long enough. Jericho didn't want me, and nothing I did or said would ever change that.

Not even restoring his family home, which meant it might be time to admit defeat to both Jericho and Matilda.

5

JERICHO

"What kind of business do you think she meant?" I couldn't stop staring after Madeleine's car, couldn't stop feeling as if my chest was about to implode on itself. Why did her driving away feel as if she was *leaving*?

Kingston—dragon shifter and all-around pain in the ass even if I did like the guy—sounded awfully cocky as he said, "Perhaps her mate should already know that."

"I'm not her mate." Lie. One that suddenly hurt more than it should have. Even my inner bear whimpered at the brutality of the deceptive words.

And Kingston didn't believe me anyway. "Could have fooled me."

I sighed and turned to glare at the reptile, not sure how far I could trust him. Not sure if anyone could understand my dilemma. "I've known her since she was in diapers."

"She's not in diapers anymore."

"Don't you think I know that?" I growled and dragged my hand through my hair, pacing in front of the bastard while Madeleine's sad smile before she left stained my vision. Sad. Heartbroken, really. "I fucking know she's not in diapers anymore. I've known it since before she graduated high school when I felt like a lecherous old man for even

217

glancing her way." Her father had been one of my best friends. My great-aunt took her and her sisters in after their parents' death. They'd both asked me to take care of the girls, but I doubted either ever saw the fates stepping in to decide what *care* meant with one of them. And I had no idea if they'd approve, considering the life I'd be subjecting her to. "I still feel like a lecherous old man."

"I'm likely hundreds of years older than my mate, and you're the one feeling like a dirty old man for the gift the fates have given you." Kingston's big, slightly cold hand landed on my shoulder. "I'd love to stay and make you see how stupid you're being, but I have a mate to track down."

"How'd you lose her, anyway?"

"Fell asleep."

I grunted—I hadn't gotten a good night's sleep in weeks. Not since Spencer had announced he'd be running against me. Not since Madeleine being mine had started looking even less possible. "Sleep is good."

"Mates are better." The dragon shifted forms, taking flight with his broad wings and leaving me behind in the alley. A pressure built in my chest, one my bear and I both reacted to. One that couldn't be stopped.

Need.

For our mate.

I couldn't do it. Couldn't let her drive away from me. Not again. Not after seeing how sad she'd been when she'd left. How hurt she'd been. Everything else—every little detail holding me back—no longer mattered. I needed to make sure my mate was okay.

I hopped in my truck and tore out of the lot like a man possessed, roaring through the streets until I saw her little red car just one intersection ahead of me. The pain in my chest eased, and I nudged my foot off the gas so I could follow at a conservative distance, hoping she wouldn't notice me. Wanting so badly to know what the hell she was up to. Business outside of the bakery? What business? What the hell was going on, and why didn't I know about it?

Because you refuse to accept her as your mate, dumbass.

I huffed and changed lanes, keeping her little sedan in my sights. My inner bear paced inside of me, growling and grunting as his mate slipped further away. Our mate. Not that I could keep her. Not that I should.

But I wanted to.

Fuck, how I wanted.

Madeleine pulled into a spot in front of the bookstore I had seen her at just the day before. The one where she'd seemed nervous and distracted. The one where I had smelled her on another man. Was she dating someone? The thought nearly suffocated me, stealing my breath in an instant. She'd always been there, even as I'd told myself she couldn't be mine. Even as I'd kept far too much space between us. If another man had come into the picture...come between us. If I'd lost her before I even had her...

My inner bear practically mewed his sorrow.

"I hear you, big guy."

I waited until Madeleine walked into the store to follow her, needing to know what was going on. Dreading the truth but in too deep to stop myself. An old lady with wild hair sat behind the counter.

"Can I help you, Mayor?"

Yeah. No hiding in Kinship Cove. Might as well be honest. "I thought I saw one of the women who owns the bakery in town come in here."

"Oh yes, Madeleine is here." She smiled and nodded toward the rear of the store. "Why don't you check out our local history section. I'm sure the young lady will be down in a few minutes."

"Is she not shopping?"

"Oh no. Miss Madeleine doesn't buy many things these days, though she used to be one of my best customers. It's unfortunate how that old house has taken over her life."

The old house—my family's home. The one she'd bought even though I'd known it should have been demolished. "Taken over her life?"

"Well, of course, I don't know all the details. But last week, she was going on about a problem with the new roof and how the roofer wanted more money to fix it. She was looking up construction books to do some research. I told her she shouldn't have used that Peterson Roofing company."

Peterson Roofing. Coyote shifter, former boyfriend of Parker's, and an all-around cheat in every sense of the word. I'd been trying to get his construction license revoked for a couple of years, though something always ended up stealing my attention away from that particular issue. Madeleine had hired him? I could have told her a better company to use. What had she been thinking? What had she—

A man walked down the stairs, looking unlike any book-reader I'd ever known and yet oddly familiar. The man from the day before—the one who'd met with Madeleine in this very place. He hurried toward the door with his shoulders hunched and his head down. Hiding. Wanting to be invisible. Fuck that noise. I took two steps toward the staircase when a hard voice stopped me.

"Don't go up there just yet." The old lady gave me a stern look. "She'll be down."

"He looked shady."

"He likely is, but Miss Madeleine does just fine. That's why she comes here to conduct her business. It's a safe place."

So the old lady knew more about what was going on than I did. That stung. "What kind of business?"

"I believe you'd have to ask her that."

Maybe. That could be tricky, though. But there was someone else who knew what Madeleine was up to. Someone who'd likely not left the lot just yet.

I raced for the door, ignoring the old lady's cry of my name and hauling ass for the man who'd just reached his car. Who looked even guiltier than in the store.

"Hey, you." I quickened my pace when he looked up, the fear in his eyes a sure sign he would try to run if he thought he could get away from me.

He couldn't, but he didn't know that yet.

"I was just leaving." His voice wobbled, fear making him sweat. At least, it had better have been fear.

"Hold up a second. I want to know why you were at the bookstore."

"I needed something to read."

Sure, he did. I wanted to say more, to ask him a hundred questions about how he knew Madeleine and what they were doing together. But at that moment, the wind shifted, and a scent that made my bear stand on two feet and roar met my senses.

Madeleine.

He smelled like *my* Madeleine.

I practically leaped in front of him, pinning him against the hood of his own car. "What did you do to her?"

He fell backward, his eyes wide and panicked. "Nothing. I didn't take anything she didn't want me to."

"And what did she want you to take?"

"Look, man, it's just a little trade. I give her the cash she needs, and she gives me…what I need."

"What's that?"

He licked his lips, his eyes darting back and forth. "It's not illegal, you know."

By the fates, this guy and his half answers. "What's not? What is it you buy from her?"

His hand shook as he reached into his pocket and pulled out a piece of fabric. Bright pink, satiny, and small enough to fit in his fist, the object stole every bit of my attention. My inner bear sniffed, nearly busting through my control as the scent of Madeleine compounded. Grew deeper, stronger, more luscious. As it made my damn mouth water. But then he opened his fist, and my heart nearly stopped.

Panties.

Pink with white lace trim. Smelling of my mate. In some other man's hand.

My vision sharpened as my bear surged to the forefront of my mind, almost breaking through my control and taking over. I had partially shifted before I grabbed the reins again, had begun to sprout fur before I stopped myself from letting my bear take over. But that animal side didn't retreat as quickly as I needed it to. I snatched the fabric from his grasp, scraping him with my claws. Cutting his palm open and not feeling one bit guilty about the blood welling against his pale skin.

Rage filled my words as I asked, "What the fuck are you doing with these?"

He opened his mouth to answer, but a soft response came from behind me.

"Jericho?"

I spun, a snarl rumbling out of me as the only woman I would ever love, the only one who would ever truly matter to me, obliterated my control. My bear snapped the leash I'd been keeping him on, breaking the tether of my humanity and taking over with his animal desires. *Mate. Mine. Want.*

I tossed the man to the side and stalked toward Madeleine, not taking my eyes off her for a second. Not giving her a moment's reprieve from my gaze.

She glared right back at me. "Why are you out here scaring people?" She looked over my shoulder as a car door slammed behind me, likely the man I'd thrown. "Ryder looks sick with worry."

Ryder. As if that was his *real* name. He looked more like a Eugene.

"As he should be." I held out the pink fabric still clutched in my hand. "It's dangerous to take what isn't yours in a town of shifters."

She stared at the ball of fabric, her face going flat even as her eyes looked ready to burn me alive. "How did you get those?"

"I took them from that kid."

"You ruined my sale. Now I'm going to have to issue him a refund."

"You sell your...undergarments."

If her cocked eyebrow could talk, it would have said *Duh, you moron.* "Panties. I sell my panties, yes."

No hesitation. No fear. No...reserve. Little Madeleine suddenly seemed even more grown-up than she usually did, and I found that epically attractive. Still... "Why?"

"That's not your business." Head up, she turned as if to walk away. Not that I was going to let her.

"The fuck, it's not." I grabbed her elbow and twisted her around, the man inside of me battling with the beast. *Be gentle. Take her. You can't have her. She's mine.*

Madeleine glared. "Let go of me."

"Not until you listen to me."

"That's really not how any of this works."

"And this is?" I held up the pink panties. She tried to snatch them from me, but no fucking way was I letting them out of my hold. "What the hell are you thinking, Madeleine? Selling something of yourself that should be saved for—"

"For what? Or should I ask, for whom? Because right now, no one seems to want what I have to offer unless they're paying me for it."

That hurt. A lot. "I want." The confession rocked me to my soul. Too truthful, too honest. Too terrifying. But I did want her—wanted her so badly my bones ached with the need.

And I was tired of not having her.

Without another word, I grabbed her by the hips and picked her up. She squeaked but didn't pull away. Didn't tell me to stop. In fact, she grabbed my arms and held on tight. Clinging to me.

"Jericho, what—"

"I'm so tired of fighting this." I sat her ass on the hood of my truck, pushing her skirt up her slim thighs and spreading her knees so I could stand between them. So I could move closer to that secret place, the one I shouldn't have been looking at. The one I needed more than air or water or life.

Madeleine should have been shocked or scared. Instead, she seemed steady. Calm, even, as she whispered, "Then don't."

I practically whimpered as her legs came around my hips and tugged me into her. By the fates, the woman was just so *small* compared to me. Fragile, almost. Someone for me to take care of. "Don't say that."

"Why not? I'm yours, Jericho. Always have been. Why do you fight that so hard?"

I couldn't answer her question, but I could kiss her. So I did, deep and hard and hungry. I kissed her with the fire of too many years of resisting. Kissed her with my entire body, wrapping her in my arms as my lips devoured hers. As our hips notched together in a way that was meant to be. So good, so soft, my sweet Madeleine. Everything about her felt perfectly made just for me. I wanted more. I wanted everything.

But beast that I was, I wanted her taste on my tongue most of all. Not just her mouth—oh no. Even though her tongue sliding against mine was about the greatest thing that had ever happened to me, it wasn't enough. Breathing her air wasn't enough. Bending her backward over the hood of the truck until she lay underneath me wasn't enough. I needed to touch her, taste her, watch her come apart at my command. I needed, and nothing but her telling me no was going to stop me.

I broke the kiss, growling low at her whimper. "Want more."

"Anything," she said in a husky sort of whisper that sent chills down my spine. "I'm yours."

And though I knew she couldn't mean those words, though the idea of her accepting me as her mate made my bear want to celebrate his power, I held back. She didn't know what that sort of thing meant to shifters. She was human and so many years younger than me. I would need to tread carefully.

After I snuck a little taste.

Without another word, I lifted her up and carried her around the side of the bookstore. Shadows ruled back there, an almost empty parking lot coming into view just past the entrance from the alley. It wasn't perfect—wasn't at all what she deserved—but it was secluded enough for me to get what I needed. To give my mate a little tease of what could be. What *would* be. Someday.

"What are you doing?" Madeleine asked as I sat her ass on top of a lonely picnic table. It rested under an awning that created a quiet, shady nook against the building. Perfect for what I wanted to do.

"Taking what I need," I said. I worked my way down the length of her, pressing her knees apart to open her for me. Finding no resistance in her body. Only want and need. The girl was willing. So damn willing. And mine.

Just a few more months.

"Jericho," she whined, as if I wouldn't give her what she needed. What she craved. Silly girl.

"I've got you, sweet one. I'll take care of you."

Without pausing, without hesitation or delay or any other word that meant taking my damn time, I dove in, dropping down with a growl to lick the exposed flesh of her pussy. My entire body shivered at the flavor of her, the heat against me. By the fates, I'd never get enough of her. Not her scent, the feel of her skin against my tongue, the taste of her. I could eat her all day every day and *still* be hungry for her.

Fuck the election and the town. Making my mate come with my mouth would be my legacy.

Madeleine moaned long and loud as her fingers clutched my hair and pulled. Yanked, really. Demanding little thing that she was. I enjoyed it, though. Grew harder and needier as she proved how much I pleased her. I licked her over and over, growling softly, shoving her thighs apart and giving her not a second of reprieve from my greedy tongue. Once, twice...back to front. Great, wide laps against her flesh before zeroing in on her little clit and flicking my tongue against it. Madeleine arched and groaned, yanking me against her pussy as her legs spread even wider. Opening herself for me. Giving herself to me. And I took—by the fates, did I take. Her taste on my tongue, her wetness coating my fingers as I slipped them inside, her sweet moans forever recorded in my head. I took it all.

And when she came, when she cried my name to the world and pulled me impossibly closer, when my cock practically leaped out of my pants in need of its own release, I whispered a quiet "Mine" against her soft, wet flesh. I didn't know how or when or what would come from it, but I'd be claiming her as my own eventually. Publicly. Permanently. Likely after the election so Spencer couldn't target her or use our mating against me. It would be hell to wait, but I'd do it to keep my girl safe and out of the public eye. Just for a few more months.

And then, all would be right with the world.

But as I stood over her little body, as I fumbled to open my zipper and pull out my aching cock, I went stupid. Absolutely, terrifyingly stupid.

Because right as I slipped the tip of my cock inside my mate for the very first time, I asked, "Why have you been selling your panties to other men?"

6

MADELEINE

Wrong, wrong, wrong. Everything was so wrong, even though nothing had ever felt so right.

"Please," I heard my voice whisper. Not that I begged like that. No. Not possible. Not after what he'd just asked me, and yet the word had to have come from my mouth.

"Answer me, Madeleine."

Oh my, he used my full name. No childish nickname as he rocked his hips and thrust his cock deeper inside me. As he forced his way into my willing body. I was so full—of him, of joy, of hope—but that question, those ten words, were more than I could deal with.

"Jericho, please. I need..." I groaned and let my head fall back, arching into the sensations overtaking my body as he slid deep and froze. I tried to pull him closer, tighter, to force him to move, but he might as well have been a mountain in that moment. He simply refused to budge.

"Fuck me, you're so tight. Why are you so damn tight?" Jericho leaned down and planted a kiss on my lips, a soft, gentle one, before inching out of me slowly. Too slowly. "Is this okay?"

I choked on a laugh and tugged him closer, suddenly needing to feel his warmth all over my body. "It seems pretty okay to me."

He growled and moved a little faster, thrust a little deeper. And me? I took it. All of it. Every push and pull, every slide of his cock inside of me, every brush of his skin against mine. I took it all and filed it away for later. I'd replay these memories for years—would enjoy every second of rewinding this moment to focus on the details. The rough wood behind my back, the scratch of Jericho's chest hair against me, the little grunts he gave on every thrust. The sun burned bright behind the trees, and the sky looked to be a deeper blue than I'd ever seen it. Somewhere farther away, a car door slammed. And my dream man—the only person I'd ever wanted to do this with, the only one I'd ever felt comfortable giving myself to—was on top of me. Inside of me. Completely wrapped around me. And I loved it.

"Oh fuck, Madeleine. You're so perfect. I always knew you'd be so fucking perfect." Jericho grabbed my thigh and pushed my leg down, opening me wider for him. "Dreamed of this, you know. Of taking my mate. Can't believe I have you."

I didn't. I didn't know, so I shook my head and clutched at his arms as I whispered a pleading, "Jericho."

"I know, sweet girl. I know." He pushed harder, bending over me to kiss me again, deeper this time. Longer. He only broke the kiss to murmur against my lips, "I've dreamed of this every day and night for years, my sweet girl. Every single one. I've wanted you for so long."

I'd wanted him to say those words to me forever, and there they were. Laid out and raw and whispered during such an intimate moment. My heart wanted to soar. Wanted to fly high into the clouds and celebrate. Instead, I wrapped my legs around Jericho's hips and told him the only thing I could. The only truth I had. "I've loved you for so many years. I've never wanted another man, and I'm so glad my first time is with you."

"Ah, fuck. I can't…can't believe. Mine. All mine." Rhythm broken, he thrust deeper, growling my name on every push, burying his face in my neck as he slipped a hand between us to find my clit. And find it, he did. One brush with his large, rough finger and I broke, my body bowing, my mouth falling open, and my legs shaking as every inch of my body locked down and focused in on the pleasure washing over me.

Jericho groaned and followed me, stiffening as he came. As he grunted and growled and thrust deep inside me. Still, he held me, though. Kept my body covered with his. Kept me in his arms, safe and warm and covered from the world.

"Mine," he grunted, his body giving one last tremble.

I ran my hands through his hair, enjoying the warmth of him. The weight pushing into me. "Yours."

He didn't respond with words, simply kissed my breast and licked a path up to my neck. Tasting me. Savoring the moment.

At least, until he opened his mouth.

"I know my timing sucks, but I have to know. Why have you been selling your panties to other men?"

Exposed. I had never felt so exposed. I couldn't even look up at him as I said, "Men pay a premium price for them."

"Why?"

"I assume because they can't get girls of their own."

Jericho nipped at my neck and tugged me tighter against him. "No. I can guess why they *buy* them, but why do you sell them?"

Because you said men would come sniffing around, and they did. Because I needed someone to find something about me attractive. Because trying to hold on to an imagined connection to you is far more expensive than I could have imagined. All truths, but all things I couldn't say. So I fudged a bit.

"The house is old, and I needed more money than the bakery could provide me to fix it up. Every month, there was something else—repairs to be made or things to replace. A second job wasn't really an option because of my hours, and this fits into my schedule nicely."

"I will never understand why you bought that old house."

"Someone had to save it." I ran my fingers up and down his arms, blinking back something that felt like tears. "It was where I finally felt safe again after the death of my parents. Where you showed me your bear for the first time. I have happy memories there."

Jericho pulled away just enough to meet my eyes, his amber ones so dark and wide in the shadowy light. "Why didn't you ask me for help?"

"You weren't there."

"I've always been—"

"Not like this." I tugged him closer and ran my hands over his chest. "Not in this way. You've always been a friend but never indicated you wanted more. In fact, you had made it clear you didn't want more. From me."

He slipped from my body, easing the loss by covering me once more and dropping kisses all over my face. "I've always wanted you. Always. I never thought I could have you, though. But I always, always wanted."

"I didn't know."

"That's my fault, sweet girl. All mine. But I'm going to fix this. I just need—" His phone ringing stopped him in mid-sentence, a rough growl ripping from his chest as he cursed and dropped his head to my shoulder. "I have to answer that."

"Okay." And it was. The man was mayor. A tough job in the best of circumstances. I straightened up and watched as he yanked his phone from his pocket and took off across the lot. Back into the sun where people could see his tousled hair and half-unfastened fly. The man looked sexed-up and debauched, just the way I'd always pictured him in my fantasies. No, not the same. Better.

At least, until he frowned my way.

Something in that look, in the expression on his face, told me he was talking about me. And he wasn't happy.

By the time he hung up and made his way back under the awning, I was half panicked. "What is it?"

"Emergency campaign meeting."

"Something wrong?"

"No," he said, but his eyes screamed yes.

"Would you like to come over afterward? To talk or something?"

He shook his head. "It'll likely be late."

Late. Of course. Too late to put energy into making his mate happy. Too late to do anything other than what he wanted to do.

Too late for my happiness.

"Well then." I pushed off the table, shoving past him. "You should get going."

"Maddy, I—"

"Don't." I whirled, anger burning hot and bright in my chest. "Don't call me Maddy. I hate it."

He raised his hands and took a step back, looking all sorts of confused. "Okay. I'm sorry—I had no idea."

"Of course not, because you never took the time to ask me."

"Madeleine, I—"

"Need to go to your meeting. I got that. So, go."

But he didn't go. In fact, he grabbed my arm and pulled until my back pressed against his chest. "I don't know what just happened, but I don't want to leave things like this."

His phone rang again, making him growl. Giving me the chance to pull out of his hold no matter how good it felt to be in it. No matter how much it hurt to walk away. "You should get that. It might be important."

"Stop," he said as he reached for me again, growling when I pulled out of his grasp. "Damn it, woman. What the hell is going on?"

And I broke. "What's going on is you just fucked me on a table but can't wait to get away from me. What's going on is I'd like to figure out what just happened between us other than fucking, but you don't have the time to give me, even when I offer to work around your schedule. What's going on is I'm beginning to think this crush I've had on you all these years isn't good for me, after all."

"Madeleine, stop. It's not—"

His phone started ringing again, and I sighed. "Answer that. Go to your meeting. Do whatever you want. I'm going home."

I turned and rushed to my car, too angry to walk calmly. Too frustrated not to squeal the tires as I backed out of my spot. I raced home like a demon was chasing me through the streets of Kinship Cove. I shouldn't have been so afraid—there were no demons in town. Heck, not even a bear shifter had followed me. I'd been all alone on the road.

When I finally opened the front door to my house, Matilda had a surprise of her own for me. Water. Everywhere. Leaking through the ceiling from the attic over the two-story foyer, pouring down the stairs, and flowing out the front door. I tried to rush up the stairs to see what was happening, but my foot went right through the first tread, and I fell instead. In the water. The cold, dirty water.

"Fine," I screamed as I lay in the grossness that now coated my wood floors. "I give up. You win, okay? I'm done."

Done with the house.

Done with Jericho.

Likely done with Kinship Cove altogether.

Just...done.

7

JERICHO

Meetings sucked.

This upcoming election sucked.

Not being able to kill Spencer sucked.

This stupid wedding I was being forced to go to sucked.

In short, my life sucked.

And it certainly didn't get any better when Parker slipped into the seat beside me. We sat in silence as one of the social media analysts she'd hired droned on about some post Spencer had put up. A post that had warranted this meeting of my entire team to make a plan for a counterpost. *This* was what had been so important as to pull me away from my mate after I'd finally—*finally*—given in and stolen a taste of her.

Social media sucked.

"Can you stop?" Parker whispered, stealing my attention from the suck my life had become. "You're glowering so hard at the poor guy. You're going to scare him."

"He should be scared. Who gives a shit about this stuff?"

"Almost every single resident of Kinship Cove, that's who."

I looked over the screen again—a presentation of some social media platform I'd never joined but had a mayoral account on for other people to

233

post stuff to. One Spencer had used to call me weak, soft…a coward. He'd been posting all afternoon, each statement more outrageous. He'd dragged my family through the mud and also called out the fact that I'd hired my sister, saying it was nepotism at its finest. Never mind the woman had a master's degree, had experience running far larger campaigns than mine, and worked for peanuts so as not to put a strain on the town's budget. Spencer couldn't be bothered to actually find out the truth about a situation—he simply posted some inflammatory statement on social media and got the locals all worked up over nothing. The shifter didn't have the balls to say any of that shit to my face, but put him behind a keyboard, and he became one mouthy motherfucker. He'd even brought up the Chance sisters and their bakery—questioning why I went there every day. Implying there were untoward things happening there. He hadn't named any sister in particular, but I still took the statement as an attack on Madeleine.

In my day, I'd have beaten the shit out of him and tossed him back to his pride to deal with.

This was not my day. So instead, I had to listen to forty-five minutes of copywriters and social media experts argue what words to use in my rebuttal. A written, posted rebuttal instead of an ass-kicking.

My life = the suckiest.

Parker huffed and inched closer in her seat. "Seriously, what is wrong with you?"

I glanced at my phone screen—the same move I'd made at least a hundred times in the past hour—to see if Madeleine had texted me back. No dice.

Which meant I might need help. This was going to hurt. "I think Madeleine's angry with me."

"As she should be. You've been keeping her at a distance for years."

"Yeah, well…not tonight, I didn't."

Her head whipped in my direction. "What did you do?"

Fucked my mate on a picnic table under an awning in an alley behind a bookstore. It sounded so wrong and yet so right at the same time. "I gave in and told her she was my mate."

I could see the moment when Parker figured out I'd done something horribly wrong along the way. Her smile stopped growing, and her eyes widened for just a second before her entire face shrank into the most evil glare she'd ever given me. "What. Did. You. Do?"

I sank about six inches into my chair and stared down at the desk. "I sort of claimed her."

"Sort of."

"I mean…we…fuck, Parker. Don't make me say it. To *you*."

"So you had sex with your mate—congrats, by the way—and then what? Please tell me you don't have her waiting in the car."

"Of course not. I'm not that bad."

"Prove it. What did you do?"

"I told her I had to come here, and that it would be late when I got out."

Parker cocked her head and blinked, her lips settling into a thin line that looked more dangerous than her snarl. "Let me guess. She wanted to see you tonight, and that's when you said it would be late when you got out."

"No. I mean—that is what I said, but I hadn't meant it the way it sounded."

"Well, good, because it sounds like you brushed her off. Like you took exactly what you needed, then decided she wasn't worth your time. Is that what you did?"

By the fates, I was the biggest idiot in the world. "Fuck me."

"She did and got hurt for it. So you're going to her house after this, right? To fix this mess you made?"

"Yes. Of course. Late or not."

"And you'll be groveling?"

No way around it. "Deeply and sincerely."

"Good boy." She patted my arm then pointed at the screen, redirecting my attention. "Now, about this post—"

"Who the fuck does this guy think he is?"

The others in the room all quieted and turned my way. Apparently, my whispering had failed me. Oops.

"Not you," Parker said, smiling at the owl shifter who'd been taking us through various social media platforms and their demographics so we could make the most impact with our rebuttal. Or something.

"Not you," I reiterated, agreeing with my sister. "That jackass, Spencer. Who the fuck does he think he is?"

The owl shifter adjusted his glasses. "He thinks he's the next mayor of Kinship Cove."

Which couldn't happen. "A man like that divides a community—he doesn't bring it together. He doesn't strengthen it. He doesn't have what it takes to run this town."

"Which is why we're all here." Parker stood, walking around the table and across the floor to take control of the room. In her element, for sure. "Spencer is the worst sort of adversary—he's brash and dishonest. A liar and a cheater, completely ignorant of the decorum of an election and too lazy to learn it. He sees no value in hard work, not wanting to put in the hustle to win. He wants the glory without the effort."

I snorted. "What fucking glory?"

"Exactly. He thinks your job is all pomp and circumstance. You make it look easy, brother. You keep your cool at all times and stay the course of what's best for the Cove and its residents."

"That's my job."

"Yeah, well—it's time to lose your temper."

And even though I missed my mate, even though I knew I'd fucked up and that I'd be heading to her house as soon as the meeting ended, things had just gotten a lot more interesting. And two hours later when I rushed out the door, I was almost in a good mood. Almost. I needed to find Madeleine first, to apologize. To get down on my fucking knees and beg her to forgive me for being such an idiot. Then I could bask in the glory that was hope and possibility. That was a light at the end of the long, dark tunnel I'd dragged her into.

But Madeleine wasn't at home. In fact, the old house sat dark and quiet, looking empty of all life. I circled it for a long time, running my fingers along the wood siding, seeing every fault in the exterior of the old place. How could Madeleine take care of such a house? And why did she want to?

The house practically sighed as I stepped onto the back porch, the old structure settling in a way I remembered. Noisy—she'd always been a noisy building. She'd never looked so lost, though. So abandoned. Perhaps, like Kinship Cove, she needed someone from my family to keep her running true. Perhaps Madeleine had so many issues with her because the house knew there was a piece missing to her family.

Perhaps the old place missed me as much as I missed my mate.

8

MADELEINE

There was something about waking up with icing in your hair that would likely seem wrong to most people. I wasn't most people. But sleeping on a stainless-steel counter in the bakery had done horrible things to my neck, and the stickiness clinging to my skin made everything that much worse. As did the burning around my eyes from all the crying I'd done over Jericho. And Matilda. Mostly Jericho.

And yet, when I finally found the strength to lift my head and look at what I'd done—what I'd made—nothing else mattered. The cake—a bear on its back legs, roaring to the world—stood close to four feet tall and likely two feet in diameter. Massive was one word to describe it. Impressive, another. I didn't usually brag on myself, but I'd really pushed my limits. I'd created a cake that easily rivaled the lacy delicacy of the actual wedding cake. Every aspect of the beast rang true—every detail carved or built with precision. And it wasn't just any bear—it was Jericho's bear. I hadn't seen the animal in years, but I remembered. Every person in town would know it, too. Golden brown with darker tones of umber along his head and ears, streaks of silver decorating the hair on the tips of his ears just like in his human form. Paws the size of frying pans and a glare in its amber eyes that would send lesser men scurrying completed the overall look.

239

Yeah, there was no denying the identity of that beast.

I'd started baking the cake out of hurt, then anger, but in the end, the piece had become a love letter to the man who would never want me the way I wanted him. Perhaps a last goodbye of sorts. Letting him know I saw him—all parts of him—and had loved each one.

"What the hell did you do?" Misty closed the door behind her, eyes locked on the bear cake.

I could only shrug, having not expected her to come in and yet not surprised by her appearance in the kitchen. "I made a cake."

"Uh, no. This is not a cake. It's a work of art. Madeleine, you've outdone yourself." She tore her eyes from it to look my way. "Does he know?"

And that was when the tears began to fall again. "He knows."

"Yet you're here alone."

I couldn't deal with that truth, with questions and answers and deep-diving into my non-relationship with Jericho and what the cake meant. I just couldn't. "I have no idea what to do with it."

The cake. The man. The house. That really could have been for any of them. Thankfully, Misty stuck to the issue at hand.

"We'll take it to the wedding with the other cake."

"It's a bear."

"You don't say?" Her eyebrows arched in a definite statement of *Are you kidding me?* "I never would have guessed."

"But the wedding is for wolves."

It was her turn to shrug. "Food is food and art is gorgeous, no matter the subject. The townspeople are going to love this."

Townspeople. Locals. Friends and family and… "They're going to know it's him."

"They might pick up on that, yes. Does it matter?"

Did it? If they knew I'd fallen for the mayor, would they care? His opponent had been stirring up a lot of trouble lately—a quiet sort of negativity in his speeches and social media posts that had been consistently growing louder and more divisive. A sort of…anti-Jericho but also anti-anyone other than shifters sort of sentiment. He'd even questioned our bakery last night—claiming Jericho came into the shop every day for more than just baked goods. And maybe he did—he'd basically admitted as much under that awning yesterday—but did it matter? If the town figured out I was in love with Jericho, but he didn't have it in him to want me back, would it change anything? Would it stop me from leaving or make me run all that much faster?

Only time would tell. "No. It doesn't matter."

"Then we take it. Now, go clean yourself up—you're looking a little hobo-ish."

Vicious. Always so vicious. "I'm not a hobo."

"Really? Then you might want to explain why you have green icing all over the left side of your face." She laughed as I shot a hand to my face to feel—yup, sticky. "Now, go wash, you filthy animal. These cakes won't deliver themselves."

The cakes had been heavy. Even on rolling carts and with two of us, the lifting, tugging, pulling, and sliding of two mountains of sugar, flour, buttercream frosting, and fondant had been more of a workout than my sore body had been prepared for. My back hurt, my hips screamed, and my feet were not happy to be trapped in four-inch strappy heels, but I still walked into the wedding of Nico and Fiona with my head high, my lipstick bright, and no tears in my eyes. I had tissues in my clutch just in case, though.

"Oh, don't you look lovely." Parker, Jericho's sister and campaign manager, snagged me by the arm. "He's going to be thrilled to see you."

I had to stomp on my heart a bit to stop the hope from making it beat. "I don't know what you're talking about."

Her wicked eyebrow raise told me that she knew I was lying. "Look, I figure we've got about two minutes before this shindig starts, so let me cut to the chase. My brother's an idiot."

"He's not—"

"Hush. He is. An idiot trying really hard to live up to a family legacy no man should have to shoulder, especially not alone. He's also dealing with that asshole Spencer, who seems to like picking apart Jericho's life and dissecting each piece."

"Why are you telling me this?"

"I know you don't see it yet, but he's protecting you." She smiled at someone walking by and lowered her voice as she led me toward where my sisters were sitting. "If Spencer finds out you're Jericho's mate, he'll dig into everything about your life and put it out there for the entire Cove to see. He'll twist the facts to fit his agenda, then toss the bones out for the wolves to descend on."

"That sounds horrible."

"It is, and Jericho would be out for blood if it happened. So, while he's an idiot—don't argue that he's not—he's an idiot doing all the wrong things for the right reasons. You may be seen as the sweetest Chance sister, but we both know that's not true, now don't we?"

My heart stuttered. "I don't—"

"Yeah, you do. And don't think I'm judging you because I'm not—a girl's gotta make that money. But if Spencer finds out, he'll crucify you for it, and Jericho will go berserk that the man had the balls to attack his mate. Then Spencer will say Jericho is too weak to control his mate and his bear, so how can he possibly control the town. See how this plays out?"

I did. I totally did. And I hated it. "What should I do?"

"Stay strong, get ready to defend yourself, and if you happen to have it in you, prepare to go on the offensive."

"But won't that just make things worse? Make this Spencer guy even more angry?"

"Angry men make mistakes, and guys like Spencer are usually pretty good at showing their asses when confronted by smart, bold women. He has no idea how to argue against us because he doesn't see us as worthwhile opponents. It's the cock-and-balls playbook—we don't have them, so he doesn't plan for us." She stopped us at a row of chairs and leaned in for a hug. "I hope you have a little patience in you. I'd really like to get to know a new sister."

And with that, she walked away, leaving me with *my* sisters. Ginger sat next to her dragon mate, the two leaning into one another and whispering softly back and forth. Coco held the hand of her wolf shifter mate, both looking slightly stiff. I couldn't blame them—Coco had dated the groom, and her mate was the groom's father. Every person in the room could put two and two together on how that all played out. And I thought my life could be awkward at times.

I took the chair next to Coco and gave her a shoulder bump. "It's good to see you."

Her smile seemed forced. "You too. Everything okay?"

No. "Sure. It's good to see you again, Magnus."

Coco's mate—with his gorgeous smile and salt-and-pepper hair—reached for my hand. "Madeleine. You're looking lovely."

"Stunning, I'd say." Kingston—dragon shifter and definite silver fox—smiled my way. "If I weren't mad about your sister, I'd definitely be trying to get you out of that dress."

Charmer. Before I could respond, a heavy weight shook the seat next to me. "The only person getting you out of your dress is me."

Jericho, in all his suited, muscled glory. His hair wasn't as gray as Kingston's, but there was still quite a bit of silver in it. A fact that wasn't lost on me—my sisters and I obviously had a thing for older men. Too bad mine didn't have a thing for me.

"I believe I'm the one who gets to decide such things, Jericho. Shouldn't you be with all the other elected officials?"

"I'd rather be here."

"What if I don't want you sitting next to me?"

His amber eyes stared into mine, something practically on fire behind them. "Then I'd be duty-bound to leave you alone. Is that what you want, Madeleine?"

I couldn't answer him, couldn't even attempt to lie and say yes. Not with him looking so broken beside me. So I turned to the front instead as the music began to play and women came slipping down the aisle in support of the bride.

But Jericho wasn't done with me yet. "Madeleine, I know—"

"You know nothing," I whispered. "Now, please—the ceremony is about to start."

"I went looking for you last night, but you weren't home. I need to talk to you."

He looked for me? That made my heart leap a little bit, but I kept it tied down. Controlled. Under wraps. "You've had a number of years to want to talk to me, but you've done nothing. I'm tired of always waiting for you."

And with that, the bridal march began, and all eyes turned to the back of the room to watch as Fiona, smiling radiantly under her white veil, began her slow walk to the dais where Nico stood waiting for her. Both of them looked deliriously happy, both fresh and young and in love. Ready to start a new life together, to move past old grievances and work toward a shared future.

To start anew.

If only we all got that same chance.

9

JERICHO

Growing up, I'd never really enjoyed weddings. Sure, they were places to catch up with people you didn't see much and eat cake, but I didn't care for the ceremonies or the showiness of them. I'd never actually given my own wedding any thought. But sitting next to my mate, my sweet Madeleine, as a ceremony generations old went on before us? Totally different story. I watched every moment, took in every detail. Planned for a day when it would be us up there. Because that would happen—eventually. I just needed to get her to forgive me first.

A hard goal when she wouldn't even look at me.

At about twenty minutes past when I figured we should have been served cake, otherwise known as I was getting grumpy from a lack of food and too long of a ceremony o'clock, I leaned close to Madeleine and whispered, "Shouldn't they be done by now?"

She jerked a little, as if I'd surprised her. "Hush. It's almost over."

Not enough. "But it's been so long."

Finally, my girl turned my way, her teeth buried against her bottom lip as if biting back a grin. "You're so impatient today."

I never had been one to turn down an opening when I saw one.

245

"I want cake. Your cake." Inching closer, I brushed her hair off her shoulder and pressed a kiss to the base of her ear. "Your sweetness."

"Stop it." But she didn't mean it. Her cheeks flushed a soft pink, and her eyes were soft. Kind. A little wanting. At least, I hoped for that last part.

"I know I have a lot of making up to do, but—"

"Please rise," the preacher called, his voice booming through the speakers and cutting me off. "Let us welcome the newest couple of Kinship Cove. Mr. and Mrs. Nico Bertolf."

We rose, we clapped, we cheered as the newlyweds hurried down the aisle. Ceremony done—time for cake. But before I could ask Madeleine if I could escort her to the reception area, I got hit with an unpleasant surprise.

"Jericho. So happy to see you up and about." Spencer stood at the end of the aisle, a small woman by his side. I didn't even need to glance around to know Parker was headed to me. No way was this douchebag here to be friendly.

And all I'd wanted was cake and a little time with my mate.

"Spencer." I stood and stepped toward him, clearing the pew and forcing him to turn toward the front of the church. Away from my mate and her sisters. "I hope you enjoyed the ceremony."

A wicked sort of grin crept over his scraggly face. "Oh, I definitely did. Though, you seemed a bit distracted, what with the youngest Chance sister practically sitting on your lap."

Now that was a way to make a wedding ceremony better—put my mate on my lap and slip my hands under her pretty dress. But he didn't know Madeleine was my mate, and his words implied something that made my blood boil.

"There was no one on my lap, Spencer."

"Could have fooled me. You two seemed awfully…intimate."

And just like that, I saw how this would go. Spencer would imply Madeleine was a whore or that I was having some sort of taboo affair with a girl half my age. He'd dig into our relationship, see that she'd lived in my family's home, and likely claim we'd started crossing lines all the way back then. I doubted anyone would believe him, so punching him in the face for even looking down that road seemed fair and just. But there was one snag in my plan.

If he dug into Madeleine's history, he'd likely find her secret—that she sold her panties on the internet for money.

Having the entire town know that would likely destroy her.

Having her hurt because my job made me have to deal with assholes like Spencer wasn't about to happen.

I needed a distraction. "I have to apologize," I said, directing my attention to the woman at Spencer's side. "We haven't been introduced. I'm Jericho—"

"She knows who you are." Spencer yanked the woman—I had to assume it was his mate—against him. "And she doesn't need to talk to you."

Treating his mate like an object instead of a person. I'd say I was shocked, but that fit his persona. "I'd think the lady could make her own decisions on who to talk to."

"And I say I get to decide who my mate is worthy enough to speak to."

The women around us—shifter and human alike—all seemed to take a visible breath and step back, as if his words had slapped the lot of them. Good. Let them see him for what he was.

This might actually be worth waiting for cake. "I'd say your mate is plenty worthy to speak to me. In fact, I'd say she's worthy of having her own opinions of the people around her and to make her own decisions. Aren't you, miss?"

"Do not speak to her." Spencer's face had gone red, and his eyes burned with rage as he stepped between me and his mate. "I don't want some man who thought it was a good idea to rub up all over some hussy during a religious ceremony sullying my mate."

See now, there were a few things wrong with his statement. My actions couldn't sully another, I hadn't gotten the opportunity to rub all up over my mate—though I'd take that opportunity if she'd give it to me —and he'd called Madeleine a hussy. It was the last one that made me lose my temper. Because, of course.

"Don't you dare call that woman such a name. I won't have you disparaging her."

"If she's willing to let you be so brazen during a wedding, then that's what she is. Perhaps you should spend your time finding a mate instead of—"

"He has a mate." Madeleine stepped beside me, her back straight as an arrow and a hard expression on her beautiful face. I suddenly understood Spencer's desire to tug his mate behind him, though I wasn't about to do that. Madeleine would kill me...as would her sisters...as would *my* sister.

Though, if he dared to step even an inch in her direction, all bets were off.

Spencer glowered at Madeleine, looking almost furious that he was forced to speak to her. "That's a lie—the mayor has no mate—and you have no business speaking to me, little girl."

My growl came unbidden, and that urge to step before my mate was one I battled to control. Sort of. I mean, I may have inched to the side so I could at least block her with my shoulder. "Don't you dare—"

"I'm no little girl, and I'll speak to you if I so choose." Madeleine practically pushed past me, staring down Spencer with a steely look on her face. One I knew could only lead to trouble.

I tugged her behind me again, not taking my eyes off the lion shifter for a second. "You need to back off, Spencer."

He pointed at Madeleine as he spat, "And you need to control this little slut before I do it for you."

Madeleine gasped along with every woman in the crowd, but the sound was nothing compared to the snarl that thundered out of me. Rage unlike any I'd ever experienced exploded inside of me, nowhere near a level I could control. My bear practically burst through my skin, roaring long and loud at the piece of garbage before me. Making the entire room shake as our paws hit the ground and we jumped toward our foe.

Spencer stumbled backward, dragging his mate with him. His eyes were wide and filled with fear. I didn't shift often anymore—especially not in public—so Spencer likely had no concept of the beast that lived within me. The power the animal exuded. He'd only seen my human side because I had an image to uphold, a town to support. I needed to be seen as someone people could talk to even though, at almost seven feet tall, I towered over them. Spencer likely had no idea that people tended to think my bear was scary simply because of his size.

A fact that came in handy as I stalked all the more closely to his retreating form with my teeth bared and my claws clicking on the floor.

At least, until my sister stopped me.

"That's enough," Parker said, slipping in beside me and directing quite the glare at the lion shifter. "You've insulted a respected member of our community and made implications about my brother and his mate that are simply not true. I think it's time for you to leave."

"He's lost all control," Spencer said, sounding near panicked as he stared my way. "You can't even rein in your beast. You're not fit to lead."

I leaped closer to him, landing with a thud that nearly knocked over three pews as a roar ripped through me. Spencer took the hint, rushing for the door and dragging his mate behind him. *Behind him*—as in, between himself and me, the thing he saw as a threat. What a coward.

"C'mon, big guy," Parker said, shoving me toward the back of the room once Spencer had disappeared. "We need to find you a private spot where you can shift back and re-dress."

I whined but followed her, swinging my head back and forth as I looked for Madeleine. She was nowhere to be seen, though. In fact, none of the Chance sisters was. A fact that didn't sit well with me.

Parker found an empty room and led me into it before rushing outside to grab a change of clothes from my car—occupational hazard. Bears couldn't shift with their clothes. Only dragons could. Lucky bastards. Once she returned, I shifted and dressed, rushing through the motions. Unable to focus on anything other than my mate.

"Where's Madeleine?"

But Parker was too giddy to focus at all. "That was amazing. Did you see those women watching? Even the men looked disgusted by Spencer's actions. Who treats their mate that way anymore? We didn't even have to do anything—he made himself the asshole in a matter of seconds."

"Yeah. Cool. Great. Where's Madeleine?"

"Gone."

"Gone?" She'd left. Without me. "I have to find her."

Parker nodded and tugged on my shirt as she rebuttoned it. "You do. She was amazing as well, wasn't she? So strong and sure. I didn't think she had it in her. So yes, you need to find her. Right now."

"Really? I thought you'd want me to do…cleanup."

"Brother dear, you just set yourself up as the biggest alpha in the room to every woman in Kinship Cove. You showed everyone why you're not just mayor but clan leader, and you did it with a strength no one could ever deny. I think you're good on cleanup. Now, go get your mate."

So I did. Cake could wait.

But when I walked out into the hallway, it was a cake that stopped me. No, not just a cake. A goddamned work of art in cake form.

"It's you," Parker said, her eyes wide as she stared at the mountain of confection staring back at her. "She sculpted you. From cake."

There was only one her who could have done this. Only one woman with the talent and the attention to detail who could have made such a glorious work of art. Madeleine. She must have worked for hours on the standing bear with the mountain behind him. Must have stayed up all night crafting such a thing. A crowd had gathered around the cake, all oohing and aahing as they inspected the details. As they glanced my way and whispered to one another.

"They all know it's me."

"They do," Misty said as she appeared beside me. Sneaky fox. "And they're all talking about you and Madeleine Chance possibly being mated after all these years."

A growl rumbled through me. "They'd better not—"

"They're not."

"You don't know what I was about to say."

"Doesn't matter—they're not. They want to see you settled, and they all love the Chance sisters. Quit worrying so much about appearances."

"I'm more worried about assholes like Spencer using her as a weapon and hurting her."

"Yeah, well…I'm pretty sure she can handle herself, as she just proved in that room. And you just showed all of Kinship Cove what happens when you imply Madeleine Chance is anything other than an amazing woman. Well done, by the way."

"Thanks." I ran a hand through my hair, looking around at all the people. "Any idea where she is?"

"Matilda."

"Ma—what?"

"Matilda." Misty sighed when I stared blankly at her. "It's what she named that shitty house she bought. She went home."

"Perfect." I turned to leave, but Misty stopped me with a hand on my arm.

"You know you fucked up, right?"

"Yeah, I know." And I did. Knew it with every fiber of my being. And was ready to fix it.

"You need to make it up to her," Misty said as if reading my mind. But her words gave me an idea—this woman knew my mate better than most people. Had been with the sisters every day since they'd opened their bakery in town. She was an untapped resource in my war to win over my mate.

And I was not about to turn my back on such a gift. "I do need to make it up to her. In a big way. You got any ideas?"

Misty's grin turned a little evil, and she crossed her arms over her chest. "I just might, Mayor. But first, I'm going to need you to answer a few questions."

I could do that. "Shoot."

"Know anything about roofing?"

10

MADELEINE

Circles. I'd been walking in circles for what felt like hours. How dare that jerk Spencer call me a slut? Who did he think he was? He was lucky Jericho had pushed me back. Otherwise, I would have smacked that lion right on the nose. Dorothy Gale style. Who knew cowardly lions were actually a thing?

But Jericho—in all his ursine glory—had defended me. Had shifted right there in front of all those people and bared his teeth. Literally. That had stunned me a bit. The man had always been so controlled, so even-keeled. He rarely showed his more aggressive side. At least, I'd never seen him react like that. Like something he truly cared about was in danger. Viciously aggressive and ready to fight.

Deep down, a little glimmer of hope thought maybe—just *maybe*— that violent reaction was for me. Was in defense of me. Of his mate. He'd called me that, and I'd believed him even though he certainly didn't treat me as a mate should. Or, as I assumed a mate should. Perhaps I'd been wrong in expecting more from him. Perhaps he was giving me all he had to give, and it was my job to figure out if that was enough.

I'd never wished to be a shifter more than in that moment simply so I would have some sort of reference for what I was supposed to do in this situation. Being human had left me wholly unprepared.

But as I turned the corner on my street and headed home to a still waterlogged Matilda, all thoughts of my mate and weddings and jerk shifters who needed better vocabularies—seriously, who used "hussy" anymore?—slipped away. There was something on my roof. A big, hulking something probably causing a ridiculous amount of damage right by the chimney of the only working fireplace in the house.

This was so not what I needed.

I quickened my pace, dollar signs flashing as I started wondering exactly how much removing whatever the something that had fallen on my roof would cost. Hundreds? Thousands? Would I even be able to pay it? I was already deep down in a hole because of the roof and the latest plumbing issue in the house that had caused the flood the night before. Wood floors and new drywall had been added to my list of necessary updates, along with a toilet that had decided to explode for no reason. I couldn't take another repair. Couldn't bear to think about how much more this house would take from me before I finally gave in.

As I came closer, though, the realization that it wasn't some*thing* on my roof but some*one* slammed into me like a pile of bricks. Like a car with no brakes. Like—a bear shifter enraged.

Jericho.

"What are you doing?" I yelled, shading my eyes and looking up at him from the sidewalk. All of him. Miles and miles of tanned skin and hair and muscle.

My lord, he didn't have a shirt on.

"Fixing this roof."

That wasn't what I'd expected to hear, not that I'd ever experienced coming home to the bear shifter of my dreams shirtless and on my roof before.

Alternate reality—table for one, please.

"But...why? I was going to call Ralph Peterson for it."

"Ralph Peterson, and therefore Peterson Roofing, is no longer licensed to work in Kinship Cove. He's a cheat." Jericho paused in his banging to give me a look that I could feel all the way from where I stood two stories below. "Besides, a man should take pride in caring for his mate."

Mate. Me. Taking care of Matilda for me. Of my house for me. For… us? That hope deep inside me peeked out, wanting so badly to grow warmer, brighter, and bigger.

Fear and doubt kept it dark, though. Kept me from being willing to accept his words at face value. "Stop it, please."

Jericho banged a few more times on something up there, then crawled to the ladder propped against the side of the house, descending it faster than my heart could handle.

"Don't fall," I whispered, unable not to. His husky laugh greeted me from behind the house, but then he was there. Turning the corner and heading right for me. All shirtless and muscled and…glistening. And so damn big, my brain practically trembled like a newborn foal on wobbly legs.

Don't drool. You'll only embarrass yourself.

Jericho didn't seem fazed by my blatant ogling at all. In fact, if anything, I'd have called his smile cocky as he watched me fight my instincts to touch and taste and scratch.

"Two feet on the ground," he said when he finally came to a stop before me.

"Good. Now—"

"I meant what I said." He grabbed my hand and pulled it to his chest, joining us. Tugging me closer to him as he gazed down at me with the most delicious expression on his face. "A man should take pride in taking care of his mate, and I failed at that."

"Jericho, you—"

"Madeleine Chance, you're my mate. My one and only. The reason my heart beats and the light brightening my days. I've known for far too long but fought it, thinking I was doing the best thing for you. That was wrong of me. I want to fix what I've screwed up. Want to show you I can and will be a good mate to you."

Heart. Stopped. "Don't say that just to take it back."

"Never. I will never let anything come between us again." He inched closer, pressing all that warm skin and muscle against me. Looking at me with such an earnest expression on his handsome face. "This is me apologizing—my grand gesture. I'm sorry I was an idiot. I'm sorry I didn't trust in your strength enough to tell you about people like Spencer so we could deal with him head on. I'm sorry for making you wait for me to pull my head out of my ass and claim you as mine. But mostly, I'm so damn sorry I wasn't paying enough attention to know you needed me. I failed my mate, and I will work extra hard for all my days to make that up to you."

Hope was a wily thing. No matter how hard I tried to hold it back, that glimmer managed to escape. It grew big and bold, so warm my entire body heated. So large even my heart felt the pressure. Hope and Jericho were a deadly combination, though. "You don't deserve me."

His lips twitched into a half smile. "I will never argue that point, and my sister would totally agree with you. But I'll try, my sweet. I'll try every day to earn your love if you'll let me."

I wanted to let him, so I inched that much closer. Pressing the length of my body to his even as I said, "Maybe."

Hands on my hips, Jericho gripped me tight. Held me in place as the hard ridge of his cock pressed into my stomach. "Maybe?"

"Depends on if that roof repair holds."

"It'll fucking hold."

"We'll see," I said with a shrug, enjoying the way his brow furrowed and his eyes darkened. "Matilda is tough."

"I'm tougher."

"Stronger than my roof?"

"Yes."

"Prove it."

He picked me up with a growl and carried me to the front porch, taking the steps two at a time as I laughed in his arms. My big, strong man. But as he opened the door, I had to stop him.

"You might want to wait."

"Why?" he asked, looking not at all interested in stopping.

"A toilet exploded."

"Pardon?"

"A toilet. On the second floor. Exploded. Everything's likely still wet."

"The only thing I care about being wet is you, sweet girl."

Welp. Damaged wood floors be damned. "Then feel free to proceed."

He chuckled and headed inside, but his hold tightened as he crossed the threshold of Matilda's front door, and his growl turned darker. Deeper. Almost scary.

"There's one more thing, Madeleine."

My full name. I liked that. "What?"

"Your panty-selling days are over."

"Jericho—"

"No. I can't handle the thought of some other shifter getting off to the smell of your cunt. That's mine to enjoy." He pushed me against the wall and dropped to his knees, ignoring the creak as the saturated wood bowed under his weight. He slid his hands up my thighs to lift my dress so he could see the piece of fabric in question. Running his fingers along the lace edges I'd worn just for him this time. "Fucking beautiful."

"Yours," I said, knowing he needed to hear that. Needed the permission. His answering growl told me I'd chosen the right word as did his hurried hands as he ripped the sides of my panties and yanked them off me.

"All mine." He leaned in closer, lace trapped in his hand as it rested against my hip, nose teasing along my pussy. "I'd kill for this scent, my sweet. You have no idea how close I came to doing just that when that guy at the bookstore smelled like you. The idea of another man—"

"Just you," I said, tugging on his hair to get him to look up at me. "Only you."

"Only me...and I couldn't even be man enough to bring you someplace special for our first time together. I had to take you on a picnic table."

"I liked it."

He pushed my legs apart, a wicked grin on his face as he looked up at me. "Me too. But you deserve more."

"I just want you."

"You've got me." A kiss. Soft and gentle but right on the mound of my pussy, his chin putting pressure where I needed it most, his hands bracketing me and holding me in place. Such a tease. "If this house needs a repair, I'll take care of it. I'm moving in the second you say I can, so it'll be me taking care of our home as I should. And if you need money for other things, you can sell those panties to me."

"You want to buy my panties?"

He bit the fabric in question, making his point clear. "Every last pair."

"I'd give them to you for free, you know."

"So long as you're not wearing any."

"That can be arranged."

"Good. Because I have a feeling I'm going to want this flavor on my tongue every fucking day." He spread my lips and licked me from opening to clit, growling softly as he dove in. As he pushed my body against the wall and made me stand there and take his attack. And I took, all right—I took his licks and his vibrations and his suckles until I broke right there in the hallway of my home. Of the house we would share together. In the place where I had first met the bear shifter I'd always known would be my perfect match.

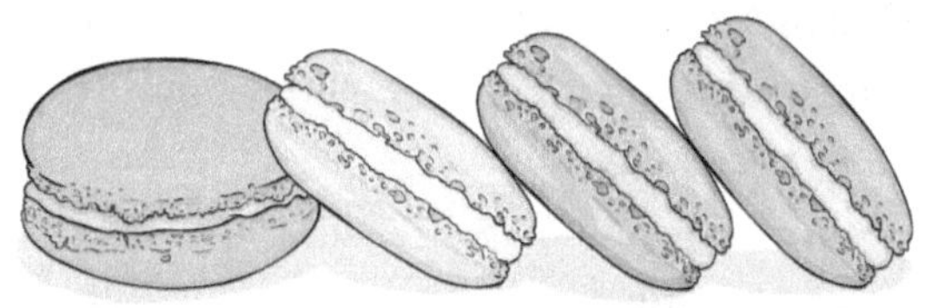

I pulled up outside the bookstore and put my car in park. It had been a long time since I'd been there for anything other than buying books, but when your favorite customer asked for something specific, you did it. *Customer service is king.*

I glanced at the clock before stepping outside. I had about two minutes until our scheduled meeting time. Talk about cutting it close, but there was simply no time to spare, what with the election coming up, the remodel happening at Matilda, and the upswing in business the bakery had seen over the last few months. My sisters and I were quite busy, as were our mates. Not a moment to spare.

I nodded to the old lady behind the counter—the same one I'd been nodding to and buying books from since I was a child—and hurried to the stairs. Up here, in the used books and antiquated research materials sections, was where I'd once sold my panties for money to a man not named Ryder. His real name was actually Clark, and he had a thing for toffee bars, sweet coffee, and snarky fox shifters.

But that was a story for another day.

Footsteps on the stairs set my heart pounding. My two minutes seemed to be up, which meant it was time to put on my show. I slipped into a shadowy corner and waited, knowing that he'd find me. That there was no escaping a shifter's sense of smell. That I didn't want to escape anyway because, this deal? It was too rich to pass up.

"I can practically taste your excitement." That voice—it did things to me. Always had. He didn't need to say dirty words—though I liked that too—he simply had to let his voice roll over my skin, and he owned me. Always.

"Come find me and turn practically into literally."

Jericho's rich laugh met my ears just before he came into view. He'd worn his blue suit today, the one I thought made his eyes seem even more vibrant than usual. The one I'd hung in a special corner of our shared closet so he'd know it was my favorite. The one I'd had him bring to the bakery so I could match the shade of blue perfectly for his election cookies.

Bakers gonna bake. Politicians gonna… Well, today, he was going to buy the panties right off me.

"Hey there, handsome." I grinned as he whipped in my direction, his eyes lighting up when he saw me. I'd also chosen an outfit from a specific spot in the closet. One that he'd hung with care. That he'd selected as one of his favorites. A knee-length dress with flirty polka dots and a deep V for a neckline. One that wrapped and tied around me. That offered him easy access for moments like this.

"My sweet girl." Jericho grabbed me and pulled me against his broad chest, lifting me off the ground as he kissed me deep and hard. So perfect.

I gasped as he moved on to my neck. "How much time do we have?"

He already had his hands on the tie of my dress. "Twenty minutes, tops."

"We should have done this at home—we didn't need to waste the ten minutes driving."

"True, but I like a challenge." He grinned at me before tugging my dress apart, groaning as he saw the blue lace bra and panty set I'd worn just for him. The one that also matched my favorite suit of his. "Look at you. What did I ever do to gain such good favor from the fates?"

So many things, but this wasn't the time to lay them all out. I needed my mate, and he needed to finalize our transaction. "Did you bring the payment?"

His lips kicked up a notch, and he reached into his back pocket with one hand, even as the other slipped down to tug on my panties. "I am a man of my word."

He was. He really was. "Show me."

The glint in his eye turned wicked. "You show me yours, and I'll show you mine."

I wasn't exactly one to back away from a challenge. I arched a little, giving myself room to hook my thumbs into the lace around my waist and tug down. I kept my eyes on his as I leaned over to pull the panties from one leg then the other, kept our gazes locked as I brought the fabric up to hold in front of his face, letting it dangle from one finger.

"I'm a woman of my word."

"My woman."

"Yes."

"My woman who wants a cat."

"Also yes."

"Matilda might eat him."

"Matilda loves you and is happy as a clam now that you're living inside of her walls once more."

"She does seem to favor me."

Understatement. The damn house adored him. If the lights weren't going to work, it would be when I walked into a room. If the hot water was going to cut out, it would be when I was taking a shower. Never Jericho. The only special treatment I seemed to get was when I was planning our upcoming wedding. Matilda liked that and would brighten the lights for me and make these happy, groany noises as her old frame settled. The house wanted us married, as did the town.

Soon. Very, very soon.

Jericho pulled out his phone and scrolled through a couple of screens before turning it my way. "This little guy has been at the shelter over the mountain for six months. No one seems to want him because he's skittish and has a bad leg. He's on his way to Kinship Cove now for you to meet to see if he's the right one for us."

I grinned, jumping at my mate and wrapping my arms around him. "Thank you."

Jericho grabbed my ass and lifted, forcing me to wrap my legs around his waist. "Thank me with more than your words, sweet girl."

I giggled as I slipped my hands between us, holding my hips away from his so I had room to unfasten his pants. And then I did thank him —long and hard and energetically until he couldn't take my mouth anymore and yanked me up the length of his body. And then he thanked me, making me come three times before he roared his release. Before he panted my name as he rocked into me one last time. Clinging to me in the dusty stacks of books, with my panties locked in his grip.

"So," I said once I'd finally caught my breath. "This was fun."

He chuckled, burying his face in my chest so he could kiss and lick the swells of my breasts. "We should do this more often."

"I'm not sure you could afford to buy my panties any more than you already do." Because he did—he bought them from me weekly, paying for them with little gifts and surprises, with repairs to Matilda and experiences for me. Those were my favorites—when he paid me with his time. It was so limited with the election coming up. Spencer hadn't given up trying to dehumanize my mate, but he hadn't been very successful about it either. Especially not when he'd attempted to use me to break down Jericho. My mate had shown his true alpha side, thundering through town and laying down the law to all the residents of Kinship Cove—I was off-limits.

He'd gotten more than my panties for that.

Jericho kissed me sweetly, his hands still roaming over my curves. "Two more weeks until the election."

"And two weeks after that until the wedding."

"I'd marry you now. Today. This second."

He would. "After the election. I want your full attention for the honeymoon."

"You've got it. Always."

And I did. For six more minutes.

"Think you can make me come again before you have to go?" I asked as I rocked against where he was already growing hard for me.

He growled and dove in for a kiss, shoving me against the bookshelf and pressing his body into mine.

Where we stayed for the next five-and-half minutes.

The man never had been one to back down from a challenge.

Paranormal romance with a dangerously ever after.

FERAL BREED MOTORCYCLE CLUB

Wolf shifters, motorcycles, witches, and a threat lurking in the shadows.

Novels

Claiming His Fate

Claiming His Need

Claiming His Witch

Claiming His Beauty

Claiming His Fire

Claiming His Desire

Claiming Her Heart

Collections

Claiming Their Forever: A Collection of Shorts

The Feral Breed: Volume One

The Feral Breed: Volume Two

The Feral Breed: The Complete Series

FERAL BREED FOLLOWINGS

Stand-alone stories of characters first met in the Feral Breed Motorcycle Club series. Featuring cage fighters, dragon shifters, second chances, and young love.

Claiming His Chance

Claiming His Prize

THE GATHERING TALES

Come and enjoy tales from the biggest shifter event of the year as wolves from around the country fall in lust, in love, and in fate at The Gathering.

The Gathering Tales

THE DEVIL'S DIRES

There's no escaping a Dire Wolf on the hunt...

Savage Surrender

Savage Sanctuary

Savage Seduction

Savage Silence

Savage Sacrifice

Savage Security

Savage Salvation

MOTOR CITY ALIEN MAIL ORDER BRIDES

Where the men aren't human and the women are uninformed.

Cutlass

Hudson

Maverick

KINSHIP COVE: MATES & MACARONS

When shifters and humans mingle, the fates like to have a little fun.

Candied Wolf

Sugar Dragon

Honey Bear

Frappé Fox

Espresso con Eagle

Caffé Wolverino

Reindeer Ripple

STAND-ALONE ROMANCE

Masterson: A Vampire Sons Story

Fox Hunt: A Reverse Harem Romance

Sign up for Ellis Leigh's newsletter for release information, promotions, swag opportunities, and early access to free reads!

Free Reads…News…Good Stuff!

For new release announcements only, follow Ellis on Bookbub.

collar community know exactly what it is to have to rise from the ashes. Never giving up is part of life, like second base, second gear, and second chances.

POP THE CLUTCH

REV THE ENGINE (Coming Soon)

Sign up for Kristin Harte's newsletter so you never miss out on news and updates.

www.kristinharte.com/newsletter

Are you a Bookbub subscriber? You can follow Kristin there as well so you never miss a new release!

www.kristinharte.com/bookbub

ABOUT THE AUTHOR

A storyteller from the time she could talk, Ellis grew up among family legends of hauntings, psychics, and love spanning decades. Those stories didn't always have the happiest of endings, so they inspired her to write about real life, real love, and the difficulties therein. From farmers to werewolves, store clerks to witches—if there's love to be found, she'll write about it. Ellis lives in the Chicago area with her two daughters and a German Shepherd that never leaves her side.

When she's not writing paranormal romance, Ellis Leigh can be found writing romantic suspense as Kristin Harte and erotic shorts as London Hale.

Sign up for Ellis Leigh's newsletter for release information, promotions, swag opportunities, and early access to free reads!

www.ellisleigh.com/newsletter.

For new release announcements only, follow Ellis on Bookbub.

Come join my reader group for fun, snippets, secret handshakes, and discussions of what I'm working on and when that next book will be out.

Ellis' Elite Reader Group

Let's be social!
www.ellisleigh.com
ellis@ellisleigh.com